One of the traps of meth addiction is that the users don't take care of themselves. This is one of the many ways I will be different from the average user.

I go to a Wal-Mart far away from our neighborhood. Not that anyone cares what I buy at the McSuperCenter, but I need to get accustomed to being sneaky.

I buy cherry Chap Stick. I buy the vitamin supplements pregnant women take. I need something powerful enough for two people, even if one of them hasn't yet been born. I buy canned tuna fish for the protein and tryptophan, a loaf of whole-wheat bread for the complex carbs, and a huge bag of Jolly Ranchers because meth makes you crave sugar. I get saline nose spray and a package of straws in case I decide to snort. The idea of shoving a rolled-up dollar bill up my nose sounds both painful and unsanitary. Even with the straws, I doubt I'll snort. Still, you never know what you are capable of doing when you are really messed up on drugs.

I don't want meth mouth, so I buy a case of bottled water and some of the most expensive fluoride toothpaste I can find. That's the real problem. Addicts don't brush their teeth. I will always brush my teeth, no matter how fucked-up I am.

D0061868

HIGH BEFORE HOMEROOM

MAYA SLOAN

GALLERY BOOKS

NEW YORK   LONDON   TORONTO   SYDNEY

G

Gallery Books
A Division of Simon & Schuster, Inc.
1230 Avenue of the Americas
New York, NY 10020

First Gallery Books trade paperback edition June 2010

GALLERY BOOKS and colophon are trademarks of Simon & Schuster, Inc.

For information about special discounts for bulk purchases, please contact Simon & Schuster Special Sales at
1-866-506-1949 or business@simonandschuster.com.

The Simon & Schuster Speakers Bureau can bring authors to your live event. For more information or to book an event contact the Simon & Schuster Speakers Bureau at 1-866-248-3049 or visit our website at www.simonspeakers.com.

Designed by Kyoko Watanabe

Manufactured in the United States of America

10   9   8   7   6   5   4   3   2   1

Library of Congress Cataloging-in-Publication Data is available.

ISBN 978-1-4391-7129-5
ISBN 978-1-4391-7163-9 (ebook)

With love to my father and mother,
Stephen and Roberta Sloan.

ACKNOWLEDGMENTS

There are so many people I love. And I will try to name them all, even if the acknowledgments end up longer than the book itself.

To Thomas Warming, because you make me happy. I love you, Dejlige.

Margaret Reynolds Fredrickson and Emily Johnson, because I am completely myself when you are with me. You are the most extraordinary women I have ever met.

Greg Sloan, my brother, best friend, and one of the most amazing people I've ever known. Thank you for helping me with this novel. Thank you for having my back, and know I've always got yours.

My family, I adore you all: Chris Sloan, Carla Kaufman Sloan. Caleb Finiz and Calder Jacob Sloan. Robin, Arnold,

ACKNOWLEDGMENTS

Gaby, and Josh Kanarek. Aaron, Elan, Vivian, Larry, and Zena Miller. Jon and Julie Gold. Shira and Jason Raider.

Because, somehow, this short, loudmouthed Okie girl found the most brilliant mentors in the universe—Donald "Skip" Hays, who made me love stories and taught me to tell them, and who makes so many lives richer with his wisdom, huge heart, and guts. To the brilliant Leslie Epstein, who called me "lazy" and then taught me how not to be. You are a gift both to the literary world and also to me.

My friends. I cannot wait to see your luminous talent explode on this world: Stephen Sanders, Matthew Goldberg, Matt Yost, Randa Tantawi, Alex Ankrom, James Kaelan, Kodi Scheer, Brooke Cheshier, Anastasia Kolendo. And, of course, Nate Warren Lane.

My Bulgarian family: Silvia, Sara, and "Burn Brother" Zack Karabshlieva. My extended Bulgarian family: Svetlozar Zhelev, Alexandra Chaushova, Alexander Shpatov, Yanitsa Radeva, Maria Doneva, Yordan Kostourkov, Milena Deleva, Pavel Gonevski, Josip Novakovich. And Elizabeth Kostova, for her boundless generosity.

Matt Bialer, because you are, above all, a really great friend. Katie Arnoldi, for teaching me to be strong, even when faced with (literal) bears. I love you, Katie. Gonzalo "Pepe" De Mendoza, because you are my family.

Thank you so, so, so much to my extraordinary editor, Megan McKeever. You took a chance for me, and I will be eternally grateful. Thank you to Gallery Books.

Lindsay Ribar, for your talent, guidance and friendship.

Hilda Willis. Carol Koss. Debbie, Buzz, Natalie, and Nicholas Lane. Janelle Taylor, Coco Ferrari, BJ Pettigrew. George, Ann, Mayan, and Melissa Lopez. Candace Muzny. Anahi, David, and the Sorias familia. Keith Fredrickson. Kent and Brenda Johnson. Jennifer Haigh. Francis Cathcart III. Jason Sitzes. Julianna Baggott. Zachariah Horton. John Provatas. Anne Hathcoat. Katie Walton. Sarah Jacoby. Mari Mari Narvaez. Gemma Martin. Sabine Schmidt. Leslie Gilkeson-Shrum. Davy Rothbart. Zack Goehner. Jerry Kalajian. John Rechy. Rachel Wolf. Brently Reynolds. Gary Scott Dean. Charles, Ry, and Natalie Arnoldi. Ken Roberts. Molly Giles. Ellen Gilchrist. Ha Jin. Nazy Baskin. Sheryl Lee Ralph. James Rahn. Rilla Askew. Mandy Aaronson. Will Smith I.

Judith Pierson. Because, in all the words I've ever said to you, there would never be enough to thank you.

E. Lynn Harris, who said it would happen. I can feel you smiling on me at this very moment.

The Elizabeth Kostova Foundation. Richard Burgin and *Boulevard*. Yogi Bair and the whole Bear Paw backcountry crew. Laurie Meadoff and the CITYKIDS Repertory. Maire Mullins and Pepperdine University. Alicia Thomas, Marion W. Roydhouse, and Philadelphia University. The Honorary Mayor of Canal Street, Dr. George Solomon. Eli Goldblatt and Temple University. Robert Pinsky and the Boston Arts Academy. Kate Snodgrass and the Boston Playwrights' Theatre. The University of Arkansas Writers in the Schools Program. The Hi-Lo Club of OKC. Michael Sanders. Bob Vernon and Westminster

ACKNOWLEDGMENTS

School. The Writers Retreat Workshop. The Rittenhouse Writers Group. The Los Angeles S Factor. The crew at the Chelsea Hotel—Jefferson Courtney, Willem Van Es, and the ghost of Dylan Thomas. Tattoo artist Dan Smith. Dramaturge Dan Smith. Sister Janice Powers Home for Orphaned and Wayward Girls. The UARK Creative Writing Department. The BU Creative Writing Department. Loui Dobin and Greene Family Camp of Bruceville, Texas. The entire Bishop McGuinness class of 1995.

Oklahomans, because they are the nicest people in the world. And Oklahoma itself—I may mock you, but you will always be my home and the state I love. And, yes, you really are okay.

All my students. Past, present, and future. Because you keep me going, inspire me, make me laugh, and remind me why I love stories. Because I can only hope I've taught you as much as you've taught me.

HIGH BEFORE HOMEROOM

CHAPTER ONE

Laurilee's legs are bare and faintly bluish beneath the pleats of her plaid jumper. She once told me that it is the same one she wore in Catholic grade school. A lot of guys would get a stiffy if a girl told them that. I'm one of those guys.

Laurilee and I crouch behind the Dumpster at the back entrance of Penn Square Mall. We lean against the concrete wall and smoke unfiltered Camels. I used to smoke Parliaments until I met Laurilee. I like the Camels. I like how the shreds of tobacco get stuck to the end of my tongue. I cock my head to the left and spit them out and it makes me feel like a man.

We keep an eye out for Terrance, the six-foot-four,

pockmarked, probably undiagnosed-schizophrenic mall-security Nazi. By regulation, all employees are required to leave mall grounds when smoking, but we only have fifteen minutes and it's cold. Laurilee has a scab across her knee. I want to run my fingertips around the jagged edges. I want to touch each of her flaws—the slightly stick-out ears, the bitten-down nails with chipped silver polish. I want to bury my face in her unwashed hair, the turquoise streaks fading at the temples. Instead, I pick at a zit on my cheek. It's one of those you can't see. Right under the skin. Those hurt the worst.

"Yesterday he was harassing these poor baby wank-sters," says Laurilee. I can hear her teeth chattering as she wraps her chapped lips around the end of her Camel. "They weren't messing with anyone, just killing time by the fountain. They were probably twelve or something. He took them outside, made them take off their bandan-nas. 'Gang wear,' he told them. Ha. Twelve-year-old Okie Crips. Please."

"Terrance must have been a crack baby," I tell her. "Hey, you want my coat?" Nothing would make me hap-pier. Laurilee wearing my coat, her smell seeping into the lining, wearing Laurilee for the rest of the day. Being inside Laurilee. I feel my dick stiffen. I cock my head, spit, and think about my grandmother naked. My grand-mother has been dead for fifteen years, which makes this an even more effective mental exercise. Almost immedi-ately, my boner goes away. Laurilee has pulled her legs to her chest and rests her cheek on one plaid knee.

"I like the cold. It wakes me up," she says. I suck on my cigarette, imagining my lungs blackening and shriveling up with each inhalation. It makes me feel like I'm doing something that matters. I figure it's the same reason some people cut themselves or puke up their food. At least you have control over something, even if it is your own annihilation. Besides, you never hear of sixteen-year-olds getting lung cancer. Cancer is for old people. Sixteen-year-olds get some rare, undiagnosable neurological disorder or leukemia. They lose all their hair and the whole football team shaves their heads in solidarity and then *People* magazine writes an article about it. I wonder, if I got an incurable disease, if the Make-A-Wish Foundation would get me a high-class whore so I won't die a virgin. I look at Laurilee. Her turquoise streak matches the faded blue of the Dumpster.

"If you were about to die, and you could meet one famous person before you did, who would you pick?" I ask. Laurilee wrinkles her nose in concentration. Most girls would just roll their eyes and go, *Ew, stop being so weird.* Laurilee isn't most girls.

"Living or dead?" she asks.

"Either."

"Mythological or real?"

"Whatever you want. It's a theoretical question."

"Jesus," she says with a big grin.

"Jesus?"

"Black Jesus for sure. Young, sexy black Jesus. Is that racist?"

"Nah, but you can't pick Jesus. Too easy," I tell her.

"I didn't know theoretical questions had rules. How about Satan, then?"

"Your final answer?" I say, in my best *Who Wants to Be a Millionaire* voice.

"Wait!" she says, sitting up straight. "David Bowie. That's who I'd pick. Circa Ziggy Stardust. When he was all pretty and, like, sexually ambiguous." David Bowie is Laurilee's new obsession. Before that, it was Kurt Cobain. Then everyone else at school discovered him, so she had to move on. Old-school tormented musicians are making a comeback. Even better if they died from a suicide or drug overdose. Laurilee figures, since Bowie is still alive, she's got him to herself for at least another couple of months unless he pulls a Michael Jackson.

"You'd pick David Bowie? Out of anyone?"

"Sure," she says. "It'd be a nice way to go. He could sing me a lullaby as I drifted away. He could do my makeup. I'd be kickin' it in my casket, all glammed out with glitter and false eyelashes. What about you, kid?"

"I don't know." Laurilee has always called me *kid,* even though we are both sixteen.

"You're not dying, are you?" she asks.

"Not yet."

"Good. I don't want you to die. Who'd I smoke with on break? I'd have to smoke with one of the makeup-counter girls. Or those assholes from Hot Dog on a Stick. They don't even give mall-employee discounts, those Stick dicks. Don't die, okay, kid? I'd miss you." She attempts, then fails, to blow a smoke ring.

I don't hear anything after *I'd miss you.* Laurilee would miss me. That means she thinks about me when we aren't together. I do some quick calculations in my head. During the average mall shift, we usually spend our two fifteen-minute breaks smoking by the Dumpster. Sometimes, if she isn't too busy stocking headbands, she'll clock out at the same time as I do for dinner break. If there are around 168 hours in a week, and I'm spending at least two of those hours with Laurilee out here smoking cigarettes by the Dumpster, and she says she'd *miss me,* then at some point during the other 166 hours of the week she must be thinking about me. You have to *think about someone to miss them.* And, at some point during those 158 hours, she must be naked. So at some point in the week there is an off-off-chance that Laurilee is naked and thinking about me *at the same time.* The thought makes my dick hard again. I can see her white body slick with soap, her hair wet, running one of those pink bath puffs down her body, *missing me.*

Then again, girls like Laurilee don't spend their free time thinking about guys like me. *I'd miss you* is just a figure of speech. *I'd miss you, it fucked me up good, I almost died, pass the salt.*

As if she can read my mind, she sighs. "I'm spent. I went out last night."

"Where'd you go?" I ask, my jaw tightening. Laurilee goes out every night. My jaw tightens every time she tells me about it.

"Infinity, down near Twenty-third. It used to be a

church. You know the one? They gutted it, put in some strobe lights, wah-la. They still have those stained-glass windows, I mean, I think they do. I was pretty fucked-up, kid. I'll have to ask Daniel."

"The guy from El Reno?" I say, knowing perfectly well the guy from El Reno is named Marcus, drives an Oldsmobile he calls the pimpmobile, and spent two years in juvie for check forgery. Laurilee blows a raspberry.

"Please. Marcus is a douche. I'm over him. Now, Daniel. Daniel is on a whole other plane. He's a Buddhist. And he's got a tat on his neck. Of a dragon. Blowing fire and everything. God, I want a tat so bad. Someday I'm gonna get a tat. Somewhere you can't even hide it. Daniel doesn't give a fuck what anyone thinks. He's opened my eyes to a lot of shit. Buddhism is pretty cool."

"Does he eat meat?"

"Fuck, yeah." She gives a fresh shiver, even though the wind has died down. Her pale, goose-pimpled collarbone juts out like a coat hanger from the ragged top of her sweatshirt where she has unevenly cut out the collar. It kind of defeats the purpose of a sweatshirt, but it looks good on her. When I tell her I like it, she tells me she was inspired by a late-night rerun of *Flashdance* on TNT. *It was two in the morning and I cut the neck out of every T-shirt in my closet,* she tells me. *I can't explain it. I just felt like those collars were holding me back. My Mom was superpissed when she found out, half of them were these cashmere J. Crew sweaters she ordered out of a catalog, which made her twice as pissed. It doesn't matter, I like pissing her off. Besides, they look better my way. I should be on one of those reality shows where you, like, make a dress out of banana peels and they give you a hundred thou and tell you what a damn genius you are. The eighties are back, anyway.* When I remind her she wasn't even born in the eighties, she grins at me. *Past life,* she says. *Silly boy.*

According to Laurilee, in her past life she was an Egyptian queen, a beggar girl on the streets of London with only her wits and pickpocketing prowess as a means of survival, and the descendant of a plantation owner and his slave mistress. When I mention that these revelations seem to coincide with cable reruns of *Cleopatra, Oliver!,* and *Roots,* she punches me in the arm. "Stop being so literal," she tells me. When Laurilee grins at me, nothing else matters. There could be an earthquake, a tornado, the release of a fatal viral strain extracted from Asian monkeys that will eventually kill off the human race as we know it, and I wouldn't notice. I'd just grin right back at her.

Now she's cold, and if I had any balls, I'd put my arm around her shoulder.

"He's a modern Buddhist. It's all in how you define it. He believes in the four noble truths and all that, but he'll still eat a steak. I couldn't date a vegan, you know that. They have the stankiest breath. Besides, there's nothing better than a big-ass juicy steak, don'tcha think? Like down in the stockyards? My mom took me once when I was a kid. You can get beer in a boot, how quality is that? I mean, I got a Shirley Temple, of course, because I was just a kid. But they still let me keep the boot. Then we went to that cowboy store across the street and my mom got me this kiddie-pink cowboy hat with a pink ribbon that tied under the chin. I thought I was cowgirl Barbie for the rest of the day, that's how pretty I felt. I don't know where that hat is now. I think we sold it in a yard sale. I wish I still had it." She laughs.

I want to tell her that we can go back to the stock-yards. I'll buy her another pink hat. I'll buy her the biggest steak she's ever seen, one of those seventy-two ouncers. I'll even cut it into bite-size pieces and feed it to her. And she can be naked while I do it.

"Hey," she says, sitting up straight, "what time is it?"

"Four ten."

"Uh-oh," she says, running her hands through her hair as she stands. "You should have told me. Can't leave Denise in charge for too long. She'll probably pierce some third grader's septum or something."

If I lean my body across the Aunt Betty's Cookie counter and look to the left of the food court, I can see Laurilee through the window of Trinkets. I've watched her pierce hundreds of ears. She rests her hand under each tiny chin and whispers as she lifts the piercing gun. The little girls rarely cry. I wonder what she says to them. I wish she'd whisper to me. Anything. A grocery list. The table of elements. After she pierces them, she holds up a mirror and they smile at themselves with baby teeth and rotate their heads from side to side, the tiny gold balls flashing in their earlobes. Her mouth moves. Sometimes I can make out words. *Pretty,* she tells them. *Beautiful thing.*

Laurilee stubs out her cigarette on the side of the Dumpster and puts the butt back in the pack. "You ever want to do something drastic?"

"Sure." I imagine myself pushing her up against that blue Dumpster and shoving my hands under her skirt and between her cold thighs. I imagine her eyes fluttering, her low moan, the rhythmic clanging of metal against her back. Then I realize how retarded this fantasy is, not to mention unsanitary.

"Well, I'm gonna do something drastic. Just wait, kid. I'm gonna do something irreversible."

"Like what?"

"Oh, you'll see. It will be a surprise." She grins at me.

She's beautiful. Not the kind of beautiful those asstard guys at my school can see. Not prom-queen beautiful. She's a classic beauty, like a chick in a silent film. She's got those big, liquid eyes that talk even when her mouth isn't moving. Those dumbass farmboys at my school wouldn't take a second look at a girl like Laurilee. *A butter face,* they'd mutter to each other. *Her body is okay, but-ter face ain't all that. A six out of ten. If I had on beer goggles.* They could have been manufactured in a lab, those clichéd dicks at my school. Take a beaker and put in some reality television, whatever song is on MTV rotation that week, mix in some middle-class, white-boy poser slang—*Ya, nigga, me and my boys was chillin' with some smoke and a forty in the Wal-Mart parkin' lot*—shake it all up, and dump it in a petri dish. There you go: you've got every guy who ever went to Classen High. They are science experiments. They are Pavlov's dogs, salivating at big cheerleader boobs, blond hair, the smell of hair spray. I'd almost feel sorry for guys like that. I mean, if they didn't make my life suck so bad.

"I've got something for you," I say, trying to keep my voice calm. *You're cool, man. You're fine.* I reach nonchalantly into the front pocket of my Aunt Betty's apron, wishing to God I hadn't been so eager to see her that I'd taken it off, wishing to God I didn't have to wear an apron in the first place, and pull out the copy of *Leaves of Grass* I've been carrying around for two months. "Here," I say, holding it out for her like it was a stick of chewing gum. "I thought you might like it. He was this crazy, bearded hippie. Before there were hippies, I mean. Kerouac loved him. Remember that guy I told you about? Kerouac? The one who took those road trips?" I hear the urgency in my voice. *Shut up, fucktard. Just shut up.* "He was bisexual, too. Before it was, like, cool. I mean, he tried everything. That was his philosophy. Girls, guys, it didn't matter. He probably even did it with animals. Just kidding. He loved animals. As pets, I mean." I laugh. *I am a fucking idiot and I want to die.*

She takes the book from my hand and looks down at it. She smiles, and then I do too, because she's like an infection. The kind you want to get. The kind you brag about. Laurilee is the kissing disease.

In an alternate world, where I am not a pussy, this would be where I'd step close to her, wrap my arm around her waist, pull her to my ripped chest, and say, my voice sounding like Daniel Craig's James Bond, my hot, nonvegan breath on her slightly stuck-out right ear: *Little you know the subtle electric fire that for your sake is playing within me.*

But in this world, I have scrawny arms and no swagger. I look down at my high-tops, the sides of the soles scrawled with doodles. When I bought them, they seemed old-school, ironic. Now they look infantile.

"Thanks, kid," she says, and kisses my cheek. "You're sweet. I'll read it when the shop gets slow." I will feel the imprint of her frozen lips during the rest of my shift. I will think about her pussy and knobby knees and warm tongue in my mouth while I bag engorged cookies for mall-walking housewives in sweatpants. I will write *Happy Birthday, Nancy!* in pink icing on a cookie cake and think about Laurilee naked in *Kama Sutra* poses with Buddhist Daniel, his Adam's apple bouncing like a pinball beneath his tattooed dragon with each sweaty grunt. The sound system will pipe in the Muzak version of "Light My Fire," complete with eighties synthesizer and harps, like the sound track to my mediocrity. I will hum along as I cut heart shapes out of premade dough.

Laurilee smiles at me, clutching the book to her chest with one arm, as though the pages will keep her warm. Her tiny incisors are sharper than most chicks'. *I'm a vampire,* she once told me, and snarled. *Better watch out or I'll bite you!* Now she laughs, and the tinkling echoes off the cement walls and metal Dumpster, like wind chimes in a Tijuana slum. Not that I've seen Tijuana, except in documentaries. It's just that Laurilee would make a gutter beautiful.

"You're a real sweetheart, y'know that, kid?"

Laurilee gets off work before I do, leaving Trinkets to Denise, knowing no little kids come in for piercing past bedtime. I watch her walk to the escalator, clutching her ripped backpack with the anarchy patch. She stops suddenly in front of the down escalator, as though she has forgotten something, and turns toward me. I am staring at her, like a stalker. She grins and waves. I wave back like an idiot. Like she's going off to war. Then she hops on the escalator and the last thing I see, before she disappears, is the faint blue of her temples. A timer goes off, and I jump. The Snickerdoodles are ready.

It's dark when I walk from the bus stop to the split-level, ranch-style house that looks like every other split-level, ranch-style house in our neighborhood, except for the overgrown lawn. None of the neighbors has complained. They know Trevor isn't here to mow, and they probably figure I don't know how to do it myself, even though any douche can mow a lawn. Of course I wouldn't put on quite as good a show as Trevor does, getting all sweaty and whipping his shirt off, taking breaks to pour water over his head like it's halftime. And the truth is, I kind of like it like this, with the weeds growing up the side of the house and the neighbors pretending they don't see what's happening. It's like a yearlong excuse to have a brother fighting in Iraq. A get-out-of-jail-free card. I wonder what other stuff I could score if I really thought about it, like how they give you a free Grand Slam at Denny's on your birthday. It occurs to me that it's a lot easier to like Trevor when he's in a desert eight thousand miles away.

In the kitchen, my mother sits at the foldout table we used to use for backyard barbecues when the extended family came up from Little Rock. They don't come anymore, except for every third Thanksgiving, and the foldout has taken permanent residence in the kitchen. We had a real dining-room table once, when I was a kid. It was one of those extender ones that you open up for family holidays. I'm not sure where it went, but I haven't seen it in a long time. Now we eat on TV trays or standing at the kitchen counter, which is fine with me. Family dinners are overrated.

The floor is covered with half-assembled cardboard boxes and bags of packing peanuts. My mom is wearing a flannel nightgown. She hums to herself. There are stacks of candy bars, boxes of fruit roll-ups, six-packs of Hanes boxers, Juicy Fruit gum, piles of *Sports Illustrated* and *Maxim*. She has a piece of Scotch tape stuck to her bottom lip. She curls a yellow ribbon with a pair of scissors. *Yellow ribbons are for dead soldiers*, I almost tell her, except I don't want to say the word *dead* when she's thinking about Trevor. In Canada, the yellow ribbons also symbolize teenage suicide prevention, which is kind of disturbing if you think about it too hard. I googled *awareness ribbons,* figuring I could suggest another color, but they are pretty much taken. I never knew there were so many causes out there. Blue is nice, might remind the troops of the good ole American sky, but almost every shade is accounted for already. Sex-trafficking awareness is navy. In Spain, the blue ribbon symbolizes opposing the terrorism of the ETA, and in Israel it indicates support for the Israel unilateral disengagement plan of 2008. I'm not sure about the specifics of these events because they don't teach them in Oklahoma History, and we aren't required to take World History until junior year. I like the idea of ribbon awareness, though. I thought about an appropriate ribbon color for other guys like me, so we could recognize each other in the hall. Then I tried to figure out exactly what kind of guy I am, but the whole enterprise was depressing as hell, so I googled Laurilee instead. I realized I didn't remember her last name, which surprised me, considering she is the only reason I wake up in the morning.

My mom has a patch of gray hairs coming in on the front of her hairline. She used to take care of stuff like that. She used to wear pink lipstick and smear on this cream she got at the mall that smells like a vanilla sundae. She stopped doing that stuff when Trevor left. Still, she's prettier than I remember seeing her in a long time. Her face is practically glowing, or maybe it's just the shreds of silver confetti stuck to the side of her face. She puts a fistful in every package because that's just what every soldier in Iraq wants, silver fucking confetti to go with their yellow ribbons.

"Honey," she says, without looking up, "did you ask your manager about the cookies?"

"I forgot." I open the fridge. I scan for something edible that is not dehydrated, prefrozen, or shrink-wrapped. I should have stopped at Chick-fil-A. The Chick-fil-A people honor the mall discount. Probably because they are a Christian organization, and Jesus doesn't believe in stiffing fellow mall employees, unlike those ghetto asswipes at Hot Dog on a Stick in their gay rainbow hats. I take a can of Dr Pepper.

"Oh, honey, we could really use the donation," says my Mom, sounding disappointed. *Disappointed mother* is the worst sound in the world.

"I'll ask him tomorrow," I lie. I avoid talking to Roger at all costs, unless it pertains to my paycheck or a shift that coincides with Laurilee's.

"They're sending in more troops. Did you know that?" She looks up at me, midcurl. She is beaming, her cheeks flushed like a teenage girl who just made Homecoming Court. She lives for this. This is her purpose. This is why she wakes up in the morning. We have more in common than I'd like to admit.

"Yeah," I say, and chug half the can of Dr Pepper. "I think I read that somewhere."

"I called an emergency meeting for Friday."

"Are they coming here?"

"Of course."

"God, I hate those bitches. They cackle. I swear to God, Mom, I can hear them in my sleep. Like a bunch of hyenas."

"Watch it, Dougie," says my mom, holding up the scissors at me. She can't hide her smirk. She knows I'm right. My mom is the unofficial leader of the Mothers Support Our Troops Northwest Oklahoma City Chapter, not that it pays in anything other than personal satisfaction. The other northwest Oklahoma City mothers who support our troops hang on her every word, fawn over her package arrangements, argue over who will get her tea. She tells them what to do, like a sergeant, and they jump at her every command.

Since Trevor left, her days are full of lists and phone calls. It's like she's in college again, when she led a student protest against animal testing in the biology department. I can almost see that girl in her now, the art major in Birkenstocks and sarongs, with charcoal under her fingernails. At least that's how I like to picture her, as one of those arty chicks who went to poetry readings and talked about Kafka and baked stuff out of wheatgrass. Now she is an administrative assistant to a bunch of good-old-boy lawyers. They wear cowboy hats and call her *sweetie*. On Secretary's Day they pitch in to get her a gift certificate to Dillard's.

Once I found a stack of her old canvases gathering dust in the corner of the basement. The splatters are obviously derivative of early Pollock, which I know because I saw a documentary about him on PBS and was pretty impressed by any guy who'd literally piss on his own work. But there is something even better in my mom's paintings, something dark and interesting, like they were done by someone I wouldn't mind meeting. *Oh, Doug,* she said, when I showed them to her. *Put those hideous things back in the basement.* I put one on the wall over my dresser. Every time I look at it, I think about how she ended up marrying my dickhead father, and it seems like something straight out of one of those chick movies she Netflixes and forces me to watch, usually starring Emma Thompson, where all the women are desperate to get married and in the end they fall in love with some asshole tool instead of the nice, available guy who isn't as good-looking but would give them security and unconditional love and wouldn't spend their dowry on prostitutes. Of course, in the end of the movie they are old maids living in some family cottage and it is a feminist statement. If you really think about it, my mom is a feminist statement, raising me and Trevor on her own.

I don't remember my father's face. For some reason, all I see in my head is a cross between Bill Paxton and the dad on *Leave It to Beaver.* I don't think there are any pictures, and I wouldn't want to see them anyway. Only an asshole would marry someone, knock her up twice, then take off to Mexico with some mentally unstable heiress he met at the Cock O The Walk. I don't want to know anything about him, even if we do share the same DNA. DNA is as overrated as family dinners.

I watch my mom assemble packages and feel a rush

of love for her. I grew in her belly. She used to bring me orange juice when I had a fever. She's not so bad. Then I think about how there is nothing to eat in the fridge and she forgot to go grocery shopping again. "Can I have money for a pizza?" I ask.

"Just have a sandwich. Want me to heat you up a Hungry-Man?"

"Never mind," I say, hearing the whine in my voice. She shoots me a sharp look. I open a bag of Chee•tos and lean against the counter. I chew loudly.

"How was work?"

"It sucked," I say, making sure she sees my mouthful of neon orange mush.

"You got homework?"

"I guess."

"You guess or you know?" she says.

"I did most of it at work."

"I hope your grades are better this term."

"I'm getting an A in English. We just finished *The Sun Also Rises*."

My mom smiles and takes a sip of her Sleepytime tea. She'll supplement it with a tranquilizer around midnight. "Hemingway."

"The whole thing is about how Hemingway can't get a *boner*." I emphasize the word *boner*, just to see if I can get a reaction.

"I think I remember," says my mom, unmoved.

"Mrs. Wallace won't talk about that part. I don't think she knows what a *boner* is." Before Trevor left, my mother would have acted shocked at my lack of tact. *Erection*, she would have corrected me. The old Mom would have been even more pissed about Mrs. Wallace. She would have given a speech about the incompetence of the American educational system and how she wishes we had the money to send me to the white-flight private school across town where they have a pottery studio and how I'll have to make the best of a mediocre situation and why didn't I apply myself because with all my natural ability I could easily be the kind of kid who merits a school-issued bumper sticker on the back of her minivan? But now she doesn't care. Now she is only half listening. It's like when I was a kid, and I'd read an essay I'd written or act out my science-fair presentation for her. She'd worked all day and would be folding laundry or making dinner and would be this weird concoction of parent and ghost. A half-Mom phantom. When I complained, she told me she was watching out of the corner of her eye. I didn't believe her then, and I don't believe her now. It isn't humanly possible to watch someone out of the corner of your eye, unless you're some kind of animal with eyes on either side of its head, like a parrot or a fish. I can't think of any others. I'll have to google it later.

"Next we're doing the poets. Sylvia Plath. She put her head in an oven over some guy. I think he was a poet too. Poets are freaks."

My mom smiles to herself as she tapes a box closed. "I loved her in college."

"She seems kind of whiny to me. I mean, it's not like

she really suffered that much. She had a trust fund. I want a trust fund, Mom."

"Sure, honey. I'll get on that."

"Then Anne Sexton. Total child molester. Why are the poets so fucked-up?"

"I don't know, honey." I know she's stopped listening. I finish the bag of Chee•tos. Chester Cheetah smiles up at me, and I scrunch up his ugly face. A long time ago, my mother liked to read. She'd talk to me about literature. She always liked the guy books, she'd told me. *Heart of Darkness. Moby-Dick.* The stuff chicks weren't supposed to dig. The adventure stories. But that was a long time ago, when we talked about stuff like that. Middle school. It's been years since we talked about anything that matters.

"I'm going to bed," I tell her. "You should go to bed, Mom. It's pretty late."

"Soon. I've still got a lot to do. Especially now, with this thing getting worse. Poor Trevor." She roughly curls a ribbon with his name. She looks up at me. "Have you written him?"

"Sure, last week." She gives me a pointed look and goes back to the package with renewed energy. I imagine what I'd write Trevor. *Hey, Bro: You'd still hate me. We'd still have nothing to talk about. I'm still a virgin. I'll probably be one till I die, just like you said. You're pretty insightful for an asshole. Kill any babies yet?*

"I'm going to my room," I tell her.

"Good."

"Lots to do."

"Uh-huh," she says, rifling through the crap on the table. She's done with me now.

"Maybe contemplate hurting someone. Or myself."

"Uh-huh," she says, and I head for the door.

"Maybe just jack off to internet porn," I mutter under my breath.

"Sleep tight, honey," she calls from behind me.

I lock the door to my room. It smells like unwashed clothes and sweat. Along with the cooking, my mom has stopped doing the laundry, and you have to go through the living room to get to the washer and dryer, which means I'd have to pass the Wall of Trevor. I'd rather wear dirty underwear than pass the Wall of Trevor. Trevor clutching his peewee football trophy. Trevor at Spring Formal. Trevor at junior prom with his hot cheerleader date. There is the occasional school picture of me thrown in. Third grade, before I got contacts. The lenses of my glasses are so thick my eyes bulge behind them. Sixth grade, my blue period, when I decided to stop washing my hair. Trevor and me at my tenth birthday, our only photo together, his arm thrown stiffly around me, his blond hair freshly buzzed for football season. I'm scowling and wrinkling my nose. We aren't even the same species. When good genes go bad.

I once asked Mom why there weren't more pictures of me. *You won't let anyone take pictures of you,* she said. That's true. But, then again, no one really insisted that hard.

I throw my backpack on the floor and turn my iPod to "Cool Blues." I got the iPod for my fourteenth birthday. A week later they came out with one that is half the size. Pretty soon they'll just implant an iPod chip in your wrist, and you won't have to carry around anything at all.

I shove a bunch of crap off the bed and stretch out across the crumpled-up sheets that haven't been changed in a month and probably have bedbugs. Parker plays his saxophone and it drips husky sex sounds, and I imagine Jack Kerouac watching him at Milton's Playhouse in Harlem, drinking single-malt whiskey, his hand squeezing out the rhythm on the cushiony thigh of the chick next to him with torpedo-shaped tits and a tight sweater, knowing in a few hours her bare legs will be over his shoulders. I think about Laurilee's legs over my shoulders and try to imagine her pussy, but since I've never seen one live, all I can picture are the bald slits of chicks on the internet porn-site teasers, which does the job just fine. I open my fly and start to jerk off, then Buddhist Daniel pops into my head. I almost lose it, just like in Hemingway. Then I just blur out Daniel's face in my mind, like how they blur out those hillbillies getting arrested on *Cops*. I picture Laurilee getting fucked by a faceless man. Then I picture her with me. Doing things to me. I picture her doing things to herself for me. I finish the job and groan.

Not bothering to put my dick away, I turn to my nightstand and pick up my copy of *On the Road,* the pages yellowed and dog-eared, full passages underlined. Every coffee shop in America has some asshole trying to score cooter with a yellowed, dog-eared copy of *On the Road*. Only mine is like this because I actually read the book. I did buy it secondhand, but I underlined all the passages myself. I know this book like most of the kids at my school know the MTV show lineup or the pet peeves of those half-retard bitches on *The Hills*. I know just how it looks, another sixteen-year-old, outcast teenage boy obsessed with Kerouac, but I don't care. There is something soothing about these pages I've touched so many times before.

I turn to the scene where Sal, stifled by the ordinariness of his conventional life, sets out with $50 and a plan to follow Route 6 from Cape Cod to Los Angeles. Then he's on a deserted road in the black night, his huaraches drenched, unable to thumb a ride. I wonder what huaraches look like. I wonder where I could get some. I think about how much shit I already get at school without huaraches and change my mind. Sal, undeterred, heads back to New York and hops a bus to Chicago instead, because he's the kind of guy who has the guts to do that, just pick up and take off to start a new life. This is pages before he hitchhikes across America, fucking lots of small-town girls by campfires and sharing bottles of cheap vodka with transients to ward off the cold, ordering homemade pie from gaunt waitresses at highway diners before taking them out to cornfields and fucking them. Getting his dick wet in the American dream.

There is a bus station in downtown Oklahoma City, and I have saved over $800 in cookie-slave money. But I won't take a bus to Chicago, or anywhere else, because I am a pussy. Besides, I'd never see Laurilee again, and she is the only thing that makes my redundant adolescent existence bearable.

Most days I get the Gordita Supreme and two Double Deckers at Taco Bell, but during lunch hour the next day I opt for a bean burrito and the cheesy fiesta potatoes, which are pretty much Tater Tots covered in melted Cheez Whiz. I wonder if a committee of stoners is on payroll to come up with new recipes.

"Risky," says Dingo, who considers himself a Taco Bell connoisseur and peruses the menu like we are at a five-star restaurant.

"I like to shake things up," I say.

"Can I take your order?" says the voice for the second time. We are walking the drive-thru. We stand in front of the intercom.

"I would like a seven-layer burrito, two Enchiritos, a nacho supreme, and fourteen packets of hot sauce—four mild, six fire, and four hot. No, make that four mild, six hot, and four fire." There is a silence on the intercom.

"Eff you guys."

We could go inside, but we like to piss off the mildly retarded, gasoline-huffing Taco Bell employee we call Anus. We stroll around the side of the building.

"This isn't allowed, guys!" he says, sticking his head through the drive-up window as we turn the corner.

"C'mon, man," says Dingo.

"You gotta have a car," Anus slurs through jacked-up teeth. "I told ya guys that already." From behind us, a yuppie in a bloated Hummer bleats at us. He thinks we are just assholes hanging out and bullshitting, not the respectable paying customers we really are.

"C'mon, man," says Dingo, "I thought you were our buddy."

Anus snorts and adjusts his intercom mike. "This is the last time. I effing mean it. You gotta order inside like everyone else." This is the same conversation we've had with him every day of the semester. I think he looks forward to seeing us.

"Thanks, man," says Dingo. "I like your hairnet."

"Eff you," says Anus and pushes our plastic bags through the window.

We head to the park a few blocks from our school. It's usually empty during school hours, besides Homeless Fred, the guy who lives under a bench by the playground. He's wearing a purple windbreaker and his eyes are closed.

"Hey, Fred," says Dingo. He puts a wrapped Enchirito next his head. Without opening his eyes, Fred reaches for it. Dingo is all about community service.

Dingo and I climb the ladder into the hollowed-out concrete rocket ship. The blue paint is faded and chipping. I remember it as being electric cobalt when I was a kid, but then again, you always remember things being brighter. I spent whole days inside, preparing for my lift-off into space, packing and repacking my pretend supplies, checking the air-supply monitors and fuel gauges. I could name several variations of lunar surface material. I knew the chemical composition of the planetary soils and differing crater densities. I could also recite 253 species of dinosaur. I had a lot of extra time after my mom gave up on peewee football.

My mom made me join the peewee league. She was worried about me. I spent too much time reading. She loved books too, she told me, but I needed to be more *socialized*. When I did hang out, it was with Dingo, and everyone knew he was an *odd* boy. Or, as they say in Oklahoma-mom talk, "Bless his little heart. I think he might be *touched*."

I wanted to like peewee football. I wanted to make Mom proud. I tried to stick it out. I spit on the ground like the other boys, poured Dixie cups of cooler water over my face. Once I accidently doused myself in a cup of fruit-punch Gatorade by mistake. I got hell for the rest of practice, not to mention being sticky, but refused to wash off on principle. I tried, I really did. Pretended I knew what the hell everyone was talking about when they described different pass patterns. But after a week of pummelings and Coach Blair telling us, *Pain is just weakness leaving the body* and that our puke was *good for the grass,* I refused to budge from the car even when Trevor, who had just got his license and had other, more important places to go, slammed the steering wheel with his hands and said I *better get the hell outta the backseat. It isn't that hard.*

It was hard. Even when Trevor, at Mom's insistence, tried to teach me to throw and tackle in his painstakingly mowed backyard, I'd end up with bruises or scrapes and run to Mom in tears. I wasn't what Trevor had hoped for. I didn't spend weekends lifting weights in the garage. I scrawled in journals. He had a tutor who wrote term papers for him. He didn't even have to pay the dude. Trevor is the kind of guy you want to do nice things for.

Everyone in the world loves Trevor.

Even worse, you couldn't dismiss him as just another dumb jock. His grades were always good, even without people writing papers for him. He could solve algebra problems in his sleep. Trevor aced English, giving the teachers well-structured essays with precisely written answers. My essays, on the other hand, were always returned with comments like *While I appreciate your creativity, this does not follow the guidelines*. Trevor always followed the guidelines. On the rare occasion he slacked off, the teachers were perfectly willing to overlook his momentary lapse in studiousness, chalking it up to his being busy with practice. Everyone wanted another winning season. Even the teachers wanted to be state champions. Trevor gave them something to discuss over stale coffee in the faculty lounge besides district pay cuts and broken slide projectors and that Mr. Newton, who taught AP History, was rumored to be a pedophile.

At my age, Trevor was already quarterback of the Classen High Knights. He was only a sophomore, so it was a big honor. In Oklahoma, high school football is a religion, and Trevor was practically the pigskin pope. Only, instead of bowing to kiss his ring, everyone just dropped to their knees and sucked his dick instead. Both figuratively and literally, since our cheerleaders were rumored to be the biggest skanks in the division.

Trevor was man enough for both of us. He had trophies in his bedroom. He had more friends than he could count. I had Dingo, the only one who got picked after me in PE class. I still have Dingo, who, at this moment, has taco sauce dripping down his chin. Dingo says my need to read obscure writers and my obsession with travel memoirs stems from my inability to come to terms with the fact that I will never be anything like Trevor. I tell him to shut the hell up and if I wanted shitty psychoanalysis I'd go to the school counselor.

"I gave her a book," I say, and take a bite of my chalupa.

"What book?"

"*Leaves of Grass.*"

"Figures. And how'd that work out for you?" he says sarcastically. Everything Dingo says sounds sarcastic, even when he is being supportive, which isn't often.

"She said I was a sweetheart."

"And then she let you fuck her doggy-style in the mall bathroom?"

"She kissed my cheek," I say.

"You didn't even ask her out?" I look at him. "Of course you didn't," he says, balling up his wrapper and tossing it off the platform toward the garbage can, which he misses.

He leans back and stares up into the rocket funnel, his hands behind his head. "Gotta let this one go, man."

"I can't."

"Yes, you can. A girl like that, Laurilee, she's not in your league." Dingo sees Laurilee when he shows up at my Aunt Betty shift trying to score day-old cookies. "A girl like that is wild. A vixen. She's the kind of chick who'd do crazy shit. She'd be rough, y'know? She'd use her teeth, her nails. Probably try to put a finger up your ass—"

"Shut up, fucker."

"Yeah, well, you're not her type, man."

"How do you know?"

"'Cause you aren't. You gotta be realistic here, man. You aren't even in her hemisphere. You should aim lower. A fat chick, maybe. They like to suck dick. That's what I heard." He laughs, and the sound echoes around us. Dingo has a genius IQ and scored almost perfect on the PSATs, though you wouldn't know it. Even though we are only sophomores, he's already getting letters from Princeton and MIT. "Fat chicks," he says, and cackles.

I lean back and stare up into the funnel with him. My classmates come here at night to get wasted and hook up. The inside has been scrawled on with pens and markers, the backs of pennies and Swiss-army knives. Years' worth of words dissolving into each other. Every day there is fresh writing. Everyone wants to leave a mark.

"It doesn't matter anyway," he says. "Every belief is false."

"Don't start with that—"

"When you finally accept the pointlessness, you'll be a shitload happier." He turns and smiles at me.

"Can you stop with that nihilist bullshit?"

"It's not as bad as that beatnik shit. C'mon, man, I expect more of you. Really. You and every other sixteen-year-old outcast in Shitsville, America, getting a hard-on for Kerouac and then going home to eat his mommy's tuna casserole." He sighs. "Fact is, Laurilee is not gonna fuck you." I hate hearing her name come out of his mouth. "She dates badasses. She's got low self-esteem. It's a form of self-punishment. You're too nice, man. You're, well, you're—"

"A loser."

"Yeah." He picks at a ripe zit on his chin. This one is so big it practically has an area code. *Proactive is the greatest lie in America,* he once told me. *Proactive is a government conspiracy.* "Just wait it out, man. Wait till we graduate and get out of this futile city. Just look at those Google guys. It's all about money. Make a lot of money, you can fuck anyone you want. Anytime. Two at a time. After I make my first million—"

"I'm going to ask her out."

He looks at me, and for just a moment, I think I see something like tenderness in his eyes. Then, just like that, it's gone. He shakes his head. "I wouldn't."

"I got to do something."

"Why?"

"Because I'm in love with her."

"There is no such thing as the institution of love," he says with finality.

"I have to do something," I say again, more to myself than him.

"She's gonna take hold of your guts, pull 'em out, and grind them on the floor with her cute little combat boot. I'm only telling you this because you're my friend."

I take out a cigarette and light it. I blow smoke into the funnel. We stare up in silence.

"Now, if you want a real woman, I should introduce you to some of Felicia's friends. There's this one chick, Destiny, she's Asian, thirty-six–twenty-four–thirty-six, stacked, leather, whip, really into all that shit—"

"No."

"She's a law student, man."

"She's an avatar."

"Nah, man. She goes to UPenn—"

"She's probably some three-hundred-pound, bald dude who lives in a basement in, like, Bulgaria or something. Not to mention Felicia. I don't even want to think about her real identity."

"Felicia is getting her Ph.D. in microbiology."

"I don't date cartoons."

"They aren't cartoons," he says, and pouts.

In the virtual universe, Dingo is hot shit. He is a legend within the Second Life hemisphere. He owns property and his own theme park. He has a fully furnished virtual mansion and hosts a weekly rave and a nihilist meeting society. He looks like an attractive version of himself, with pecs and a swagger. He gets fucked regularly by hot avatar chicks, but Felicia is favorite. *Felicia and I went to Amsterdam last night,* he'll tell me. *We got really messed up on 'shrooms and I ate her out under a waterfall in Rio.* When I ask him how a virtual person gets stoned on virtual hallucinogens, he rolls his eyes at me, as though the answer should be obvious. When I ask him how he can be having an affair with a woman whose real face he has never seen, he tells me I don't understand. *She's incredible. She really gets me. It's not about something as frivolous as a face. It's not even about the sex, though the sex is pretty fucking sick, man.* I want to tell him that rubbing a quick one out while typing *Ooooh, baby* with your other hand isn't exactly sex, but it's not like I've got any credibility. Laurilee may be flesh and blood, but I'm too pussy to accidentally brush her when she's inches away.

Dingo spends seven hours a night online. There are times I wonder if he has mild Asperger's. Still, he's my best friend. He's the only one I've got.

"Come over tonight," he says. "My mom is making cheeseburger meat loaf. I'll show you the museum I'm building. There's some virtual art out there that'll blow your mind—"

"You know I don't like that shit."

"You got something better to do?"

I sigh. He knows the answer.

"No virtual stuff, okay?" he says. "I mean, I really shouldn't take a night off, but it'll be okay. We'll play Halo."

"You sure? Don't want to interfere with your virtual monarchy."

"Yeah, I guess so. I can take a night off." It is the same conversation we have every Friday. I may not have virtual double D's, but even Dingo gets lonely for someone with an actual heartbeat. And it's not like I've got anything better to do.

"Okay," I say with resignation, as though it is a choice. I'd rather clean Porta Pottis on a hot August day than be near the Mothers Support Our Troops Northwest Oklahoma City Chapter during their weekend gift-box extravaganza. Besides, Dingo's Mom is a great cook. She takes white-trash gourmet to the next level. Frito pie, baked chicken smeared in Campbell's mushroom soup. I'm sick of Hungry-Man.

Dingo starts to talk about Halo and his Spartan Bungle armor and the United Nations Space Command, and I lean back and stare into the rocket ship. In fresh ink, someone has written *Doug Shafer got herpes from his mother*.

They spelled my last name wrong.

After fifth period, Ronan Applegate slams me into my locker on his way to gym class. He's so close I can see the tiny hairs growing in his chin and smell his Speed Stick. "Faggot," he says, then lets go of me. Of course I stumble and have to catch my balance on the wall. I turn back to my locker as though nothing has happened. He laughs loudly to himself as he heads to study hall. Nobody pays any attention. This is as regular an occurrence as chicken-fried steak being served in the cafeteria.

Ronan doesn't call me *faggot* because he thinks I'm gay. In the high school lexicon, it is a universal phrase for worthless; a pure waste of human existence. The gay rights people would really get their panties in a wad over that, but it is just a fact. And *faggit* is a pretty accurate description of how Ronan sees me. If my last name wasn't Schaffer, he'd probably ignore me. I'm a loser, but there are far more obvious ones he could fuck with. Johnny Eckhart with his two gay dads. Dylan Driver and his chronic psoriasis. But I've got it worse because my brother was one of the greatest quarterbacks in Classen High history, and I am nobody.

During study hall, Ronan sits in the desk behind me. He aims for the back of my neck with spitballs and chewed gum. Sometimes he'll poke me with sharp objects. *Stop*, I'll mutter, trying to dodge him. *Fucking stop. Dude, did you forget your Adderall? Stop.* We both know he won't stop. We have our routine. Coach Thompson, playing sudoku at his desk and picking his earwax with a pen, pretends not to notice. Or maybe he thinks I deserve it. Ronan is first-string defensive end for the Knights, and I wear black. Ronan is invaluable to the team. Ronan believes that my existence is a mockery to the Schaffer legacy, and Coach probably agrees.

I never fight back because Ronan is over two hundred pounds and rumored to take steroids. He's probably undiagnosed bipolar, too, but he helped lead us to a state trophy so the question of his mental stability is rarely questioned by the administration. His classes are hand-picked by Coach. Even though he isn't book smart like Trevor was, he never gets below a B. When we are having a good season, he makes honor roll. Someday I will kick his ass. I will shoot pepper spray in his eyes and punch him with brass knuckles. I will kick him when he's down, like in a bad gangster movie, and say, *Who's the faggit now, huh?* in front of the whole school while he sobs and begs for mercy, snot dripping down his Neanderthal face. For now, though, it's easier to take the long route to class and just skip study hall.

I skip many of my classes and rarely do the home-work, but always ace the tests and midterms. For this reason, I have no trouble maintaining a C− average. Sometimes I go to class, take a bathroom pass after five minutes, and never return. I don't think my teachers notice. I'm one of those kids nobody will remember at the ten-year reunion, except to ask vaguely, *Is he related to Trevor Schaffer? Man, Trevor Schaffer is a legend.* Or maybe I'll pull up in a limo with two Playboy bunnies like Hef and they'll say, *Who is that guy? Why didn't hang out with him more often?* Then I'll take home whoever was crowned homecoming queen and fuck her in a way her stockbro-ker husband is incapable of doing and make her fall in love with me. *Where were you senior year?* she'll say, after I have masterfully eaten her out. *I was there the whole time, baby,* I'll tell her. *You just weren't looking hard enough.* She'll smile. *It's been so long since I was with a real man. My husband doesn't even look at me anymore,* she'll say. *Pale pink,* I'll tell her, lighting a cigarette. *Pale pink?* she'll repeat, still flushed with the satisfaction of my having given her seven orgasms in a row. *The color of your toenails,* I'll say. *The same shade as the inside of a seashell I once found outside my beach house in Tahiti.*

I elaborate on this fantasy as I head to the football field. I'm not sure how you eat someone out, but I figure it can't be that hard. Dingo's theory is that you just *pretend it is your last meal on earth. Lick anything that sticks out.* I tell him that his extensive background in computer-generated muff diving in no way makes him an authority on real, live pussy.

I make sure to turn away when I'm passing the glass case that contains our one state championship trophy and Trevor's Most Valuable Player plaque. Trophies are plebeian. Unless they are Pulitzer Prizes or Academy Awards, and even then it is debatable. Big fucking deal. So you are the most valuable player on some stupid second-tier high school football team in some stupid second-tier state. Big fucking hoo-ha. I remind myself that the world is a big place. One day I will go to Europe like Fitzgerald and Zelda. I will sip espresso at a café and write profound insights in my journal. I will fuck Parisian girls who think my American accent is adorable. I will write them poetry, and they will translate it to French and recite my own words back to me when we are fucking, and I won't know what they are saying, but it will sound amazing coming out of their little French mouth. *You are a genius,* they will tell me. *You must meet my friend Antoinetta. She will adore you as well.*

"Schaffer," says a voice from behind me. Ronan, I think. I once googled bear attacks, thinking Ronan has about the same level of brain function. *Tip one: remain calm and avoid sudden movements.* But that doesn't work. The moment I am in the vicinity of Ronan, every muscle in my body tenses; I breathe faster and get dizzy. *Move away slowly while avoiding eye contact and speak to the bear in a low voice.* I start to walk down the hallway in slow, measured steps. "Hey, Schaffer!" he says. *Running will trigger the bear's chase response and you are incapable of outrunning a bear.* I get ready to sprint. "Doug, right? Doug Schaffer? That's your name, isn't it?"

I turn around. Mr. Prescott, the new college guidance counselor, is looking at me. He's got a bag of McDonald's in one hand, his briefcase in the other. I'm surprised he knows who I am.

"Yeah," I say.

"Shouldn't you be in class?"

"I was on my way."

We stare at each other. When they introduced him at the first assembly of the year, he looked all eager beaver, straight out of teaching school, ready to enrich the life of America's future leaders with his wisdom. He's the kind of teacher who tries to *speak our language.* He's *down with our needs.* His hair was combed down in a shiny helmet. *Kinda sexy,* I heard a girl next to me whisper to her friend.

"My door is always open to you," he'd said into the microphone. *I'm so there*, she'd said, and they'd giggled. Now, only a month later, he's morphed into a completely different person. He looks pretty rough. Both his face and hair have gone gray, and he's grown a beer belly. Now he looks like a real public-school employee.

"Doug Schaffer, right?"

"Yup."

"You haven't been in for precollege counseling."

I internally wince. With five hundred kids in my class, I didn't think anyone would notice.

"Yeah, well, I'm only a sophomore."

"You need to get started. You'll be surprised how quickly the applications—"

"Yeah. I've been meaning to get around to that. Well, I better get to—"

"You did very well on your PSATs. I looked you up after I got the results. The highest English score in your class. You could probably get advanced placement in college. Have you thought about colleges?"

"Sure," I say, looking down at my Converses. "I was thinking, like, Ivy League. Princeton, maybe."

"Oh. Well. If I remember correctly, your grades aren't quite up to—"

"I was kidding. I better get to class."

"If you're serious about that, we really need to talk about getting your GPA up to par."

I pretend Prescott is the bear. I back up slowly, avoiding eye contact. His McDonald's bag swings from his hand. I wonder what he ordered. "You better eat that or it will get cold. McDonald's sucks when it's cold."

"Just come in and see me."

"Okay."

He shakes his head. I guess I don't sound enthusiastic. "Don't you want to go to college, Doug? Don't you want to do something with your life?" His runs his hands through his messy hair. "You need college to succeed." It's like he's reciting some sort of guidance-counselor pamphlet.

"Sure. Yeah."

"Don't you want to live up to your potential?" he says, but his eyes have gone vacant. I could be anyone. Any kid who skipped his mandatory pre-pre-college counseling session and doesn't appreciate the gift of higher education.

"Yeah, of course."

"You don't sound very interested."

"I don't know, Mr. Prescott. I'm still considering my options. I might not go to college."

"Options? What kind of job can you get without a college degree? Really, Doug. With scores like that, it's obvious you are capable of more." I can practically hear the bad ABC family-programming instrumental rising behind him. It really pisses me off. "Don't you agree?" I wish he'd shut the hell up. He knows nothing about the real world.

"College is a cesspool of academic elitism," I mutter.

"What was that?"

I look him in the eyes. "College," I say firmly, "is a

cesspool of academic elitism. It's the fast track to a life-time of mediocrity."

"Is that so?"

"Yup. Sorry, Mr. Prescott. Not to dis your career choice, but that's how I see it. I really appreciate your interest, but I prefer to avoid the trappings of the bourgeois."

"Is that so?" he says again, flustered. I nod. Two red spots have bloomed in the middle of his gray cheeks. "Oh, really, Doug. I see. Well, obviously you have intelligence. And what do you expect to do with that when you graduate, if you don't mind me asking? Be a sandwich artist at Subway?"

"The Aunt Betty Corporation," I mutter. "Much more opportunity for advancement."

"Well, if you ever intend to do something with your life, my door is—"

"I might go somewhere. Europe or something."

"Well, some colleges have exchange programs."

"You don't get it," I say, frustrated. "I'm just not college material." I know I'm right. I don't have the grades to go out of state, and I don't plan on trying for them. My only options are in-state colleges, which would just be an extension of high school. Something like 90 percent of OU students are in fraternities or sororities. And even if I did pledge one of the loser houses, and they actually wanted me, no fucking way I'm gonna let them haze me. I won't fuck a sheep just for the opportunity to live in a glorified dorm with other outcasts for four more years. Prescott stares at me with pity. I wish his eyes would shut the fuck up. "College is pointless," I say with finality. He shakes his head and sighs, defeated.

He used to come to school early to work out in the football weight room. I'd be there early to avoid Ronan, who often stakes out my locker before first period to get in his early-morning quota of harassment. I'd smoke cigarettes in the alley by the athletics storage room. I'd watch Prescott emerge from the gym into the deserted parking lot, Nike duffel slung over his shoulder, his face glowing. Ready to change the public educational system one lost soul at a time. Poor fucking tool, I'd think, blowing a mixture of smoke and my own frozen breath into the morning air. That was a long time ago. I haven't seen him there in a long time.

"Well then. I suppose, if we were to follow your line of thinking, a job like mine serves no purpose, does it?" We stare at each other. Maybe he sees the answer in my face. "Well, if you change your mind, my door is open to you."

"Good to know. Guidance counselor. Door. Open to me. Got it."

Prescott stares at me with distaste. He shakes his head, like I am just another example of the education system gone to shit, the future of America gone to hell, the government and economy and environment all imploding because of guys like me who don't care enough to go to pre-precollege counseling. Then he smirks.

"Hey," he says, his voice suddenly calm and collected, the red spots faded. "You aren't related to Trevor Schaffer,

are you? The quarterback? Damn. That kid is a legend."
He doesn't let me answer. He gives me a wry grin and
turns on his scuffed loafers. He walks down the hallway
toward the faculty lounge, whistling, his McDonald's bag
swinging with each step. *Enjoy your lunch,* I want to yell
after him. *Cold Big Macs suck ass.*

I go to the grass beneath the bleachers. It's one of those
weird days, sunny and cold, and I'm glad I have my parka.
The light comes through the slats in bright stripes on the
grass, and I settle in one of the dark gaps. I like how the
autumn air stings the insides of my nostrils.

I take out my copy of *Dharma Bums* and skip to the
last section. Ray Smith, having triumphantly reached the
top of Desolation Peak, is euphoric. He will live in a hum-
ble cabin, with the mountain as his companion. He will
relish the isolation. No one will be there to criticize him,
call him a faggot, or flick sharp objects at the back of his
neck. No one would do that because he's a real man, and
things like football trophies and algebra quizzes are inconsequential here. He is a man, and this is his mountain.
I close my eyes for a second and imagine my own cabin,
only Laurilee is there too. I shoot a deer for fresh meat
because in this fantasy I'm the kind of guy who shoots
things without wincing, and she makes us stew. I know
how to use a gun, get maple from a tree, light a fire with
two sticks. I wear a red flannel shirt, just like Kerouac, and
I'm ripped. Laurilee fucks me on a bearskin rug, strad-

dling me, leaning forward, her small, silken breasts resting on each side of my face. She smells faintly of sugar cookies. She says, *Oh, Doug,* and moans, her eyes rolling back.

I sit up because the moan is real. I crawl a few feet under the bleachers, wondering if I've finally gone over the edge and am hearing things. Wondering if I can diagnose my own schizophrenia on WebMD, I duck under the lowest riser and look to my left. A way down, a dark shape is falling and rising beneath a coat. A streak of light slants across a scrunched eye, the tip of a nose, a scowl. I know who it is right away. Peter Wilkenson, his teeth clenched, jackhammers into some girl. She could be any girl because he is Peter Wilkenson, and since he got back from rehab, the girls love him like flies love shit. He swaggers down the hall with new muscles, his eyes heavy-lidded, glaring at something the rest of us can't make out. He knows something we don't. He's seen the world, and it's gross and messy, and the girls all line up for the opportunity to fuck his pain away.

The girl squeaks like a hungry kitten as he pounds into her. She can't be enjoying it. She can't be wet. In *Dharma Bums,* Japhy Ryder teaches Ray Smith the Tibetan art of *yab-yum*—he sits in lotus position while a girl named Princess straddles his lap. They sit there for hours. They are seeking enlightenment. Peter Wilkenson is looking for a warm place to splooge. If I had Laurilee, I wouldn't fuck her under bleachers. I'd spend months running my hand over her body, licking every part of her. I'd climb inside her pussy and take up residence. But she is a fantasy, and

Peter Wilkenson is getting his sword sharpened with a live, breathing girl. The world is a really twisted place.

I check my watch. I pick up my backpack. I want to keep watching, but I only have a few minutes to make Chemistry and will have to take the long way to avoid Ronan. I have my priorities.

CHAPTER TWO

"I'm going on break in fifteen," I tell Roger, who hovers behind me while I roll the peanut-butter-chip-and-oatmeal dough, marking on his clipboard.

"How are we doing on cake orders for next week?"

"Six, same as when you asked me an hour ago."

"We really need to get those orders up, dude," he says, adjusting the collar of his button-up pink shirt. It's in style for guys to wear pink shirts, but I still think it looks gay.

"What do you want me to do? Walk around and ask shoppers if they want to order a cookie cake? Pimp cookie cakes outside Dillard's?"

"You're being funny, right?"

"Yeah." I sigh. "Isn't it your day off?"

"Yes."

"Why are you here?"

"Initiative, dude. You have to be proactive in the business world. By the way, have you thought about what we talked about?"

"No." I never listen when Roger talks. His voice is white noise. Television static.

"Well, I really think you should consider it, dude. The thing is, and I've done some research on this so I'm not pulling it out of my butt, y'know? Black is a nonverbal indicator of lackluster receptivity towards the clients."

"So?"

"You wear a lot of black."

"There isn't any rule about it," I say, taking off my latex gloves and filling a Styrofoam cup with Coke. I lean against the counter and drink. Roger watches me, trying to decide whether to pursue the issue of my wardrobe or move on to the moral repercussions of illicit soda intake by employees.

"I know there isn't a dress code, per se," he says, still eyeing the drink. He'll probably just deduct it from my paycheck. "But it is about the image you want to portray to the clientele."

"I don't think they care, Roger."

"But they do, dude! I mean, maybe it's on a subconscious level, but it has a direct impact on how much they buy. For instance, navy and gold create a sense of camaraderie and trust." He gestures to his blue-and-yellow tie.

"Yeah, and they look really fucking great with a pink shirt."

He shakes his head. He looks sad. For a minute I feel sorry for him. Roger believes in his work. Roger believes his mall managerial position with the Aunt Betty's Cookie Corporation, which he was promoted to right after high school graduation, is putting him on the fast track to a position in the home office and, after four or five years of kissing ass, a high-level rank and spot on the board of directors. He's memorized the two-hundred-page Aunt Betty's customer-service manifesto, or *Mein Cookie Kampf* as I call it, and recites key passages at length when lecturing employees on proper workplace sanitation, customer relations, and which directions the napkins in the dispenser should be facing.

"Sorry," I say, because he looks so defeated. Roger believes in Aunt Betty's the way I believe in Laurilee, and we all need a reason to wake up in the morning.

"You got so much potential, dude."

"Thanks," I say.

"I mean, you're a smart guy. You could have a lucrative future in the food-service industry if you showed a little drive." I fight the urge to roll my eyes. First Mr. Prescott and now Roger. They can both take all my so-called fucking *potential* and shove it up their fucking asses. I crack my neck and wipe excess crumbs and peanut chips onto the floor. Roger watches them fall.

"Roger?"

Roger lifts his chin to look at me intently. I wonder

if he practices intimate and meaningful eye contact in his bathroom mirror. I wonder if he recites the table of contents of the *Mein Cookie Kampf* while he jacks off. He smiles at me with confidence and warmth. He smiles like a man who knows what the hell he wants out of life.

"Yeah, Doug?" he says, his eyes glassy with faith in me.

"I'm gonna go on break now."

A large black woman is holding two banana clips up to Laurilee and saying something, and Laurilee nods, takes one, and opens and closes it like a giant mouth. She spots me outside the window, leaning against the rail by a fake potted plant that is for some reason, planted in real dirt. Her eyes widen and she grins. Instantly, my body throbs, my pulse quickens, my dick tingles. She is an injection of adrenaline; when she smiles at me, it is like being submerged in ice water. For that moment, nothing in the world sucks. She holds up two fingers and cocks her head toward the parking lot, then goes back to the black woman and the clip.

By the Dumpster I pace and smoke a cigarette. I thump on the side of the Dumpster and the sound echoes against the concrete walls. I wish I could play the drums. If I could play the drums, I could be in a band. Girls love that shit. Or maybe the guitar. Yeah, it's gotta be the guitar. Like that old joke, *What do you call someone who hangs around a band? A drummer.* No one fucks the drummer. I'll play the bass. I can't sing for shit, but then again, neither can Bob Dylan. But he's Bob Dylan, and I am Doug Schaffer. For the millionth time, I wish I had talent. I feel something cold on the back of my neck and jump.

"Hiya," says Laurilee.

"Your hand is cold," I tell her, wishing she'd touch me again. Just for a second.

"Told ya I was a vampire," she says, taking a half-smoked cigarette out of her pack. I light it for her, and my hand shakes.

"You need a coat," I say. We lean against the wall. She is wearing tights. She has leg warmers she made from cutting off the ends of her jeans. Her T-shirt is riding up on her belly, and I try not to stare at the edges of her sharp, white hip bones. *Fuck muscles,* Dingo calls them.

"I feel like this shift will never end. We got in a new shipment. If I have to stock one more scrunchie, I might just hang myself with it."

"Can you actually hang yourself with a scrunchie?" I ask.

"Well, they do it with shoelaces in prison all the time. I'll bet I could. I'm pretty crafty. Anyway. How about you?"

"Roger came in today. He's not even scheduled. Just to hang out."

"Poor Roger." She laughs. "We talked once, did I ever tell you that?"

"No," I say with a pang of jealousy.

"At the manager Christmas party last year. I don't know why I went. I snuck in some whiskey, put it in my eggnog. I was pretty trashed. He kept talking to me about Aunt Betty. I think he was trying to flirt."

"What a fucking tool." My voice sounds hoarse and angry, so I laugh, which makes me sound like a twelve-year-old whose voice is breaking. "What did you do?"

She smiles and dips her head down. She gives me a sexy look from under her lashes. "I said, 'I really, really love cookies, Roger. Especially those really, really ginormous ones you guys sell. I like to lick the icing off first.'" Her voice is husky and seductive. I'm instantly hard. She turns away, laughing, and sucks on her cigarette. She always chews the end, like she's going to suck some nutrition out of the filter. It's the hottest shit I've ever seen. I try to play it cool. I try not to stare at her lips.

"And what did he say?"

"He thought I was serious. He started talking about cookies. I swear to God. He named all the kinds you sell. Maybe he thought it would impress me."

"Did he tell you all twenty-seven varieties?" I ask, relieved.

"Pretty much." She giggles. I light another cigarette. "I read some of that book you gave me."

"Did you like it?"

"Yeah, I did. I googled him too. He's got balls, that guy. I mean, kind of perverted, but sexy too. Hey, do I have a booger?" She tilts her head upward. I look into the dark hollows of her nostrils and wish I had the guts to kiss her. I can check the inside of her nose for mucus, but I don't have the sacs to touch her lips to my own.

"I think you're clean," I say.

"Speaking of clean, I heard a rumor Trinkets was going to start drug testing. If they knew all the shit in my system, they'd confiscate my piercing gun."

"I didn't mean to, like, imply anything or—"

"I know what you mean, kid." She giggles. "Whitman wouldn't care, would he? He'd tell Trinkets to fuck off and go roll in the grass, right? He wouldn't put up with that crapola. He wasn't a scaredy-cat."

"Neither are you." I look at her, leaning against the wall, smoking. I am awed by her. She is perfect, from her sharp, tiny teeth to the tips of her combat boots. I want to fuck her until she can't see straight. But it wouldn't be like that at first. I know. I'd come quick my first time. That's what happens in the movies. I'd come quick, but it would be okay, because then I'd be calm. I could take my time. Spend eternity with my hands on her body. Laurilee's body. I'd read her like a map. I'd find all her cities, every single one. Discover entire universes behind each knobby knee. I'd tell her she is beautiful and sink into her like quicksand.

"I'm afraid of everything, kid," she says quietly.

"Nah. No way. Afraid? Afraid of what?"

She shakes her head, grins, and looks across the parking lot. Her eyes are sad. "The girls at my school who wear too much lip gloss. Their big, shiny lips scare me." Laurilee never talks about her school. I know she goes to Heritage Academy across town. It has gates on every side and the parking lot is full of BMWs. I can't imagine her there. "And their big white teeth. They look like Chiclets. Sometimes, when they laugh, it looks like they are about to eat you." She lights another cigarette and chews the end. Something is different today. We usually talk about work, Terrance, mall bullshit. Laurilee's eyes are glassy. It occurs to me she might be fucked-up. If she's fucked-up, she might let me kiss her. Or is that a form of rape? Maybe she wants me to kiss her, and this is my chance, right now, when her defenses are down. I inch a little closer. I don't say anything. I don't want to break the spell. I want Laurilee to tell me everything that has ever mattered to her, and then I want to kiss her until her lips bleed.

"My mom is an attorney. Did I ever tell you that?"

"No." In my mind, Laurilee doesn't have parents. She sprung fully formed from the head of Zeus. She is an island, a haiku. She stands alone.

"She makes lists, kid. Lots of them. On Post-its. She puts them everywhere, I swear to God. On the fridge, by the washing machine. She puts them on my bedroom door. *Change your sheets. Take laundry out of machine. Casserole.* Just the word: *casserole.* That's a funny word, isn't it?"

"Casserole," I say, and she laughs. We are closer than we've ever been. I am inches from her face. She doesn't move away. I know our break has ended, but I want her to keep talking.

"She left a Post-it on the kitchen table yesterday. You know what it said?"

"What?"

"*Make to-do list.*" Laurilee shakes her head.

For a moment, we are silent. No one else exists. Just me and Laurilee in our cocoon of Camel smoke behind the Dumpster.

"I'll tell you what, soon as I graduate, I'm getting the hell outta Dodge, boy."

"Where will you go?" I say.

"I'm not sure. I heard Montana is nice."

"We could get in a car and just take off. Like Kerouac did. We could go anywhere. 'My witness is the empty sky.' That's what he said."

"'My witness is the empty sky.'"

"We could go to Mexico," I say, getting excited. "We could do it. We could take off. Who's stopping us?"

"I like tequila. But we need a car. You don't have one, and mine is a piece of shit. We won't make it past the Panhandle."

"I'll find one. I'll steal it if I have to. We can make it happen. We can." She smiles. She looks tired. The skin under her eyes is translucent, the greenish blue shade of a healing bruise. "You said you wanted to do something drastic, right?"

"Yeah, I guess I did," she says, almost to herself. She looks at me for a moment, like I'm someone she's doesn't quite remember, someone she can almost place. "You know what? You're really easy to talk to. Sometimes I think you're the only one who actually listens to me, Doug."

We look at each other. *Do it,* I tell myself. *Do it, you pussy. You faggot. Do something. Do something right now.*

"We should hang out more," I say. "I mean, I could

take you somewhere. I could, I don't know. I could buy you a steak. A big-ass, juicy one. I mean, I could take you out sometime. Like a date."

There is a long silence. My pulse is pounding in my ears. I said *date*. I said *date* to Laurilee. I asked her out. I think that's what I did. But she isn't answering. She's chewing her cigarette. She's scrunching her eyebrows together and looking at the ground.

Someone honks in the parking lot.

She stubs out her cigarette on the Dumpster.

"I wish you hadn't done that," she says, so quietly I can barely hear her. She drops her half-smoked cigarette to the ground, not bothering to put it back in the pack for later. She crushes it under her sneaker, grinding it into the ground. She steps toward me. She puts a hand on my cheek. She doesn't look at me. Her hand is warm now, her palm harder than I expected, callused.

"You're too good for me, kid. Way too good." She drops her hand, and there is empty space where it was. Just cold Oklahoma air. "We better get back," she says, still not looking at me. "I got scrunchies to stock."

Roger is waiting for me, his hand on his hip. He is glaring at his watch. "That was a forty-minute break. I had to ring up eight customers, which is really not my job, dude."

We stare at each other. I can see Roger's future, graphed out like one of his Aunt Betty's Corporation improvement charts, the ones he does for fun on Microsoft Excel. Home in the suburbs, job security, a vapid yet satisfactory wife, yearly trips to resorts in the Bahamas where you never have to interact with actual locals. Golf clubs, blow jobs on his birthday. I know what he's seeing. I am empty space. A black hole. And he's right. I will never go on the road. I will never write like Kerouac. I will be stuck in the rocket ship with Dingo for eternity, waiting for something to happen, staring at the words *Doug Shafer got herpes from his mother*. I take off my apron and drop it on the shiny floor. Roger's had his way with the mop.

"I'm going home," I tell him.

"You still got two hours on your shift."

"I don't care."

"You sick?"

"Nope," I say.

"This is completely inappropriate behavior, dude. No one else is scheduled. I expect more of you." He tugs at his hideous tie. He is the only manager in the mall who wears a tie. "Look, I really don't want to have to fire you."

I snort. "You won't."

"Why shouldn't I?"

"Because only a retard or parolee would take a shit job like this for six twenty-five an hour."

"Is this about pay?" says Roger from behind me. I'm already headed for the escalator. The Musak version of "Like a Rolling Stone" is playing, and I fight my way through preteens killing time after school, housewives on the lookout for sales racks, mall walkers pumping their fists in the air as they stride by, white-trash children with chocolate stains like caked shit circling their mouth. I'm no different from them. I like to pretend I am too smart for this southwest suburban hell-division life, that somewhere else I'd be appreciated for my deep insight and intellect, but I've been fooling myself. I am just another kid in another mall with ripped jeans and doodles on his Converses and sad little jack-off fantasies about a girl who would never really consider him other than as a smoke-break time killer.

I try not to look, but I can't help but glance through the window of Trinkets as I'm going down the escalator. Laurilee attaches a fake blond ponytail to the back of a little girl's head in front of the full-length mirror. The little girl is wearing a pink sweatshirt that says PORN STAR in silver sparkles. They are laughing. Their reflections laugh right back at them.

When I get home, I go straight down the hall to my room. I lock the door behind me. I think about what kind of music would be most appropriate for this occasion. The sound track to my humiliation. I put on Lou Reed's *Berlin*. I read somewhere it is considered the most depressing album ever written. I stretch out across my bed and acquiesce to my mediocrity. I think about crying, but tears don't come. For the fifty-millionth time I think about slitting my wrists in the bathtub or downing a bottle of peroxide, though I know I'd never do it. Not really.

Once last year, Ronan Applegate had the audacity to

throw me against the locker and give me a wedgie, because he doesn't even have enough creativity to think of something he hadn't seen in a teen flick. Everyone in the hallway laughed like it was goddamn *Showtime at the Apollo* amateur night and I was the white guy trying to rap. After school, I went so far as to look under our kitchen cabinet for some bleach to drink, not that I'd actually do it, but still. All I could find was liquid Cascade, and I couldn't see myself with my head thrown back, squirting the green liquid down my throat.

Besides, suicide is way too cliché. The kids at school would say they saw it coming or play depressed enough to get out of class and see the grief counselor the school district keeps on staff in case of lonely, outcast suicides. There would be a full-page memorial in the high school yearbook with my eyes-half-closed class picture and student quotes about how *I really wish I'd gotten to know him better.* Unless, of course, someone more attractive died in a drunk-driving accident, then I'd only get half a page, and probably the bottom half. It wouldn't make a dent on the world. Dingo would be sad for a while, but then he'd have more time to build his online empire. My mom would be upset, but she'd get over it. She'd still have Trevor.

I roll over and stare at my mother's abstract painting. I think I see something in the thick black splatters. Hopelessness, that's what it is. It was there all the time. I was delusional to think a girl like Laurilee would even consider me. I've seen the guys she goes out with. They pick her up when the mall is closing, wait outside Trinkets with their hands deep in the pockets of their baggy pants. They have tattoos and weird configurations of facial hair, like a shaved line from their sideburns to chin, or a small, gay-looking patch of fuzz under their chins. *A flavor saver,* Dingo calls it. They stand there, too good for the mall, too good for Oklahoma, with *Fuck you* in their eyes. This is the Okie caste system. These are the possibilities: you can be like Laurilee's boyfriends or Peter Wilkenson out of rehab, one of those guys who strides the hallway untouchable in his angst, not giving a fuck what anyone thinks. Or aim to be Trevor, golden and beloved. Then there are the rest of us, just filling space, like an extra in the movie of our lives.

I sit on the edge of the bed. I stand up and take off my clothes. They smell faintly of raw dough and flour. I kick a pile of clothes out of the way and take the wet towel off my mirror. The room is dark, my body half lit up by the artificial orange glow of my halogen lamp. I look at myself like a specimen, as though I were in a museum behind glass. AVERAGE AMERICAN TEENAGER, the plaque would say. CIRCA 2IST CENTURY.

I'm skinny. In this light, my ribs stick out like a Holocaust victim's in a film reel, my stomach bathed in darkness. My skin is pale, my legs scrawny. My face isn't bad or good, just ordinary. Flaccid, my penis is the same length as the average American male's. I know because I looked it up on the internet and measured it with my geometry ruler. I'm not ugly or pretty. Physically, I don't look that much different from the guys that pick Laurilee up. Not as built, maybe, but it's hard to tell with their clothes on.

I run my hand across my belly and chest. Last month I counted forty-eight chest hairs. At least they are all in one place and haven't migrated to my back. I squeeze my biceps, which isn't much, and tighten my calves. I turn around and examine my ass. It's pretty fucking white, but not much different from any other asses I've seen in the shower after gym class. Not that I was looking on purpose, but sometimes you can't help it.

Before Peter Wilkenson went to rehab, no one knew his name. He might have been in my English class, but I'm not sure. Now he gets snatch beneath the bleachers during sixth period.

I look at my average body, my average face, my average existence. For the first time, it occurs to me that maybe it is a choice.

The plan just pops in my head. At first it seems silly, implausible. I make a hypothesis, just like we did for freshman science fair, only this time I am not proving Pavlov's theory with goldfish and a flashlight. I am the experiment.

If Laurilee only fucks guys with reputations, and Doug Schaffer develops a reputation, then Laurilee will surely fuck him.

The question is, how do I get a reputation? I could be one of those guys who is always looking for a fight, but I'd probably get my ass kicked and end up in the hospital with multiple stitches. I could get a gun and rob a liquor store, but then I'd go to juvie or jail and get raped or end up someone's bitch. I've seen reruns of *Oz*, I know how that one works out. I can't impress people with a badass car because I don't have money for insurance, let alone the car itself. I can't throw wicked underground parties because no one besides Dingo would come. I can't become a DJ because I don't have the equipment and I hate that fucking bullshit mix crap anyway. Unless I want to pull a Virginia Tech, there aren't any options. For a moment, I understand those Columbine guys. At least someone noticed. At least someone gave a damn.

I think about Peter Wilkenson. All it took was rehab.

The plan comes to me in a fury. At first it seems impossible, but the more I pace the room and think about it, the more perfect it sounds. It makes sense. I put on Nine Inch Nails, which are just having a comeback at my school. I like them despite that, and they seem like the right choice. I have a plan. It's crazy, but at the same time it makes more sense than anything else has in as long as I can remember.

Jack Kerouac was just a poor kid from provincial Lowell, Massachusetts, with an alcoholic father and an overbearing mother. Even though he was brilliant, most people saw him a shy kid who pretty much kept to himself, his face in a book. He could play football, but he hated it. In college he failed chemistry and skipped classes to read novels. He got drafted into the navy, but was put under psychiatric evaluation because he lacked discipline and was later discharged. He wrote *On the Road* in three weeks while fucked-up on pot and bennies.

The average American would have considered him a loser. Now he's a legend.

I think about Jack while I surf the net and make notes. I tell my mom through the door that I have indigestion and don't want a Hungry-Man. I smoke three packs of cigarettes, making sure to blow out the window and put a wet towel against the doorframe. I never put on my clothes. I jack off to the teaser videos on porn sites to help my focus, take two No-Doz, make an outline, chew off my nails, and, for the first time in as long as I can remember, feel a flicker of what I figure must be hope.

By dawn I know the eleven most commonly abused drugs and many of their variants. I know that cannabis is the easiest to get, but, in the end, it wouldn't make a significant statement. One in three Americans over the age of twelve has tried marijuana, and there isn't substantial evidence that it is physically or psychologically addictive. In other words, any kid with twenty bucks can smoke a blunt behind the 7-Eleven, gorge himself on Honey Smacks, and pass out on a couch somewhere.

For a while, cocaine seems like a viable option. The high gives you confidence, and the withdrawal isn't as dramatic as with heroin or opiates. I imagine myself chain-smoking after a four-day coke binge, my face drawn, my clothes sweat-stained, my hair greasy and disheveled like that of those guys in the cologne ads. But coke is hard to come by in a place like Oklahoma, and even if I aim for a low purity level, I couldn't afford many lines with my cookie money.

I consider prescription drugs like OxyContin. First I'd have to injure myself to get the prescription, break my arm by slamming it in the car door or something, but knowing me I'd just get a sprain. Besides, it's hard to imagine getting any street cred for being a pill popper. Pills are for bored housewives. There's nothing rebellious about jacking bottles from some old lady's medicine cabinet.

Ecstasy is too clubby, and I'm not sure anyone does it anymore, and heroin would be trying too hard. I picture a skinny white boy like myself going down to Martin Luther King Boulevard and trying to score some crack and mark that off my list immediately. I don't want to end up the drugged-out honky tool to a badass Bloods dealer, running his errands in South Oklahoma City and sucking dick at the downtown Greyhound station for my next fix.

In the end, every possibility is crossed out except one.

Meth is cheap. You can get a quarter gram for around thirty bucks, and Oklahoma is one of the biggest markets in the country. Anyone can make it. Cooks whip up batches in their basement with Sudafed, fuel, Kitty Litter, and the strike pads of matchbooks. It's one of the most addictive drugs, so I'll get dependent quick.

I know it does some nasty shit to your body. I try not to think too much about that. I won't be on it that long, anyway, just long enough to get sent away and cleaned up. I'm different from the average user. I have a plan.

The only thing that freaks me out is that it makes you ugly. Your skin gets messed up with sores and you lose a lot of weight. But I figure my face will clear up in rehab after they put me through a medical detox. They'll probably have gym equipment. I'll go on a strict weight-lifting regimen. I'll eat lots of protein. I'll come back in thirty to sixty days well rested, cut, maybe even with a tan. It will be like an extralong spring break. When I walk down the hall at school, everyone will really see me for the first time. They'll be shocked by how they underestimated me. Lots of girls will want me, but I'll only want Laurilee. I might even take her to Spring Formal.

Laurilee will be the most surprised of all. She'll hold my hand and stare at me with awe. She'll say, *I had no idea. Are you okay? How was it?* I'll tell her, *There's a lot of bullshit that goes down in rehab, a lot of meetings and time-consuming crap to keep you from using. Here,* I'll say gruffly, and hand her a bracelet with her initials I made in Art Therapy. *I never stopped thinking about you.*

When my mom knocks on the door in the morning, I pretend to be sick. She puts her hand on my forehead. "You do feel warm. Let me tuck you in." She pretends not to be disgusted by the state of my room and doesn't even mention the mix of stale cigarette smoke and the Febreze I used to disguise it. I'm sure she knows I smoke, and she knows that I know that she knows, but we never mention it. It's the same way they run the government.

"Honey, I know I've been busy lately. We haven't really had time to talk."

"It's just a cold, Mom."

"Okay, honey." Before Trevor left, she might have tried a little harder. She might have asked about school, or Dingo, or how my job was going. I wouldn't have said much, I never did, but I liked that she asked. Now she looks preoccupied, and I know it has more to do with packing tape than me.

She leans over me in her flannel nightgown. She smells most like herself right now, in the morning. For a moment I want to nestle my head against her breasts, like when I was a kid and had a bad dream. It was enough then, the feel of the fabric against my cheek, her voice rough with sleep telling me everything would be fine, just to close my eyes and think of something nice. I used to believe her. When she told me I was special and unique, a gift to the world. But that's just the crap all parents are required to tell their kids. Then one day you wake up to truth: Of course you think I'm extraordinary. I came out of your womb. But to the rest of the world I'm television static, a lost golf ball, the crusts you cut off a sandwich.

"I think I have the flu," I say, and give a fake cough, which tastes like coffee and three packs of Camels Lights and leads to a real round of hacking, which is cool because it adds authenticity.

"Okay, honey," she says, rubbing my back until the noise subsides. "Just rest, then."

For an instant, I feel like a horrible person. She's suffered enough, with a son in Iraq, and now she's going to have a drug addict to top it off. She'll probably have to take out a second mortgage to send me to rehab, unless insurance covers my stay. I forgot to check on that, but it's too late now.

"I think we have some soup in the cabinet. Chicken and stars. You like that. You just have to heat it up," she says, before she closes the door. I did like chicken and stars. When I was six.

"Thanks," I say.

Maybe she can start a Mothers of Addicts group.

CHAPTER THREE

I call Roger and tell him I won't be coming in after school. As much as I could give a fuck about Aunt Betty's, I'm the only one scheduled, and if Roger gets fired, I'll feel pretty guilty for fucking up his life agenda.

"Dude, this is completely unacceptable. Listen, I've been thinking about our conversation, and I'm worried about your well-being. Is there anything you need to talk about? I know stuff happens. Life isn't easy." I imagine him flipping frantically through *Mein Cookie Kampf* for the chapter on employer/employee interpersonal relations. "Tell me how you feel."

"I just need a couple of days off."

"Can you give me a reason why?"

"Nope."

Roger is silent, probably scanning the page for an affirmative yet sympathetic response that will open a dialogue to further reinforce workplace camaraderie.

"I'm not sure how to tell you this, Roger. This is really hard. Let's just say . . . I'm having an identity crisis."

There is a long pause. "Okay, dude," says Roger, his voice cracking. "I'll mark off your shifts for the rest of the week."

I find Mitchell Dwight Thompson III in the phone book. Instead of loaning me his car, Trevor sold it before basic, because that's the kind of guy he is. I have to take two transfers on the bus and walk four miles. Mitch lives in one of those subdivisions that have sprouted in the farmland past Quail Springs Mall. You have to be pretty loaded to afford one of the huge-ass houses, but money was never an issue for Mitchell Dwight Thompson III.

Mitch's family is old oil money. The Thompsons were one the first families to claim land after they passed the Homestead Act. Walking through the dried-up farmland, still a mile away, with sweat pooling in my armpits, I wonder why anyone would want to claim 160 acres of a shithole like Oklahoma. The ones who wanted it bad enough snuck in illegally and marked their territory by moonlight. We even named our football team after them: the Sooners. Basically, our state was founded by criminals, or at least that's what I got out of a semester of required Oklahoma History class.

Mitch's family were some of these first settlers, and proud of it. When Mitch's father ran for local congress, it was part of his campaign: *Mitch Dwight, Sooner to the Bone*. When President Harrison officially opened Oklahoma to settlers, I bet the Thompsons were already there, smug in their staked-out property, probably sunbathing in lawn chairs and drinking six-packs of Pabst.

I made the mistake of asking our teacher, Coach Langton, about the Native Americans who were already here. He told me to look at a paragraph in chapter 4 that made vague reference to our "proud" heritage and Indian reservations, none of which are actually in Oklahoma. Besides, everyone knows reservations are made up of poor, blue-paint-huffing alcoholics living off public assistance, but that wasn't in the chapter either. Instead, there was a detailed explanation of the symbolic nature of a dream catcher.

In high school, Mitchell Dwight III was hot shit. Besides having a politician for a father, he played fullback and was president of the Future Business Leaders of America. His State debate trophy still stands in a glass cabinet outside the cafeteria. He was one of those guys who could get away with being smart because he was athletic and rich and threw big keggers when his parents were out of town, which was almost every weekend since his mom was having an affair with some guy who made belt buckles in Santa Fe and his dad commuted to Nevada, where he had invested in a casino.

After high school, Mitch went to OU. He was in the best fraternity, the one that caters to the spawn of the oil-money, debutante-escort crowd. He dropped out after fall semester to follow Phish. "Cool," I said, when Trevor relayed the news at dinner to my mother's query of why he didn't come around anymore.

"It's not cool. He's wasting his life. He's a meth head," said Trevor, giving me one of those looks he had perfected, as though I was not worth the energy it took to speak.

I could feel the distaste rising off him, and it wasn't really for Mitch.

"He really messed up. Just goes to show you," said Trevor with authority.

"Goes to show you what?" I asked.

"That some people don't know a good thing when they have it."

"What does that mean?" I asked. Trevor was visiting from Oklahoma State for the Mother's Day weekend. It was his second semester, and college, for him, seemed to be an extension from high school without the lockers. He was on full scholarship, and still playing football, and he was still good. He was still popular. He was majoring in business, making friends with the offspring of the Okie elite, spending the weekends at their cabins on Bear Lake, being invited to the country club to play golf with their fathers. He pledged a fraternity and got in, even though he didn't have the same familial credentials as the other brothers. Trevor had something better—football prowess and that aw-shucks, corn-fed grin that made the mothers want to feed and/or fuck him, and the fathers want to give him internships. Trevor had a firm grip when he shook your hand. Trevor seemed genuinely interested when he asked a question. Trevor radiated warmth and looked good in khaki pants. My mother was proud. She might not have graduated college, she might be a secretary to a bunch of good-old-boy lawyers who called her sweetie and stared at her breasts when she brought them coffee, but she had produced the miracle that is Trevor.

That Mother's Day weekend, Trevor stabbed his chicken and flipped back his hair. He could be one of those poster boys for Abercrombie & Fitch, suntanned and worthy of all your admiration, looking like the outcome of a Nazi experiment to create the perfect human male. It didn't matter that, even with my sucky grades, I was obviously the smarter one. No one cared that I knew all the great philosophers, could have a meaningful conversation about the themes in Salinger's lexicon, and could quote Ezra Pound, even if it was only a stanza and I wasn't quite sure what it meant. Somewhere else, on the East Coast maybe, in an alternative reality, I would be the prized son for my insight. My parents would nurture my intellect, send me on a semester abroad to see the art of Rome and get fucked by Italian girls who found my accent charming. I might not be the hottest guy, but women would flock to me, unable to resist my self-deprecating charm and sharp insight. I've seen Woody Allen movies.

I know these things can happen. They just don't happen in Oklahoma City.

"Listen, Doug, a situation like that, Mitch, I mean that's real unfortunate. He's a smart guy. He coulda done some big things, with a dad like his. There is nothing cool about him being a burnout." Trevor chewed roughly. "I know you and Dingo think that kind of thing is, I don't know, *rad* right now, but it's time to wise up. The guy is a loser. I'm not saying this to be mean, but he—excuse my language, Mom—really screwed the pooch on this one. He had every opportunity in the world." Trevor nodded, comforted in his vast knowledge of the inner workings of the universe. "The thing is, Doug, he got kicked out of school. He had a good future ahead of him. You gotta take the bull by the horns."

This was his new thing. Magically appearing on holiday weekends and giving me life advice now that he'd seen the great, vast world and all it had to offer. If the great, vast world consisted of a fraternity in Stillwater, Oklahoma, then he could have it. "You got to be ready, Doug. When opportunity knocks."

"God, can you speak in something other than clichés?" I asked, clanging my fork against my plate. I shuddered at my own teenage whine. Trevor stared at me with disgust. He was actually speaking to someone of my plebeian status, and here I was, rejecting his deep and meaningful insight.

"Whatever," said Trevor. "Hey, Mom, this chicken is great." Across the room, my mother smiled vaguely from the oven where she was sticking a toothpick in the Double Fudge Mother's Day cupcakes. They were Trevor's favorite. I knew for a fact she preferred vanilla.

"Listen to your brother," said my mother. "He's got a lot of good advice."

"Why? 'Cause he's in college? 'Cause he went an hour away to some bullshit state school?" I knew I was being an asshole, but I'd had to vacuum the carpet for his arrival. I'd had to clean my room, as if he'd ever been within ten feet of it. When Trevor visited, it was like we were preparing for a foreign dignitary.

"Watch it, Doug," said Mom distractedly.

"Why you gotta be like that?" asked Trevor. "Sometimes you act like a real brat. I mean, can't you be normal for once? For Mom, at least? On Mother's Day?"

I looked at my mom. She was washing a dish with a vague smile on her face. Later she'd do the garbage bag of laundry Trevor had brought with him, then she'd start to work on dinner.

"What you gonna do for Mother's Day? Big plans?" I asked him. "Who's throwing the kegger in their backyard tonight?" We stared at each other. I could see I was right. There was a kegger, and he would be going, while Mom and I sat at home and watched Mother's Day programming. *When Harry Met Sally* or some other vagina movie. And I'd sit right there with her and watch the whole thing. Because that is what you're supposed to do on Mother's Day. And also because I'd have nowhere else to go.

Trevor shook his head. He looked me up and down

and smirked. "Fag," he muttered, his lips barely moving, the words almost inauditable.

"Fuck you," I said, dropping my fork.

"Hey!" said my mom. "Watch it, boys."

"I got a 3.9 this semester. How are your grades, Doug? You're kind of a genius, right?" I glanced over at my mom. She'd shown him my report card, even though she'd promised not to. Even though I'd promised to try harder.

"Grades are not an indicator of—"

"By the way, nice outfit," said Trevor, and snorted. I was wearing black. I always wore black. "Really, it's depressing. What are people supposed to think when they look at you?"

I wanted to tell him that in Japanese culture black is the color of nobility. I wanted to tell him midlevel Christian sects believed black to represent perfection. I wanted to tell him that intellectuals and philosophers and beatniks have all worn black. I want to tell him that black is the color of objects that do not reflect light, and I am one of those objects, and it is his fault. There is nothing here beautiful to reflect.

"'Cause I'm not retarded enough to spend eighty dollars on a gay-ass, fucking powder-blue shirt from *the Gap*," I muttered, but he wasn't listening. He was telling my mom about all the girls that were after him at college, and she was laughing. She was proud. She understood why the women would flock to him, as handsome and charming as he was. I stabbed a spear of broccoli with my fork like I was murdering it.

Still, as my mom passed by me with a fresh beer for Trevor, she smoothed down the back of my hair with her warm hand. She did it so quickly that nobody could have noticed but me.

Later, she came to my room with a piece of cake. "Thought you might want a second helping," she said, carefully avoiding piles of crap as she crossed the great divide of my bedroom. She set the cake on my dresser. She stood there and stared at me. I waited for her to tell me what I'd done wrong. That I should be nicer to my brother, wear nicer clothes, raise my GPA, get a hobby, get a life, plan a future.

"I was thinking," she said, "maybe we could go somewhere. Just you and me. On Christmas break, after Trevor goes back. I have some sick days I can call in. We could go, I don't know, to Dallas. To Six Flags. You always loved Six Flags."

I hate Six Flags. All those endless lines for a two-minute ride, sticky bodies and overpriced snack stands, but it didn't matter. "That sounds really cool, Mom."

She nodded. "Good." She weaved through the minefield of shit. She paused for a second. She looked at me. "My boy. You know I'm proud of you, right?" Before I could think of an answer, she smiled and closed the door.

By the time I reach Mitch's condo, I am soaked with sweat and thirsty. He lives on the far side of the subdivision, the poor side, where the young professionals stay until they get their first big job promotion or trophy wife and can afford one of the monstrous McHouses across the golf course. The community is done to look like small-town America, with old-fashioned streetlamps and fake-looking antique trim bordering the windows. The shiny Lexuses and Hummers lining the driveways are anachronistic, a word I just learned in sophomore English.

Next to the other immaculate condos, Mitch's stands out like a sore thumb. The Mercedes in the driveway is beat-up and the grass is overgrown. The pastel paint is peeling, and his old-fashioned brass mailbox is hanging at a weird angle, like it was hit by a car, the front flap swinging open like a gaping mouth.

I knock on the door hard, like someone with a purpose. A minute passes, and I knock again, hard enough that my knuckle stings. Suddenly, the door opens wide, and I stumble backward and squeal. Then I wince because I sound like a six-year-old girl.

I barely recognize the scrawny figure in front of me. He looks vaguely like Mitch, kind of like a distant, white-trash version of him with hygiene issues. This guy, Mitch-but-not-Mitch, is so skinny I can see his ribs through his white T-shirt. His eyes are sunk deep in his skull, with canyons beneath them. He looks like shit, but I admire his baggy, stained jeans and the yellow sweat stains under his armpits. That's what I was going for when I smudged dirt from the yard across my pants and squirted barbecue sauce across a ripped windbreaker I found in the garage. Now I feel like I'm wearing a Halloween costume.

"Who the fuck are you?" he asks, his beady eyes squinting at me.

"Doug Schaffer," I say, my voice too high. I cough. "I'm, uh, Trevor's brother." I remind myself that I'm supposed to be fiending for a fix so I maniacally pick at a zit on the side of my face that still hasn't surfaced with the stubs of the fingernails I chewed off last night. He steps closer and examines me. He smells like the powder shit my mom uses to clean the kitchen counters. The chemical lemon makes my eyes water and my nose sting, but I force myself not to flinch. "Doug Schaffer," I say again. "Trevor's brother."

Then he steps back and laughs. His laugh hasn't changed. It's the big, warm, deep sound I remember from when he used to sit at our kitchen table and drink Orangina after football practice. He and Trevor would rehash drills while my mother cooked dinner and hummed. She'd ask how he wanted his meat, and he'd say something that made her giggle and blush, and she'd eat it up, so proud to have these two strapping guys in her kitchen, one of them a local celebrity's son as the cherry on top. Mitch had even been nice to me, and I was just some stupid kid. *How ya doing, buddy?* he'd ask, grinning at me. *How those middle-school girls treatin' ya? Enjoy it now, buddy, 'cause they're only gonna get worse in high school.* Then he'd whisper so only I could hear, *Ya think you get cock-blocked now? Just wait.* I'd had no idea what he was talking about, but I felt really cool that he'd talk to me at all. Then he'd laugh, and I'd feel like I was in some special club.

"Doug Schaffer," says this different Mitch with the same laugh. "Doug motherfuckin' Schaffer. How do you like that? I haven't seen you since you were a kid. Schaffer's little bro. Well, shit." His eyes dart behind me. "Get the fuck in here quick, okay?" He grabs my wrist and pulls me in the house and locks the door behind us. It's so dark, for a moment I can't make out anything. I hear Mitch messing with the door lock, clicking it open and closed, then open and closed again. The chemical smell is everywhere. I try not to gag, and Mitch says, "You didn't see anyone lurking around out there, did you?"

"Not really."

"What do you mean 'not really'? I need a definitive yes or no, buddy."

"No." I figure the Mexican guys trimming the bushes don't count. Mitch's breath is phlegmy and ragged in the dark. I can't believe I'm standing here, in Mitch Dwight Thompson III's condo, trying to score drugs. My name is Doug Schaffer, and I am trying to score drugs.

"You sure?" he says.

"Absolutely."

"There are some real fuckos in the neighborhood, that's all. I don't want to go into it, I mean, I don't want to implicate you in anything, but the commie so-called *Neighborhood Association* is out to castrate me. This *so-called* quote-unquote *Neighborhood Association*, I mean you have no idea some of the shit that goes down around here, a whole intricate hierarchy of moneygrubbing assholes, powerful moneygrubbing assholes, that's the thing, that's even more insidious, y'know what I'm saying?"

"Absolutely."

"Yup. You know most of the people who live here work corporate jobs, right?"

"I guess." He keeps messing around with the lock, or maybe more than one, because I still can't see shit. The clicking sound is making my teeth ache.

"Well, you have no idea what some of those guys are into, really, some hard-core shit, it would blow your mind. Government shit. Since the bombing, well, I'm sure you're aware of the national attention our state has received. From more than one interested party, if you know what I mean. But you probably don't. But *I* know all about it. And *they* know that *I* know. And they keep coming over here to talk about my *lawn,* y'know, my *chipping paint,* but they have a much more intricate agenda than that. It's all about my dad and oil money, and, shit, it's way too complicated to explain right now, and like I said, I don't want to implicate you. Schaffer's bro. Whoa. Fuck." His voice is frantic in the dark, the words tripping over each other, slurring together. I wonder what the fuck I'm doing here. What was I thinking? This guy is psychologically unstable. This guy could kill me.

"They can't do crap, anyway, 'cause my dad practically owns this neighborhood." The clicking stops, and he steps away from the door. My eyes have adjusted, and I can just make out his pasty white face. He turns on a lamp, and I jump. He looks like that evil dude in those old-school cartoons. He is Skeletor in the halogen glow.

He stares at me. He is so skinny his sharp cheekbones reflect the light, making it look like there is no lower half to his face. "Schaffer's bro. Fuck. I haven't seen you since you were a kid. Wait a minute. Wait a minute. How do I know you're really Schaffer's bro? I mean, I haven't seen Schaffer in years. Since, what, graduation? Two years. So he's, what, in his second year of college? The thing is, that kid is a legend. Everyone knows him. You could be any dick dropping his name to get access to my—" He stops himself. "You could be anyone, you could be some security insider or—"

"Here." I pull my useless learner's permit out of my pocket and thrust it at him. We were required to take driver's ed, and getting the permit at the DMV was our final exam. I don't know why I even carry it. There's no reason to get a license. There's no car for me to drive. And, until today, there was nowhere important for me to drive one anyway.

Mitch swipes it from my hand and stares at it. He holds it up to the lightbulb like a clerk checking to see if your twenty is a forgery. He turns to me, his eyes narrowed. He looks funny for a second, with only half a face and slitty eyes, and I would laugh if I wasn't so freaked-out I might shit myself.

"What the fuck are you doing here?" he says, his voice suddenly gruff. His eyes are glass marbles, his teeth clenched. He's like a rabid, drugged-out junkyard dog ready to attack. "Why the fuck are you standing in my living room?" he growls. I fight the urge to ruin all his hard work with the lock, fling open the door, and sprint away as fast and hard as I can. Away from this psychotic guy and this whole ridiculous, fucked-up scheme.

Then, just like that, I imagine cupping Laurilee's soft breasts in my hands, her nipples hardening in the centers of my palms. I think about sucking the lobe of her perfect, stick-out left ear. That's an erogenous zone. I learned about erogenous zones on the internet. The back of her knobby knee. Inside her belly button.

It's too late to quit now. I refuse to pussy out. At least I'm doing something. At least something is happening. Besides, what do I have to lose? My hands are shaking with fear. I pray it looks like I'm in withdrawal. I clear my throat. I clench my face. I imagine I am Batman. The Val Kilmer Batman, not the Adam West one. I have a hard jaw, a blank stare. I am powerful and alone in this enormous, desolate world and nothing can touch me. I am immune to the cruelty of the universe. I came here for something and I'm going to get it. I'm on a mission. Laurilee's hard nipples in my palms. A mission.

"Mitch. I came here because I need to—"

"Hey!" he says, his eyes opening wide, his voice suddenly a high-pitched bubbling. "Do you like Kool-Aid? I just made some raspberry flavor!" Like he was made of Silly Putty, his face transforms into that of a five-year-old boy setting fire to something.

"Sure."

"Be right back." He drops my ID on the floor and practically skips down the hallway. I let out a deep breath, light-headed. I didn't eat. I wanted to feel weak, like a real addict in need of a fix. Method acting, just like Brando did, only it occurs to me that was a dumbass plan because I might really pass out. I scan the dim living room for somewhere to sit. I take a step forward and stumble over a pile of wires. I really look for the first time, and shit is everywhere. It isn't the hypodermic needles and piles of decaying garbage I expected from my research. Instead, there are piles of electronics and wires, power tools, hills of nails and lug nuts sorted by size. It looks like the Home Depot splooged all over the place. The sharp odor is everywhere, making me want to gag. I might not even need the drugs. I might overdose on Clorox. I try to breathe through my mouth.

"Here you go," says Mitch from behind me. I imagine him standing there with a butcher knife. When I turn, he's holding out a wineglass full of red liquid. It's the kind of glass you take out for special occasions.

"Thanks," I say, taking it from his hand, which is long and white, the nails perfect crescents. It's like he gets weekly manicures at the same Vietnamese nail salon as my mom. A rich guy's hand, I tell myself.

"Try it," he says, and stares at me intently. I take a sip, trying not to think about the possibility of ingesting roofies or arsenic or psychotic trust-fund-baby sperm. Didn't some cult leader kill his flock with raspberry Kool-Aid? The stuff is so sweet it makes my gums hurt. I don't keel over. Mitch looks at me expectantly.

"It's good, huh?"

"Yeah."

"I put in extra sugar."

"Cool."

We stare at each other for a moment, then he drops to his knees and picks up a wrench. He sets it down. He picks up a lug nut, puts it to his eye, and stares at me through the hole.

"You building something?"

"You know anything about phones?" he says, still looking through the metal hole.

"How to use them."

"Yeah, well, mine was acting funny. So I took it apart, y'know? But I can't find anything wrong with it, so I'm putting it back together." From the looks of the living room, other things must have been acting funny too, like televisions and stereo systems, the vacuum cleaner and fire alarm. He places the lug nut on the top of the lug-nut pile. "I really gotta get this shit organized." He leans back and stares at me. "How's your bro?"

"He's in Iraq."

"No fucking shit. I didn't hear that. Thought he was in college—"

"He was. He enlisted. Didn't even tell anyone. Just up and went off to war."

"Huh. Your parents must be proud. Your mom, I mean. Your dad ever come back?"

"No." *This guy is a dumb fuck,* I think. As if my dad is going to come back after all these years. Just show up at the door with flowers and a shamed grin and say, *I made a huge mistake.* Not that I haven't had that fantasy before. Many times. "Yup, he's stationed in Iraq. Mom is proud. She thinks he's an American hero."

"Y'know, Trevor always was a guy with values." He grins.

"Yup."

"Good guy, Trevor."

"Yup."

"I really hated that fucking bastard."

"Me too," I say. We look at each other for a second, then we both start laughing.

"What a fucking asshole," says Mitch. "I mean, really. Couldn't get far enough away from him. Couldn't get far enough away from all the freaking narcissistic, superficial dicks at Classen hanging out with me 'cause I'm rich and have the best parties. Or those teachers telling me about my fucking potential and societal obligations. You at Classen?"

"I'm a sophomore."

"I hated that fucking prison."

"I thought you liked it. I mean, you seemed to have a lot of friends and stuff."

"Stockholm syndrome. You heard of it? You begin to sympathize with your captors. I used it as evidence in debate. I won State, did you know that?"

"I know. They still have your plaque in the trophy case."

"My motherfucking plaque. The trophy case. Gonna change the world one trophy at a time, gonna be a great politician and social thinker and go to D.C. and make the world a better place, and by *better place* I mean figure out how to implement tax breaks for my dad's friends."

"How is your dad?"

"I have no fucking idea."

We stare at each other. He frantically begins to sort equipment into piles that, from what I can tell, are sorted based on whether the piece resembles a circle or a square. He speaks quickly, almost to himself. "'Both-the-affirmative-plan-and-the-counterplan-must-not-be-able-to-coexist-because-this-keeps-the-counterplan-pertinent-to-the-affirmative-plan.' I hated debate. You know what else I hated? Football. What a fucking joke." He takes a wire and twists it into what vaguely resembles a heart. "Football. A bunch of grown guys running around, tackling each other, naked in the locker room. It's kind of gay, if you really think about it. Half the team was probably queer, probably getting off on roughing each other up, slapping each other's asses with towels and checking out each other's dicks when we were soaping up in the showers."

"So how come you played? If you hated it so much?"

He drops his wire heart and looks at me with tiny, pinprick pupils. I think about Laurilee. I think about how she's in love with me and doesn't know it. How she looks at me with that smile and those pointy front teeth, and I see the affection in her eyes. It could be lust someday. I know it could. I just need to do one thing, this one tiny, infinitesimal thing, just take one fucking risk and change my destiny, and then she will know what she knew all along. I will clasp her wrists over her shoulders and push apart her legs with my knees and worship her. Decorate her pussy with flowers, just like the sex scenes from *Lady Chatterley's,* the only parts of the book I read. Laurilee. I'll lick every inch of her and explode all over her, then buy her chocolates and lilies and take care of her and protect her from all the bad people in the world. I remember my mission.

I pick at the zit on my chin, which has turned into a sore that is damp with blood. I lean forward and open my eyes wider. I don't blink so they water. I'm going for manic. I am Brad Pitt in *Fight Club.* I am Jack Kerouac on day three of his *On the Road* scroll. I clear my throat.

"I need a fix, man. I thought you might hook me up. All my sources are dried up, y'know, my regular guy got busted and I'm kinda in a fucked-up place right now, and y'know, I heard you might have access to some, y'know, resources. For old times' sake. 'Cause you knew my brother."

I'm proud of the speech. I wrote it out on a yellow legal pad. I did three drafts. I put in lots of *y'know*s to give it realism. I did it just how I practiced, my voice gruff, my eyes needy. I did a good job, I tell myself. I should be on *Inside the Actors Studio.*

Mitch smiles at me, and for a moment he looks like that guy who used to charm my mother. "I see," he says thoughtfully.

"Yeah. That's why I'm here."

"You need some boom shakalaka?"

I scan my brain. *Crystal, tina, shards, crank, ice, glass, speed.* I don't remember reading about *boom shakalaka.* Maybe my resources were old. There's only so much info you can get by googling *meth slang.*

"Yeah," I say. "Some of that."

"You want some chitty chitty bang bang?"

"Exactly. I got money."

Mitch smiles at me. "Little Schaffer."

"Yeah."

"Little Schaffer. You've never done a drug in your life, have you, Schaffer?"

"Of course," I squeak. He smirks at me. I sigh. I want to cry. I'm fucking incapable of anything. All that work. For fucking nothing. Jack shit nada.

"I've smoked pot," I lie. "But, y'know, I want to try something different."

"Interesting. Well, well, well." He looks me up and down. "I take it you don't play football, Schaffer."

"I don't even know the rules."

"God, Trevor must really fucking hate you, dude."

"You have to acknowledge someone's existence to hate them."

He snorts. "You're a smart guy, huh?"

"I read a lot."

"I got into Yale, did you know that?"

"I didn't," I say.

"My father wouldn't let me go. He's an OU alum. He thought it'd be bad for his rep if I went to a Yankee school. He wouldn't pay for it. He's a glorious example of the capitalist system at work, y'know? The Okie American dream right there, buddy, go Southwest, young man, claim your stake. You look at me and what do you see, Schaffer?"

Skeletor, I think. "A cool—"

"The son of the perfect American dream. I played it great too, didn't I, man? You got a politician for a dad and you learn to relate to the average Joe-fucking-schmo, I mean, that shit comes easy. The handshake. Warm, firm. Comforting. Look 'em in the eyes, make 'em believe. It's all a show. There's an art to the show. Crazy how much I'm talking, huh? I don't get see too many people. No one comes around. The asshole psychoanalyst my dad hired, but I scared him off eventually. No one bothers me too much. Except the so-called Neighborhood Association, but fuck 'em. I see straight through them. And I don't get out too much. I got so much work to do. But, then—what was I saying?"

"Son of the American—"

"So then I'm off to OU, and this is what did it, Schaffer, this was the moment, right? The moment I quit the game. You got to hear this story, Schaffer. You're gonna love this. Drink your Kool-Aid." I suck down the rest, trying not to wince. "So. We were having a party in the Sigma house. It was Thirsty Thursday. Just another party. And it had a fucking theme, 'cause all the frat parties have a fucking theme, right? It was Jell-O. That was the theme. They lined the stairs to the basement with, like, GLAD wrap and poured a pound of lime green Jell-O down, and the girls put on bikinis and took turns sliding down, and we were all fucked-up, of course, six or seven kegs. More, I think. Other stuff too. Lots of weed. Titty and weed and beer, oh my. That's college right there. In a nutshell." He pauses.

I will him to keep talking. *Trust me, Mitch. Give me what I need so I can get the hell away from this asylum, you psychotic fuck.* "What happened?"

He grins, that big trustworthy grin I remember. He's charming, beguiling. He's your best friend. Look 'em in the eyes, make 'em believe.

"I date-raped a girl."

"Oh."

"Cheryl Ann Winworth. You heard of the Winworths? Rich fucking bastards. They got a street named after them in Ada. And Cheryl Ann Winworth. Well, she was hot as fuck. Dumber than a bucket of lard, but hot as shit. Perfect fucking bubble ass. Big titties. Real ones. And they didn't sag at all. Cheryl Ann Winworth three-fourths nekkid in my little frat-house single bed. And she said *no,* just like in the public services ads, and I knew *no means no,* of course, I knew I should stop, and she was looking up at me with these scared, little eyes. And that just pissed me off. That she was such a dumb bitch. It just pissed me off. Her pretty face pissed me off. Her empty fucking head. Her incapability to have an original thought. So I just went ahead. I did it. I mean, she fought me a little, but I was pretty strong. I was jacked then, you remember?"

"Yes."

"I'd like to say I was so drunk I didn't know what the

fuck I was doing. But I wasn't *that* drunk. I knew exactly what I was doing. And I knew she wouldn't tell anyone. Because I'm *Mitchell Dwight Thompson the third*. And I picked her." He looks at me expectantly.

"Wow." This guy is sick. This guy needs his psychologist. He needs shock therapy. This guy holds the golden key to my future in his rich-boy hands.

The smile drops from his face. He's a skeleton with hair. His arms are so pale the veins stick out like TV cables. I will never get that bad. I will be in rehab long before that. I will write letters to Laurilee from rehab. Letters like Jack wrote from Mexico. To Allen Ginsberg. To all the girls he fucked. I will start them, *How ya doin', angel?*

"Okay, kid," he says.

"Okay?"

"Sure. I'll pop your cherry. For Trevor. For old times' sake. 'Cause he was such a nice guy. I was gonna make a run today anyway. Just let me freshen up, okay?" He stands shakily. "You good on the Kool-Aid? Want a refill?"

I look down at my almost empty glass. The sugar has gathered in a thick layer at the bottom. "I'm okay."

Mitch evaluates his pile of hardware. "I guess I can finish this up later." He heads down the hallway. I hear him chuckling. "Schaffer's bro," he says loudly to himself. "Motherfucking Trevor Schaffer's bro. Trevor motherfucking Schaffer's little bro wants to get fucked-up. Just wait, little Schaffer," he calls. "Just wait. You have no idea what is in store. No fucking idea."

. . .

When I was a kid, I wanted to understand how I came from the same two people as Trevor. I didn't know anything about genetics or DNA. I figured the answer was in my brain. Part of my brain, an important part, must be deranged. Misshapen. During the day, I got check minuses during science class for not paying attention, while at night I studied diagrams of the human skull. I learned that the medulla oblongata controls the things we don't think about, like breathing and pumping blood. I learned that the pons play a part in arousal and sleep, the cerebellum controls movement. I never learned what was wrong with me, but I did learn that the human brain contains 10 billion neurons. These nerve cells are connected to other nerve cells in an intricate web of electrical links called synapses.

In the next forty-five minutes, while I wait for Mitch to reemerge from the bathroom, my neurons and synapses have gone to Disney World. They are riding through Space Mountain, high on cotton candy and root beer, they are telling me a million things at once. They are all chattering, like little kids that can't make up their mind what ice cream to choose at 31 Flavors. *Get the hell out of here, bro, this is the worst idea you've ever had. But, c'mon, you're finally doing something with your life. You're finally doing something that matters. Don't be a tool. Go home now, eat a Hot Pocket, jack off to Laurilee, and tough it out. Just remember you'll get out of this rotten city one day and go somewhere that matters.*

Do something important. Look, though, you're doing something right now. Something that matters. You're making a choice. This is what a man does. A man takes risks. For the first time in your life, you're taking a risk, you're going after something that matters. You're a rock star. You're hard-core. You're an asswipe. You're a retarded fucking dipshit fag.

Mitch is standing in front of me, his eyes wide, cracking his knuckles. He looks refreshed, like he just got a long nap. He stares at me, his eyes slit, his nostrils flared, like he's trying to figure out how I got in his house. Then he laughs. "Schaffer," he says, grinning. "Little Schaffer. So you finally ready to go?"

"Sure."

"Okay, just let me close up here and we'll scram. Follow me." For the next twenty minutes, he leads me in circles around the condo while he checks to see if closed curtains are still closed and locked doors are still locked. Each room is even more chaotic than the next. One is full of paper. Ripped magazines and newspaper scraps cover the floor. "I'm working on a project. Maybe someday I'll explain it to you. It's pretty complicated, though. Pretty fucking labyrinthine, man."

Each room smells different. By the time we get back to the living room, I think I'm going to vomit from the mix of Pine-Sol, peach potpourri, and cat urine.

"You got a cat?"

He gives me a hard stare. "Why? Did you see one?"

"No. Just wondering."

After we've finally walked out into the overgrown

yard, and I've adjusted to the sudden light that makes me feel like my retinas are burning, and he's clicked the lock about a billion and six times, we are finally sitting inside his beat-up 1980s Mercedes, which smells strangely of new car. He turns to me. "I like you, Schaffer, y'know that? You're a good guy."

"Thanks."

"Put on your seat belt. Sixty percent of people who die in car wrecks are unrestrained."

I don't ask where we are going. I feel awkward. I need something to do. "Can I smoke?" I ask, thinking it will calm my nerves, make my guts stop twisting around in my stomach like garden snakes.

"Fuck no, man. That shit'll kill you." We hit the I-35 and he turns up the radio as loud as it will go. The story on NPR is about third-world hunger and this kid who is making a difference by selling jigsaw puzzles he makes in his garage. I hate that kid. We are headed toward Dallas, and we pass Falls Creek Assembly of God Baptist Camp, where the fundamentalist youth go to get saved and lose their virginity in the woods. We pass Arbuckle Wilderness, where you feed the animals from your car and an ostrich attacked me for my bucket of pellets when I was six. Since then, I can't even look at them without cringing. It isn't natural for an animal to have a neck that long and skinny. Or kneecaps. Animals shouldn't have kneecaps. After the attack, I cried, and Trevor punched my arm in the backseat. "Stop being a wuss," he said. "It's just a dang bird, baby."

Now it is all dry country field, cows, the occasional gas station and EconoLodge. The farther we get from the city, the more real this feels.

Mitch screams over the radio, "You're a good guy, Schaffer. A good listener. I wouldn't usually do this, but for some reason I trust you."

"Thanks."

"What?"

"Thanks for trusting me."

"You're a really good guy, did anyone ever tell you that? A good listener." I think about Laurilee telling me I'm the only one who listens to her, then I think about her sharp collarbone and thin ankles and about how big my dick would look in her tiny white hand. Mitch makes a sharp turn off the highway, and I know we are on our way, I just have no idea where we are going.

"I'm jealous, man. Your first time. 'You have no idea the wonders that await you.' Who said that?"

"I don't know. Dave Matthews Band?" Mitch was a frat boy, after all. Frat boys quote Dave Matthews like he's Voltaire.

"Willy Wonka, dude! Willy fuckin' Wonka. God, I love that movie. So tell me, little Schaffer, why you wanna try this?"

"I just do."

"That's not a reason."

I sigh. "I'm just sick of being ordinary." Mitch turns to stare at me with his eyes slit again, and his forehead wrinkled in concentration. He shakes his head. With a swift turn, the car screeches into the parking lot of one of those little-town convenience stores in a shack. I half expect to see extras from *Deliverance* on the porch plucking banjos and contemplating anal rape. Mitch flicks off the radio, and the sudden burst of silence makes me jump. I think I hear a cow moo somewhere. He cracks his knuckles and stares at me.

"Schaffer?"

"Yeah?" I say, drops of sweat springing up from behind my ears and itching at the back of my neck.

"Did you hear that buzzing? In the radio?"

"I guess."

"I thought so. Hey, why don't you run in there and get me some Laffy Taffy? Get as much as you can. The banana kind."

I think we are somewhere outside Alma, but it's been a long time since I've seen any signs. We are on one of those endless country roads that make me feel like the rest of the world has fallen away with, just us and acres of dried fields, the skeletons of a few decaying houses. Oklahoma must be the flattest state in America, and there's nothing on most of it. I try to push away my fear. I glom on to any sign of civilization. A haystack. Someone must have rolled it. A billboard for the Pig-Out Buffet off the I-35, TRUCKERS WELCOME. Mitch chews taffy in the silence, tapping his fingers against the dashboard, keeping beat to the tweaker sound track in his head. His right knee jiggles to a different beat. The speedometer says we are going ninety miles an hour. I want to say something, but words get stuck in my throat. I'm afraid to break his spell. I start thinking maybe he isn't a paranoid addict after all. I never actually saw drug paraphernalia. Maybe he's actually insane. All this time people just figured he was on drugs because he's so fucking nuts. He's so whacked out even his parents have disowned him. That happens sometimes. I read it somewhere. One day you wake up crazy, like a light switch got flipped in your head. Maybe I'm lost in the countryside with a psycho who plans on raping me and slitting my throat. God, I hope he slits my throat first.

For a moment I can't breathe. I'm in the middle of Nowhere, Oklahoma, trying to score dope with a possible schizophrenic, obsessive-compulsive chomping banana Laffy Taffy. This isn't me. I should be glazing cookies with buttercream frosting and craning my neck to lust after Laurilee as she pierces tiny earlobes. That's my lot in life. The fields speed past my window, fusing into a blurry golden streak.

As though he can read my mind, Mitch makes a sharp turn onto a dirt road. He drives for a mile, then stops suddenly. "Ugh," I say, bracing myself on the dashboard.

"See," he says, turning off the ignition. "That's why you gotta wear a seat belt." We are parked outside an old barn that has seen better days. A trailer is farther down the field. Based on my research, the barn is expected. Meth cooks frequently inhabit the kind of home that can be packed up and move within an hour. Mobile homes, trailers, motel rooms, abandoned shacks. Trailers. Only this trailer is different. It looks like it has been here awhile. Like a home. It's big, probably a double-wide. Lace curtains are in the window, a pinecone wreath twined with red ribbons is attached to the door. A tiny, roped-off garden is out front. Someone has stuck a bright pink plastic flamingo in the dirt by the stairs, and boxes of pink flowers are attached to the windows.

"We have arrived," says Mitch.

"Cool," I say. It sounds like a choke.

Mitch takes me straight for the barn. We stomp through mud and dog crap, though no dogs are in sight. I try to dodge the minefields of shit, then realize how pointless it is as the bottom of my jeans are caked. At least shit looks more authentic than barbecue sauce. Music is playing from inside the barn. It might be Duran Duran, Aerosmith, something vintage. Mitch stands at the front. "Hey, Pops!" he booms, with a lung power I didn't know his ragged body had the capacity to make. "Pops! Yo, Pops!"

There is some rattling, and the door slides open. A short, old man in dirty overalls peers at us over his bifocals. He's got beady eyes, and his bald head is so shiny I can almost see my reflection in it. His manicured mustache would put that guy in the *Magnum, P.I.* reruns to shame, and a beard that comes to a point in the middle of his chest. It was probably white at some point, but now it's bright green like he dipped it in a vat of pea soup.

"Son," he says, and gives Mitch a bear hug. He comes up to the middle of Mitch's scrawny chest. From a side angle, he looks a little like Walt Whitman. I wonder if it is a sign. *Little you know the subtle electric fire that for your sake is playing within me.* I cringe. It's clear to me now. Guys who quote poetry don't get the girl. Guys who score drugs do. Guys who come back from rehab with a new-found pimp status can probably quote all the poetry they want *and* get the girl. With a burst of confidence I stand up straighter. I've made it this far already. "New glasses?" says Mitch, when he and Pops disattach.

"Yup, the little lady got 'em last time she went to see her kin in Altus. Got a George Foreman grill too."

"Nice."

"They're Calvin Klein." Pops looks over at me with his moist marble eyes. "Who's the kid?" *You're too good for me, kid.*

"Doug," I say, sounding squeaky. I stick out my hand. We both stare down at my shaking fingers.

"He wants to make a purchase."

"I see," says Pops.

"He's harmless," says Mitch. "I mean, look at him." They both stare at harmless me.

The old guy steps close to me. He smells like a chemistry experiment gone bad. "You look scared."

"Yeah?" I say.

"Boo," he says quietly. He laughs, literally using the words, like a character in a comic strip: "Ha ha ha." He steps back. "Welp, I'd do anything for Mitchell."

Mitch smiles and says, "Doug Schaffer. I used to be friends with his brother. Trevor. Dude is in Iraq now."

"No shit," says Pops without taking his eyes off me. "What's he do over there?"

"He's a tank driver," I say. There is no escaping Trevor, even here, on some farm in Nowheresville, Oklahoma.

"Little guy?"

"Five feet eight," I say.

"He write you?"

"Sure," I lie.

"How many sand niggers he shoot so far?"

"I have no idea. They, uh, don't let him talk about that stuff in his letters."

"Nice thing he's doing, serving the country like that. Now Mitchell here ain't got much patriotism, we've had many a talks about it. It ain't his fault, really, it's a generational thing. But I believe in this great nation, son. Can't take it for granted. We could be in a breadline with a buncha commies somewhere, instead of right here in the greatest country the earth has ever known." Pops grins and gazes fondly across his muddy, shit-stained yard. "The land of milk and honey." He turns to me. "Y'know, I served in 'Nam."

"Yeah?"

"Best years of my life. Don't let no one tell ya different. These guys in the VA hospital, havin' flashbacks, I call bullcrap on every one of them. Milking the system. Good times, 'Nam. Good friends. And I haven't had poon that sweet since, though you better not tell the missus. Sweet-ass Chink poon, nuthin' like it. Those ladies got class. Born to serve their men, just like in the Bible. Know we gave 'em a rib. Appreciate it too. You wouldn't believe some of the stuff they can do with their pretty little mouths. Ha ha ha. You can call me Pops, son." He smiles at me. His teeth seem to go on forever. Long in the teeth, now it makes sense. "So, I guess we best getcha fucked-up, huh, boy?"

I've seen plenty of meth labs on the Web, but walking inside one is like a *Star Trek* rerun, that initial moment when the transporter beams Spock and Kirk to some alien universe and they smack head-on into the unknown. The first thing I notice is the smell, worse than anything I could think of, worse than a fresh load of diarrhea in a baby diaper, not that I've ever changed a diaper, but I'll bet it's just like this. It's overpowering, like rotten eggs and my mom's nail-polish remover, with something sickeningly sweet underneath, an overripe nectarine that has been in the sun. Mitch doesn't seem to notice. I breathe through my mouth. The place is organized. The plastic tubs of Drano are stacked in a pyramid, the metal containers of acetone in a neat line, the hundreds of empty boxes of Sudafed in sky-high stacks, like an enormous game of Jenga. This guy knows what he's doing. I know it's hard to get that many pills from my research. Since they passed the Combating Meth Act, you can only buy two packs at the Walgreens, and they keep them behind the counter. For an operation like this, you got to have people working for you, going from store to store collecting boxes. They call it smurfing. The Smurfs were gatherers. I always thought the Smurfs were kind of gay, even when I was a kid, though I did have the occasional jack-off fantasy while thinking of motorboating Smurfettes' big blue titties.

Picnic tables are covered with jars and bottles of liquid. Some have tubes snaking out of them, while others are gurgling. Some are topped in foil, and one bottle has an inflated pink balloon attached to the end. Mitch was right about Willy Wonka. The vintage one, not the Johnny Depp. I feel like I've stepped into the chocolate factory, that scene where the gigantic machine whirs and enormous levers are manned by Oompa-Loompas, and in the end there it is, that little bitty Everlasting Gobstopper that will change the face of the universe. I'm here for the Gobstopper.

I never thought I'd be in a lab. I thought I'd score a quarter gram from Mitch on a street corner, do the hand-shake pass-off you see in movies, thank him for his help, and be on my way. But here I am in an actual methamphetamine production establishment. Not the industrial superlabs of Mexico, but definitely bigger than the photos of most of the shack/motel-bathroom operations I saw on Google Images. I am standing in the middle of a clandestine lab. A *clan lab,* the cops call it. According to some reports, 15 percent of meth labs are discovered due to an explosion. Cops joke that it's easy to find meth, you just follow the fire. Meth explosions are dangerous. I could get third-degree burns, lose a limb, go blind. But the most pressing issue is not puking from the smell because that would be really embarrassing.

I stand there awkwardly, not sure what to do, willing my gag reflexes not to do their job. The music comes back on, this time Guns N' Roses, whom I know about from watching the VH1 heavy-metal retrospective with Dingo. We watched the whole four hours. We laughed our asses off at those assholes in tights smashing their guitars. It's a nice sound system. Mitch doesn't seem concerned with any buzzing now. He's where he belongs. He hops around the tables like an excited little boy. He giggles to himself. He kneels in front of a Peter Pan peanut-butter jar that is filled with a thick, pee-colored sludge. A pipe connected to the bottom is gurgling. "Look at this, lil' Schaffer! How rad is this?" He points to the jar.

I try to walk over coolly, even though my legs are wobbly and waves of nausea gurgle in my belly. "Rad," I say.

"He's gassing the mixture. See, the hydrogen bubbles are passing through the solution. Iodine and hypophorous acid. It doesn't look like much, but it's the ectoplasm. At some point he's gonna evaporate the mixture with a vacuum pump. It leaves this gooey white mud, and that right there is the nucleus of everything, Schaffer." Mitch is almost drooling. I suddenly remember that he was a National Merit Finalist.

"That's the shit that'll fuck you up good," says Mitch. "It's like mining for gold. It's an art form." He turns to Pops, who has on the same chemical goggles we are required to wear in chemistry class when we are do bullshit like make baking-soda-and-vinegar volcanoes. "You're an artist, Pops!" says Mitch. Pops smirks. He likes Mitch,

I can tell. Mitch stands, all his bones cracking. "You're one lucky little punk, seeing this. People go their whole lives without seeing this shit. And Pops, he's one of the originals. He was one of the Harley transporters back in the sixties."

"Sold that Harley long time ago," says Pops. He's swirling a beaker gently, like it's the most important thing in the world, like it's foreplay, like he's going to make hot, sweet love to it. He's holding that beaker like I'd hold Laurilee if I had the chance, he's cupping it in his palm like I'd cup her perfect white ass in my hand.

"Those guys started the revolution, took the stuff cross-country, spread the love. Kept it in the crankcases of their bikes. Crankcases. You get it now? *Crank* cases."

"Wow."

"But this goes even farther back. People don't know. Don't know anything. So quick to judge what they fear. This is the nectar of the gods. Invented by the Japanese centuries ago. Kamikaze pilots used it for bravery. You understand what I'm saying, Doug? You're gonna partake of the same substance as *kamikaze pilots*. You're gonna have that kinda bravery. To crash a plane for what you believe in. You'll have that kind of dedication. You're gonna be capable of anything. Anything you ever wanted to do, Little Schaffer, will be within your reach. You'll feel things Trevor never imagined possible."

"It's a good batch," says Pops, almost to himself. "Nice and pure. A bit of a yellow tinge, but does the job. I tried it myself." He looks at me with his watery eyes, as though seeing me for the first time. "Why don't you go talk to Majorie for a while?" he says. "I got some things to talk over with Mitchell."

Mitch smiles and nods at me. "Just knock on the door of the house," says Pops. He doesn't have to ask again. I practically jog over to the barn door, slide it open, and leap out into the yard. It has got dark out. I welcome the smell of dog shit and damp country grass. I slide the door shut. From behind me I can hear laughter and Axl Rose. He's welcoming me to the jungle. He's gonna bring me to my knees. He's going to watch me bleed.

I knock on the door to the double-wide trailer with the boxes of pink flowers. It opens, and a tiny woman looks up at me. She's so small, she's practically a midget. She's wearing one of those old-fashioned dresses with a gazillion buttons lining the front. I wonder how long it takes her to put it on. He face looks twenty years older than her body and wrinkled like a dried apricot. It's reassuring, all those folds. I'll bet it's warm between them. She smiles up at me, and I feel all the nausea and fear start to seep away.

"Pops said I should . . ."

"Oh, sweetie. You look pale. Come rest on the couch. I'll make some peppermint tea." The inside of the trailer is bigger than I imagined, and it looks like an old folks' home exploded all over it. Every surface is covered in doilies and dried flowers. Against one wall, porcelain dolls with ringlets smirk at me. "Lie down," orders Majorie. I do as she says, sprawling across a patchwork quilt. My body relaxes. I had no idea how tired I was. Majorie disappears.

On the table next to me, a stuffed bear with pearls and a purple sun hat looks down at me. I have the pussiest desire to reach for it and cuddle it in my arms like I used to do with the Cabbage Patch doll my mom bought me after I begged at a garage sale. It was pretty rough, the flesh-colored fabric covered in stains and dirt. But my mom bought it anyway. She didn't mind the doll so much. She read somewhere dolls make little boys into good fathers. Not that it would take much work to be better than mine, that's for sure. She did squawk at the price, but eventually caved.

It didn't take long for me to realize Cabbage Patch dolls, besides being outdated, were not acceptable for boys. The doll came with a birth certificate. He was named Skipper Johns, and I loved him. A few days later, Trevor caught me making Skipper a diaper out of Kleenex and clothespins. He reamed me. He told me, *Only little girls have dolls,* and asked, *Do you have a cooter or a pee-pee?* And if I wanted a cooter, I'd better just sit down to pee and start wearing ribbons in my hair and never talk to him again.

I buried Skipper Johns by an elm tree in the backyard. I had my own funeral service, like they do on TV. I pretended he had died of smallpox, because that's what our teacher said Pocahontas died of, and Pocahontas seemed like a pretty cool chick. I kept his birth certificate, though, hidden under my mattress. Our few days together had been great. I think about Skipper Johns's cushiony body all decayed in the ground and feel my body sink into the couch.

I might have fallen asleep, I'm not sure, but Majorie reappears with a china cup rimmed in a daisy pattern. She holds it to my lips. I let her. I sip like a little boy. It tastes good.

"I put in some honey," she says.

"Thanks."

"You here by yourself?"

"No. Mitch brought me."

"Mitchell. What a sweet boy. Have some more." She puts it to my lips again, and I feel the warm liquid trickle down my throat. "Like my own son, Mitchell. Rough times for a while when Pops couldn't work. He needed back surgery. In a lot of pain, and you know those HMOs. It could have been years before it was approved. Mitchell lent us the money."

"Yeah," I say, sleepy. It's like a bedtime story. HMOs. Back pain. Kamikaze pilots.

"Of course we paid him back when Pops was back on his feet. But Mitchell is a little angel. A darling. Anyone he wants to bring around . . . though I think you are the first he actually has. You must be a real special boy. Are you *his* special boy?"

"What do you mean?" I mumble.

"I just always wondered. Never asked him, though. Don't want to embarrass him. I've got nothing against boys like that. I watch that *Queer Eye* show. And that cute little muffin who hosts the *American Idol*. Those dapper suits he wears, just like the real gentlemen wore when I was a little girl. Sweet things, those homosexuals. So good with decorating. They make everything so lovely."

"No, no, it's not like . . ."

"Quiet. Just rest."

"I like your house."

"Sweet thing." She sits across from me in a flowered La-Z-Boy. She begins to knit. At some point I fall asleep to the clicking of her needles.

I wake up to a cool hand on the back of my cheek. "Wakey, wakey, *hand off snakey,*" says Majorie. She giggles. "That's how my mother used to wake my little brother." I sit up quickly. Everything has gone dark, and all the lamps have been covered in colored scarves. Mitch stands behind Majorie, his face bathed in purple light. "We gotta go, Little Schaffer," he says. "We gotta get back."

"I wish you boys could stay for pot roast." Majorie walks over and puts her hand on Mitch's shoulder. "I get lonely with Pops working all day."

"You know I'd love it," says Mitch. "Next time. By the way, Majorie, have I told you what a fucking hot-ass babe you are? Man, I get a hard-on just lookin' at you."

Majorie giggles again and covers her mouth with her tiny hand. "Oh, Mitch, silly boy."

I stand shakily. She walks over to me. She kisses me on the cheek. She smells like dried peaches, which isn't a bad smell. I never met any of my grandparents. My mom's parents were both dead before I was born. If I had a grandmother, she'd probably smell like Majorie, and she'd make me peppermint tea whenever I visited.

"Lovely to meet you." She reaches out her hand to my face. She gently picks at the inside corner of my right eye. "Sandman paid you a visit. Don't worry. I got it for you."

Mitch is even more amped up on the way home, tapping his knee against the bottom of the steering wheel and grinding his teeth. The farmland is pitch-black even with the headlights. I feel as though we are tumbling through empty space. Mitch does not stop talking from the second the ignition starts. Obviously he and the buzzing radio have established a peace treaty because he is screaming over that creepy talk-show guy who talks about aliens and crop circles.

"I love that man, Schaffer. You only meet a guy like Pops once in your life, like a gift, y'know, like a spiritual guidepost, shit, I hate to say guardian angel, but he kinda is, man, he's more a fuckin' dad than my real dad, which isn't saying much cause my real dad is a real fucking asshole, but you know what I'm saying, right? Pops, man, he's an original. A genius too. Went to Stanford for a semester in engineering. Dropped out."

"He went to Stanford?" I ask, shocked.

"That surprise you? I thought more of you, lil' Schaffer. Gotta look beneath the surface. Guy's a fucking genius. Hated that bullshit, though. Academia. Not a sell-out. Wouldn't join the establishment. Joined the army instead. Wanted to fight for freedom, not just talk about it in theory. Now me, I'm antiwar. I'm peace-loving. I'm a lover, man. But besides that, we got a lot in common, Pops and me."

"I'll bet."

"Yessir, a guardian angel." For the next hour, as I contemplate death with each 90 mph lane change Mitch makes, and wonder why the hell the cops don't pull us over, Mitch keeps talking. I tune in and out. Sometimes he makes sense. Sometimes he seems smart. Intellectual. Other times he just garbles, like he's talking underwater, or speaking another language. He probably is. When we are near his house, I say, "You can drop me off at the bus stop."

"You don't want to come over? I can show you how it's done. This is a monumental occasion, man. This is like your first erection. You probably shouldn't be alone."

I do not want to contemplate this statement too deeply, so I pretend I didn't hear it. "Thanks anyway. I think this is the kind of thing I got to do on my own, decipher my own destiny and all that, you know what I'm saying, man?" I hope he knows what I'm saying because I have no idea, my words all sound jumbly coming out of my mouth.

"Yeah, lil' Schaffer. Yeah. I getcha."

We pull over at the bus stop. He smiles at me. "Y'know, I don't take everyone I meet to Mitch's place. No one, ac-tually. But there's something about you. I wanted you to see it. See what's out there. More on heaven and earth than Trevor could even fathom. You like it?"

"Yeah. Amazing. Thanks. I mean, really. Thanks." Then he leans over like he's going to hug me, so close I can smell his sharp odor and feel my body tighten, and then shoves something in the front pocket of my jeans. My body tightens like I've been surged with electricity. I will myself not to shove him away. Besides me, no one has ever been that close to my dick, except my mom when she changed my diapers. I fight the urge to squirm out of reach. I count to three before I shove him.

One.

His face is still next to me.

Two.

I wonder what the fuck I'm going to do. He's got an animal smell to him, like deer hide.

Two and a half.

My father once took me hunting, before he left for good. Soon before he left, actually. I remember the smell on his clothes during the drive home. I don't remember much about him, but that day is clear. All of it. I was little. I had to move fast to keep up with Trevor and Dad. I remember the trees. The smell of pine. Like the little tree hanging in my mom's car, only stronger. A thousand Christmases. And other things. The flash of blood, the bottles of Coors my dad kept taking out of the blue cooler, the endless hours we sat there, silently, waiting for something big to happen. Waiting for the moment. The look of pride on his face and his whoop when the deer went down. I don't remember what his face looks like anymore, Mom destroyed the pictures, but I remember that he looked proud. He was excited. Trevor was excited. I was bawling.

Trevor was young too, but seemed eternities older than me. He knew everything about everything. He was wearing a camouflage jumpsuit. Or maybe it is just camouflage in my memory. He stood above me, bitching me out through clenched teeth for *being a goddamn baby. Goddamn* was a bad word, we both knew it. Mom got mad when Dad said it. Apparently this moment required drastic measures. Trevor kept telling me, *Shut the hell up before I punch you. Don't ruin this like you do everything else.* A few feet away Dad ripped off a thin layer of deer flesh with a knife. He did it as gently as though he were skinning an apple. *Stop crying,* Trevor said, shoving a piece of beef jerky in my mouth. He didn't want me to fuck it up, this rare moment of male bonding with our elusive father, who was either at work or silently drinking in front of the TV.

I wanted to explain myself, but I didn't have the vocabulary. I didn't know the right words. That deer had been there a moment earlier, one hoof lifted. He wasn't Rudolph or Bambi. He was real. His furry chest was moving up and down quickly as he breathed. He was looking right at me. He was smiling. Now he was limp on the ground, his head bent at an awkward angle, blood swishing from his belly. I didn't know blood could be that bright red. Mitch smells like that dead deer. Mitch is so close I can see where his skin is stretched thin over his cheekbones. His eyebrows have bald patches. Mitch says, "You know why I did this for you, right?"

"Sure. I guess." *Two and three-fourths.*

"Because Trevor is your brother. And you are nothing like him." He laughs. His voice is low. *Do something. Shove him, you pussy. Get away.* "I envy you, man. Your first time. The world is gonna crack open for you, unwrap its shroud, ooze out all the secrets you never knew you needed to know."

I feel his breath on my cheek. It smells like bananas. I'm afraid he's going to kiss me. I'm afraid he's going to suck out my soul. *Three.* Do something. *Three.* I twist around and fumble for the handle. I pull, the door pops open, and I fall on the curb, right on my ass, smack on my tailbone. The pain shoots up my back. "Fuck!" I say, and Mitch laughs. I stand up with the kind of purpose you have when you're the asshole who just fell down in front of everyone.

Mitch leans back in the driver's seat and laughs like it is the most hilarious thing he's ever seen. Like Ronan at school. He laughs for a full minute. Then looks at me with a satisfied smile on his face.

"I gotta go," I say, trying to sound calm. Trying to keep my dignity.

"No problem, lil' Doug Schaffer. I like mentoring young people." He smiles, morphing into Skeletor once again. "By the way, that'll be a hundred bucks."

I feel the tiny baggy bump through the pocket of my jeans. I know, from my research, it shouldn't be more than twenty-five bucks for a gram. This isn't even a gram. I nod at Mitch and take out my wallet.

It's midnight when I get home. My mother is at the kitchen table sorting M&M's, 3 Musketeers, Hershey's bars, and Kit Kats. A pile of half-assembled boxes is next to her. I go to the fridge and open it. She doesn't notice. I take out a carton of orange juice and gulp it loudly. She looks up at me, confused, as though she can't quite place me. "Honey? I thought you were asleep in your room."

"I was at work. We had to restock. That's why I'm so late."

"Oh. Okay." I wait for her to ask pointed questions: *Why did it take so long? Have you done your homework? Why are you wearing a windbreaker covered in barbecue sauce?* Once she would have asked those questions, but that was long ago. That was BOT: Before Operation Trevor.

"Why are you up so late, Mom?"

"Oh, honey. We have a big shipment of care packages going out. All the other ladies have finished their quota already."

"Do they have full-time jobs?"

"That has nothing to do with it. They're counting on me."

"Yeah, Mom, but they got more time on their hands than you. Half of them don't even work, right?" They are charity wives. Nichols Hills Junior League ladies who need something to pass the time, and this is their pet cause. If it wasn't magazines for soldiers who might get their brains shot out, it would be something else. Toy trucks for crack babies. My mom gives them credibility. She is the manifestation of the cause. She may not have their status or money, but everyone knows Trevor, her darling football-star son. He played pigskin with their boys. He helped them win State. He came over to their houses and drank their orange juice and was always a perfect gentleman. Of course, none of them would ever let their own sons enlist; I mean, honestly, *only white-trash boys do that*. Boys with no diploma and no other options. Trevor is nothing like those boys. He's an exception. It is the difference between those lazy Mexicans who stand outside the Food 4 Less bumming around and Marta, that lovely Dominican who has cleaned their toilets for years and is practically family. Trevor is a cut above, and now he's gonna die for our freedom. *Someone has to do it,* they suppose. Poor, sweet, brave Trevor. Poor, sweet, brave Trevor's abandoned secretary mother in last season's clothes from the clearance rack at Ross.

I sit across from her. She is better than any of them. Prettier, smarter. Without even trying. She could have been anything she wanted. And they must know that. If she hadn't met my father, she could have changed the world. I decide right then: *the truth about love is that it makes you fucking crazy.*

I open a packet of M&M's and eat a yellow one. *I understand now, Mom. I'm in love too. And I've got meth in my pocket.*

"Don't eat my supplies, Doug."

"Okay." *I'm going to go to my room with my meth. I'm going to take it out of my pocket and hold it in my hand. I'm going to change everything.* I pop a few more candies in my mouth. "Remember when you wouldn't let me eat the red ones? Said they caused cancer?"

"Well, I read it somewhere."

"Funny, worried about candy giving me cancer. Kinda funny, since you were stoned the whole time I was in your belly." My mom shakes her head, but she's smirking. I once got her to admit, after she had a spiked eggnog at Christmas, that she had tried pot. *But not on purpose,* she kept saying through her giggles. *I didn't mean to do it.* She told me she'd accidentally eaten a marijuana brownie at a party when she was pregnant with me.

"I was high in your stomach."

"Oh, Doug."

This is old routine, familiar, though we haven't done it in a while. I tell her the pot brownie is the reason I'm such a fuckup. We acknowledge I'm a fuckup together, and we laugh about it.

"Well," she says, "maybe that explains your grades." I inwardly groan. We never get into specifics during this routine. "Really, honey. I know you can do better." She's using a different script. One I've never seen. "I wish Trevor was here. He might be able to talk some sense into you."

In my mother's mind, Trevor gives a damn about me. He can reason with me and give fatherly advice. My mother's mind is a fascinating place that has nothing to do with reality. Trevor's idea of advice is asking, *Why are you such a retard? Stop upsetting Mom. Doesn't she have enough to worry about without you fucking up?*

"Have you talked to the guidance counselor? Don't you have meetings?"

"Sure," I say, thinking of Mr. Prescott walking down the hall. Eating a cold Big Mac at his desk, his smirk never fading. "I talked to him the other day, actually. He said my PSAT scores were really high."

"Well, that isn't a surprise. You always score well on those kinds of tests. But it is odd, don't you think? That someone with your obvious aptitude has such low grades?"

"Hey, I got a question," I say, hoping to distract her. "Who says, 'I want to be a guidance counselor when I grow up'? I mean, it's ironic, isn't it?"

"I don't think *irony* is the right word, Doug. It must be torture. Dealing with all those confused teenagers all day."

I have spread out the M&M's in front of me and am trying to make a picture, which never really works. You are always one candy away from finishing anything and stuck with a smiley face lacking a blue eye or a distorted heart. I know I should go to my room. I know this conversation is going nowhere good. But part of me wants to stay here, for just a moment, with my mommy.

"Yeah, well, we can't help it. We got hormones and they make us do all this crazy crap. I learned that in one of my classes, I think."

"Oh, Doug," says my mom, trying not to smile. I can make her laugh. It's the one thing I could always do that Trevor couldn't. "I know I've been busy, but you need to be thinking ahead. You've got to take steps to make things happen." *I've got meth in my pocket, Mom. You won't believe what's gonna happen.* "You have to start those applications next summer."

If I wasn't a dumbass, this would be a perfect time to say she is right and make an exit. But I can't make myself get up. I don't want to be alone with that tiny baggie. I want to hear something familiar and rational after a night of Pops and Mitch, pink balloons, beakers, and lug nuts.

Besides, she is just saying what she is supposed to say. We are two ventriloquists putting on the *Concerned Mom and Slacker Son Show*. Her puppet, the mother with a vacuum and pearls, is acting like it really matters what I do two years from now, when her real concern is if we will have enough money to make our mortgage payment this month and if my brother is going to get blown up. The son puppet, who is much more attractive than the real me, who is wearing khaki pants and a button-up shirt, is playing like he is actually concerned what the mother puppet thinks about his future.

"I'm not sure I want to go to college," says the son puppet. This is the standard puppet-son reply.

"You have no choice," says the puppet mother.

"We don't have the money."

"You'll have to take out loans," says the puppet mother, her wooden jaw opening and closing, her bright pink painted lipstick never smudging.

"You didn't finish college," says the son puppet.

"Because I got pregnant, honey. I had no choice but to quit."

"Okay," says the son puppet with resignation. "Okay. I'll look into it."

"Good." The mother puppet looks at the clock. "Oh my God, it's so late. You have school tomorrow, Dougie. You need to go to bed." The mom puppet is concerned about the son puppet having enough energy to make it through the next day of school, and just like that the show is over and the curtain goes down. I want to tell her it doesn't take much energy to be invisible. Just take the long way around. Hide underneath the bleachers. Try not to make a ripple or dent. Move without motion, sink into the crowd, keep your head low. It doesn't take any thought at all.

"Okay," I say, standing. She never noticed my greasy hair or my shit-stained jeans. She didn't see the sweat marks under my armpits or wonder what the hell I'd be stocking at a cookie stand in the mall until midnight. It's been like this since Trevor signed up for basic without telling anyone. Trevor talked a lot of shit, offered a lot of bull-crap opinions, but at least Mom was herself before he left for his desert vacation. Without Trevor to lead the troops, the mission has lost focus. I don't even remember what the mission was to begin with.

"Love you, Mom."

"You too," she says, tying a bow. That's the extra touch. She could have been a CEO, my mom, or a college art professor. Instead, she's drunk on her new mission—

the fearless leader of uppity menopausal women who think boxes of magazines are going to make the boys in Iraq forget that a stray sniper bullet to the head is right around every corner.

At least she had a kid like Trevor. That's gotta count for something.

I lean against the doorframe. I watch her, chewing her bottom lip and curling a ribbon. I've never seen her so driven. She's been happy since Trevor left. She has a purpose beyond answering phones and making Maxwell House for fat lawyers. She's important. She's in college again, protesting the administration for doing something that lacks integrity. She's at the front of the crowd, her homemade sign putting everyone else's Crayola-marker scrawls to shame. She's that girl again, the one I never met, the one who stole the heart of my charming father. The guy everyone wanted. Made him fall in love with her without even trying. Knocked her up with the miracle of Trevor. How was she supposed to know he was the kind of asshole who'd flee to Mexico with a mental-case heiress? Give up his wife and sons for margaritas and a beach cabana somewhere?

That girl was different. That girl hated violence. She hated war. Now she bakes it blueberry muffins.

I watch her slap a sticker on a package: MADE FOR YOU WITH LOVE, OMSPOT, NORTHWEST OKLAHOMA CITY CHAPTER.

This won't go on forever. The war will end and Trevor will come back because guys like Trevor don't die. Someone takes a bullet for them, or they are in the latrine taking a crap while the rest of the company gets blown up by an IED. Trevor is the kind of guy to emerge from the toilet, refreshed from his dump, to find his fellow troops in hundreds of pieces, splattered in brain matter, their blood oozing into the sand. "Luck," people would say. "Trevor has always been lucky."

Maybe it is the best thing I could do for her, this lump in my pocket. She'll have a new war to fight. The war on drugs. I'll come back from rehab, and she'll listen to my horror stories, she'll nurse me through recovery. She'll go to NA meetings, sign petitions, volunteer as a sponsor, fight for the passage of antimeth bills in Congress, speak out about her own experiences with her gifted, misguided addict son. His success story. Her part of that success, the unspoken backbone of his recovery. She's a good speaker, she once told me. She sometimes spoke at rallies in college.

Trevor will be fine. Trevor has always been fine. It'll be a new protest movement. This time it won't be about some fucking insurgents in a sand dune thousands of miles away. The fight will be right there in front of her. Me. This time, it will be personal.

In a weird way, I'm giving her a gift.

CHAPTER FOUR

In my bedroom, I take out the plastic baggie and hold it up to my halogen lamp, the same Wal-Mart lamp every other teenage boy in America has. *The people's lamp,* I'd said to my mom when she lugged the box into my room last year. *It was on sale,* she told me. *The people's* plaid comforter from Target. *The people's* $29.99 CD player.

The posters on the wall, though, are different. Posters explain everything. They show where you belong. They represent your place in the world.

The jocks at school, the guys like Trevor and the ones who aspire to be him, probably have Sooner football up there, or, if they dare look beyond the state, another team, through probably not the Cowboys, because it would be sacrilegious. Baseball is acceptable too, or even basketball, but football is king.

Besides sports, a lot of guys have music posters. Some guys at my school wear loafers, and the band is probably whatever crap band they are rotating on MTV that month. Then there are the crowds that consider themselves experimental. They'll toke up at a party and wear tie-dye with their pre-ripped Abercrombie jeans. They probably have some sweaty old-school Jimi Hendrix or Jim Morrison watching from above their dresser, his guitar strapped across his chest.

Some guys at my school, like Ronan, like rap. There aren't many black kids at Classen. Since the white flight of the sixties, they are in a completely different area of the city, one you wouldn't drive through without your car locked. So most of these guys, the ones who like rap, are white. They nod along to 50 Cent rapping about *fuckin' dat bitch* and *niggas poppin' their trunks, their two 380s, one black, one chrome, and four Glocks*. Most of them have never held a gun, but this music makes them feel hard-core. Ronan probably has a poster of Kanye West on his wall.

The other kids at school, the Students for Jesus group who wear chastity rings, put up posters of Christian rock music. They really get off on those vaguely dirty lyrics about *Jesus filling you up* and *keeping the hard rock of Christ within you*. They stare at some poster of a pseudo-edgy Christian band and sing along about how *God's holy touch burns you so deep*.

A few guys put up those bands with scrawny singers

who wear eyeliner. They embrace the angst. These guys are rare, though, because they are basically outcasts like me. Digging some guy in makeup might fly in a bigger city or on the East Coast, but this is Oklahoma City, and confessing you sympathize with satanic thoughts and approve of self-mutilation will get you a quick trip to the school counselor's office.

We all depend on our posters. It's just a scrap of paper on the wall. It doesn't say anything about anything, but it makes us feel like we matter.

The crystals are small and cloudy. They look like Pop Rocks. I am reminded of that old urban legend about frogs not being able to fart, and how if you squeeze them until their frog lips unpucker and pour a mixture of Coke and Pop Rocks down their throat, they will give a few hops and then explode in a million green, slimy pieces. I never got the guts to try it. Besides, I always liked frogs. I squeeze the baggie in my hand. It's hard to believe these puny shards will do anything to me, let alone change my life.

I put the sack under my pillow and stretch out across my bed. I close my eyes and go over one of my favorite Laurilee fantasies, an elaborate one that has her and me in a storage room of second floor of the mall, right behind the JCPenney. We are sprawled across collapsed boxes, her plaid schoolgirl jumper pushed up over her flat, white belly, her panties hanging from one ankle. Of course the panties are white, with tiny pink flowers on the edges, because as much as I'd like to believe I am capable of original thought, those are the panties that always pop into my head. I'm above her, my jeans around my ankles, my dick pushed through the fly of my shorts, my hiking boots thumping on the cement floor with each thrust inside her magical pussy, driving into that deep, warm, perfect place as the storage-room dust rises around us. She sneezes. She moans. Trying to push away the thought of meth beneath my pillow, I frantically jerk off. I cum. I don't bother to clean up.

I roll onto my side. I feel good, and I hate myself at the same time. Someone really smart once said that every orgasm was a small death. I guess I understand that. I wait for the nothingness to enter my head. I wait for that dark, blank moment, the pitch black right after the camera flashes. But it doesn't come.

I let the cum dry across my belly. I think about the morning. I can't quit now. This is for Laurilee. But now I know it is for something more. Something important. Something I can't quote from Whitman or Salinger or Ginsberg. Something I can't put into words.

Jack Kerouac, sitting in a smoke-filled coffeehouse with his lumberjack shirt and messy hair, watches me from the poster on the wall.

The next morning I drink a shake made from one of Trevor's leftover tubs of protein powder. It's called Pro Power Function and the package says that the essential amino glutamine and hyperpurified hydrolyzed whey will increase my strength and lay the brickwork for muscle recovery and physical enhancement. What the package doesn't say is that it tastes like straight-up shit. I force the thick, grainy liquid down my throat. Meth curbs the appetite, and it might be a while till I get a nutritious meal. Not that I ever had one of those before. I wonder how many of these I can chug down before tonight.

My mom flutters around in her bathrobe, putting final touches on care packages. She doesn't notice that I'm drinking a shake instead of shoving down my usual blueberry Eggo as soon as it pops out of the toaster. At least once a week I burn my tongue. I can't be late. Even though teachers don't notice when I leave midclass and don't come back, they do add up late slips, and I don't want a detention. Today I don't worry about it. I take my time. Today, there is nothing to be late for.

"What are you doing after work?" I ask my mom through a mouthful of the thick goo.

"I've got a meeting with OMSOT, then I'm going to stop by the Homeland and see if the manager will consider a donation for our next shipment. You think he'd jump at the opportunity. It's a tax deduction. IGA already said no, though." She prattles on about the supermarket hierarchy and the shelf life of Twinkies. She is talking to me without really talking to me.

"Mom?" I say, trying to distract her.

"I just don't understand the selfishness. Day old Hostess products, that's all I ask for, and they say it's against regulation, can you imagine? They're just going to throw them—"

"Mom!" I say loudly.

She almost spills her coffee. She turns to me and gives me one of those pissed-off saccharine smiles only a mom can really pull off. "Yes, honey?" she says sweetly.

"What time will you be home?"

"Eight. Maybe nine."

"Okay. I'll probably be asleep. I got a big test on Thursday. I was up till six a.m. studying. I'm exhausted."

She raises an eyebrow at me. I should have given it more thought. What a stupid bullshit excuse. Like I'm the kind of industrious guy who stays up late cramming for a test. Meth addicts are excellent liars. I really need to practice.

"Fine, honey," she says, turning away. I'm not worth the energy it would take to ask questions. "Whatever you need to do."

"I better get to school."

"Okay," she says, scanning the room for something that more urgently needs her attention.

One of the traps of meth addiction is that the users don't take care of themselves. This is one of the many ways I will be different from the average user. I go to a Wal-Mart far away from our neighborhood. It takes me an hour to get there and back by bus. Not that anyone cares what I buy at the McSuperCenter, but I need to get accustomed to being sneaky.

I buy cherry Chap Stick. I buy the vitamin supplements pregnant women take. I need something powerful enough for two people, even if one of them hasn't yet been born. I buy canned tuna fish for the protein and tryptophan, a loaf of whole-wheat bread for the complex carbs, and a huge bag of Jolly Ranchers because meth makes you crave sugar. I get saline nose spray and a package of straws in case I decide to snort. The idea of shoving a rolled-up dollar bill up my nose sound both painful and unsanitary. Even with the straws, I doubt I'll snort. Snorting would be the quickest and most effective method, but I've hated putting anything up my nose ever since a kid in my preschool was sent to the hospital for shoving a rock up his nostril. Still, you never know what you are capable of doing when you are really messed up on drugs.

Meth impedes the flow of saliva, and many users don't drink enough fluids, so bacteria and natural acids begin to eat away at their tooth enamel and gums. I don't want meth mouth, so I buy a gallon of bottled water and some of the most expensive fluoride toothpaste I can find. That's the real problem. Addicts don't brush their teeth. I will always brush my teeth, no matter how fucked-up I am. I will brush my teeth twice a day, just like Coach Walters taught in the Personal Sanitary Habits unit of our Sex Education class. We spent two weeks on Personal Sanitary Habits. We spent one day learning how to put a condom on a banana. Considering my probability of getting laid, the ratio was probably just right.

I rush through the cosmetics section, grabbing the first bottle of Oil of Olay I spot. I'm not sure why anyone would want to put oil on her face, but it's the brand my mom uses. I feel the blood rush to my face and hope the woman contemplating the tampons across from me doesn't notice. I blush again when the cashier rings up the bottle. She doesn't even look at me. I remind myself that nobody cares as much as you think they do.

It's noon when I finally get home. I haul the bags into my room and lock my bedroom door. I never lock the door unless I'm going to jerk off. My mom always knocks, but I like having the backup. What if there was a fire and she rushed in to tell me? I'd rather go up in flames than have my mom catch me with my wiener in my hand.

I make my bed and line my supplies across the mattress. I open the gallon of water, which was a fucking bitch to lug across town. I gulp and stare at the products for a long time. I rearrange them. I put them all back in the Wal-Mart bags and shove them under my bed. They fit perfectly. I stare into the murky depths beneath the place I sleep. A whole universe is under my bed— dust bunnies, a discarded collection of *Mad* magazines in their plastic sleeves, busted Transformers, disfigured G.I. Joes that had survived my wars of bricks and stolen-matchbook flames, used jerk rags, the wrapper of a 3 Musketeers bar I shoplifted when I was nine and still feel guilty about but can't throw away, and, somewhere deep in that crammed abyss, a canvas bag of my father's old clothes.

When I was ten, I found them in the basement. I was really into *The Lion, the Witch and the Wardrobe* that year, and I thought I might find a secret tunnel leading someplace better than my life. This was almost as good. Even though Mom had got rid of every garment that had touched my father's body, I instantly knew they were his. The Sooners football hat still had a ring of his sweat around the inside. I locked myself in the bathroom and put it on. It covered my entire face. I swam in his T-shirt and could pull his jeans up to the top of my chest. I stayed in there an hour, staring at myself in the mirror, until Trevor banged on the door and asked, *What the hell is taking you so long, are you spanking the monkey?* I hadn't even got my first boner yet, but I felt shame rush through my whole body. This was worse than *spanking the monkey,* even though I only had the vaguest idea what that meant.

I get up from my floor. My meth supplies belong right there, under the bed, with the rest of my secrets. Only this is a secret that actually matters.

I take out the packet of crystals. I set them on my desk and stare at them. This is the part I haven't decided yet. I consider my options.

Slamming is out of the question. I never liked shots. When I was a kid, they practically had to hog-tie me for my vaccinations. I even shunned the nurse's grape Dum Dum peace offering out of pure spite. Besides, the only person I know with needles is Dingo, because his mom is diabetic. But asking for one would blow my cover way too early.

I could go to the Smoke Shop on Twenty-third Street and get a glass pipe, but if I leave the house again, I might lose my nerve. I could booty-bump the crystals, which is a preferred method among the fag community. You dissolve the rocks in water and squirt the solution up your ass. My mom has a turkey baster in the cabinet. I think about this for less than a millisecond, cringe, and decide it is out of the question.

In the end, my only option seems to be swallowing the drugs. I could parachute them, which makes the effects last longer. You wrap the crystals in toilet paper and swallow the bundle. Something about that grosses me out. It reminds me of this messed-up kid in my fourth-grade class who used to eat reams of computer paper. I watched him do it. He'd rip off strips, fold them into neat squares, pop them in his mouth, and chew away. His family moved to Alabama during the middle of the year. Part of me missed him. He was the only one who got made fun of more than me. Still, the idea of toilet paper in my mouth makes me want to spew.

I figure I'll have to drink the stuff. I could put it in orange juice or Dr Pepper, but in the end, I decide on coffee because it is the most hard-core choice. That's how guys like Pops did it. Biker's coffee, they called it. I'm carrying on a great tradition.

I go to the kitchen and open the cabinet. There's Folgers and International French vanilla, which sounds kind of gay, so I brew the Folgers. I add five sugar cubes because I really hate the taste of coffee.

In my locked room, I measure out a fourth of the crystals. I can't find any info on the Web about the right amount to ingest, but this amount seems small enough to not kill me. I can always have another cup later if I need to. I can tell my mom I'm still cramming for that test. The key to being a good liar is keeping it going, even if it sounds outrageous. I put the baggie under my mattress, next to the wrinkled 1982 *Penthouse* I stole out of Trevor's room years ago and made excellent use of until I started to work at the mall. I still remember the perky, tan tits sported by Pet of the Month Debbie Ann from Arizona. Now Debbie, who likes Duran Duran and red licorice, seems a cheap imitation of the visions I can conjure up of Laurilee in my head.

The mug is warm in my hand. I set it down on my desk. I put *Heroin* on the people's CD player because it seems like a good choice. I pick up the cup again. I stare into the liquid for a few minutes, as though something amazing is going to happen, like a face is going to appear and start telling the story of my life. My skin feels like a tight wrapper on my bones. I think about how people say they were so nervous they could hear their heart pounding. I always thought it was a stupid cliché.

I take a sip. The liquid tastes kind of metallic, which isn't as bad as the actual coffee taste. All the beatniks drank coffee. They sat over it for hours in Greenwich Village, discussing human nature and poetry, then going home to their railroad apartments in the East Village or Greenpoint, Brooklyn, to have wild sex orgies. I pinch my nose. I chug the rest of the liquid so fast I gag. I drink the rest of my water. I glance at the clock. The drugs should take twenty to thirty minutes to settle in my system and take effect. I lie across my bed and stare at the ceiling.

I think about rehab. First there will be an intervention, I'll be sure of that. That's the best part. I'll avoid any chances of getting carted to rehab without an intervention. I'll insist I don't have a problem, I can stop anytime I want, I just like to party now and then, et cetera. I'll say that everyone else has the problem, not me. Eventually, there will be no choice, and my mom will have to bring a coun- selor in to mediate, like in the movies.

The guy they bring in will be one of those hardened, wrinkled dudes who have been at rock bottom them- selves, woken up in their own vomit in unfamiliar alleys too many times to count, who have in their time sunk to some pretty low depths to score a fix. This guy still goes by his street name, something like Big Beau or Rocky.

My aunt Lila and dickwad uncle Roger will get a baby- sitter and drive all night from Little Rock. Since the rest of the family consists of distant relatives who communicate by mass mailings at Christmas or e-cards on New Year's, Lila and Roger will be the only choice. Dingo will be there, even though we haven't talked in a while. On TV, they usually hold the interventions in hotel rooms. I pic- ture us in the Holiday Inn off the highway. It's close to the house and they give discounts to the families of soldiers.

They'll have to get a room with a sitting area. It'll cost more, but they'll be so upset they won't even be thinking about money.

Somehow they'll lure me there. I'll make it hard, of course, make them work for it. Eventually I'll show up, ragged and sick. Disheveled, unwashed, but kind of sexy, like those guys you see in MTV videos that look like they haven't showered in a few months. Maybe Laurilee will be there. I hadn't even thought about it before, but that would be perfect. She could see me like that, strung out and rebellious, saying fuck you to the status quo, making forgery Marcus and tat Daniel look like preschool teachers by comparison. Laurilee will come, and then it'll be even more kick-ass when I come back from rehab with my new muscles and badass identity. It'll be like the end of a reality show, when they have the big reveal, only the reveal isn't a spanking new house or some chick in a bikini who lost two hundred pounds. This time the reveal will be me.

There's got to be a way to get her there. I'll tell the group I won't do this without her. I need her. Dingo will tell them to call the mall. If she's not in, they'll get her number from a Trinkets employee. "It's an emergency," my mom will say, a sob behind her voice.

I lock myself in the bathroom till Laurilee arrives. I won't come out when she first shows up. I'll make them sweat it out for a while. "She's here," they'll say through the door. "Please, Doug." Maybe I'll do another hit to get me through the plane ride to detox. Finally, I'll swing open the door, slamming it against the wall, and step out into the room.

Laurilee will look up at me from the couch, her body folded into itself, her arms crossing her chest. She'll rise to her feet. She'll be scared. She'll be drawn to me. She'll be wet.

My mom and aunt will read letters they've written me. My dickwad uncle will freeze his face into a mask of worried concern while secretly wishing he was sprawled out on his couch with a Miller Lite and ESPN. This is beyond him. He always knew I was weird. He just figured I was a queer. He didn't know I had it in me, and he doesn't like being confused. The world is much simpler in his living room. Still, he'll try to act concerned, because Big Beau or Rocky told him that I might die.

The letters will be all about the good times, whatever those were. My aunt will tell stories about what a beautiful little boy I was, how I used to put on scuba flippers and goggles before I jumped in the plastic wading pool in their backyard. It'll be uncomfortable when Dingo stumbles through his letter. I'll just try to block it out. When it's my mom's turn, she will recount my first day of kindergarten, how I won the science fair in fifth grade, what a wonderful adult I might become. She'll tell how frightened she is, how much she wants back her brilliant, kind, amazing son. She'll cry. I'll tap my fingers on the sofa, fidget, crack my jaw, stare at the ceiling. "Please, baby," she'll say. "For me. I love you."

No one will mention Trevor.

Finally, I'll give in. I'll let my Mom embrace my ema-ciated body, sob on my shoulder, and tell me how much she loves me. Dingo will slap me awkwardly on the back and tell me, "It's gonna be okay, man. I'll hold down the fort till you get back. I'll email you and stuff." My uncle will give me a stiff hug, my aunt will kiss my cheek and ruffle my hair. Laurilee will walk shakily toward me. She'll put her hand on my cheek. She'll say that she'll miss me. She'll tell me she'll write every day.

"Yeah, okay," I'll say in a distracted voice.

A cab will be waiting in the parking lot. My stuff will already be packed, and Big Beau or Rocky will tell me we are going straight to the airport. "You'll like this place," he'll tell me. He'll tell me about the rehab center, which will be on a beach or in some desert lodge with cacti and fucking awesome sunsets. He'll pry off my cling-ing mother, who, at that moment, believes I am more important than anyone else in the world. As we drive off, I'll watch them blankly through the cab window. They will be gathered in a tight, sobbing huddle, clinging to each other beneath the HOLIDAY INN sign. Laurilee will be standing apart, her arms wrapped around her in a hug, her knees faintly bluish beneath her plaid jumper. Our eyes will meet. I might even give her a vague nod. I'm too far gone to trust anyone, even her.

As we hit the I-44 to Will Rogers Airport, Big Beau or Rocky will squeeze my shoulder in a rough, manly way. He'll say, his voice the growly rumble of someone who has been where I am, who is a true comrade, "You made the right choice, son. You're a brave kid." As we pass the airport welcome sign and the twenty-foot-tall mock Indian arrows stuck in the dirt outside the terminal, I'll turn to him. "I'm scared," I'll admit, my voice rough.

"That's nothing to be ashamed of," he'll tell me.

Later, he'll give me some Ativan to get through the flight.

The only problem is that I don't feel anything. It has been forty-five minutes. I have the sudden, numbing 'fraidy-ass feeling that this isn't going to work. The drugs are duds. Mitch conned me. I'm immune. I'm different from everyone else. I'm strange. They don't work on me, nothing works on me, I can't even get fucked-up right.

I look at Kerouac on the wall. Below him is Sal's famous quote from *On the Road,* the one about the only people for him being the crazy ones—*the ones who are mad to live, mad to talk, mad to be saved, desirous of everything at the same time, the ones who never yawn or say a commonplace thing but burn, burn, burn like fabulous yellow roman candles exploding like spiders across the stars.*

"Burn, burn, burn," I chant to myself, under my breath. "Burn, burn, burn," I say, like a prayer.

And then something happens.

I throw up. Like the time I ate bad crab-stuffed mushrooms at Red Lobster. Only a million times worse. I retch all over the room. I vomit in a pile of dirty laundry, in the trash can, crawling down the hall, on the dirty bathroom tiles. I puke everywhere except in the toilet.

At some point I pass out. I wake up with cold tiles against my cheek, the remnants of dried protein shake across my cheek. I'm freezing, but I'm drenched. I'm sweating from pores I didn't know I had. I heave myself to a sitting position. Since I couldn't lift the seat, the puke is splashed across the wall and the sides of the bowl. Using the counter, I heave myself to a standing position. I stagger my way back to my room. I lock my door. I collapse on my bed.

There's a knock on my door. "Honey?" says my mom. I force my eyes to open through a layer of crust, like when you get pinkeye. When I was a kid, I always thought pinkeye was kind of cool, even though it hurt like hell and made you look like Count Dracula. That you woke up with your eyelids glued shut with this body-generated shell seemed kind of incredible, like something out of a cool-ass sci-fi movie. I also liked scabs, snot, dead skin, and anything that seeped out of any bodily orifice, except semen, which I didn't know about yet. I think most little boys like that stuff. Or maybe it was just me.

Right now, I hate everything my body is capable of doing.

"Just a minute!" I say, my voice rough with phlegm.

The smell of my own puke is everywhere. The clock radio flashes 7:15. It hurts my eyes. Is it morning or night? I try to pull myself to a sitting position, but I can't move. I am an unidentified mass of flesh. My mouth tastes like something crawled in there and died.

"You're going to be late for school," she says. School. Day. Weekday. "Are you still sick?"

"Yeah," I choke.

"Open the door."

"Just want to sleep, okay?" I say, my voice coming from another continent.

"Let me check to see if you have a fever." She can't come in here. She must not enter this room. My brain is quicksand, noncoherent thoughts are pulsing through me. I know she can't come in here. I also know I'm about thirty seconds from blowing chunks again. I dig my fingernails into my belly. I will detain the vomit. Withhold regurgitation. She can't come in here.

I fall back on the son puppet. He's there, waiting to speak. He's always up for a performance. His wooden jaw clacks open and closed, his voice is high and measured. He's almost cheerful. It's morning. He's wearing pajamas with feet. "I'm okay, Mom," he says, "I just need to rest. Don't worry about it."

"Should I cancel my appointments?" says Mom puppet. Son puppet knows this is the last thing Mom puppet wants to do. Mom puppet is busy, especially lately, and a sick son puppet will completely fuck up her itinerary for the day.

"Nah. It's a virus. Dingo had it. Just gotta. Sleep it off. 'Kay?"

"Are you sure?"

"Yes," says son puppet with intensity.

"Okay, sweetheart. Just rest, then. You need Advil?"

"Already took some!" Please stop talking. Please.

"Apple juice?"

"Nah." *Shut the fuck up, Mom. Please.*

"Okay. Love you, honey."

"Yeah, me too," I croak, even though her footsteps are already at the other end of the hallway.

I'm not sure what has happened. Why does my room smell like puke? Then I remember. The clock says 6:22. Evening, I figure. My mom has meetings. Appointments. I am alone.

I took amphetamines. I drank them in coffee. There was no euphoria, no elation. I didn't feel the sudden, overwhelming assurance that I could conquer the world. It wasn't better than a thousand orgasms like they say in drug movies. There was no kamikaze bravery. I took crystal meth and it gave me the flu. I can't even do drugs right. From his poster, Jack smirks at me. *You don't deserve enlightenment,* he's thinking. *You don't know how to burn. You can't even flicker.*

My genetic code is pussy. It is preordained. It is mapped on my DNA. The room smells like vomit. The vomit is the physical manifestation of my great inner truth. My great inner truth is that I am regurgitated goods. I'm the people's lamp from Wal-Mart. I am as adequate as plastic pieces screwed together by child laborers in a third-world country. I give off just enough wattage to not make a significant impact. After a few years, you can sell me in a garage sale.

I stare at the ceiling. Laurilee was the reason I did this. Laurilee, her head cocked at an angle when she listens to me. All that work for nothing. All that work so, when I get the energy, I can scrape flecks of vomit off the bathroom wall. A sponge and spray cleaner probably won't do it. I'll probably have to hunch over with a plastic knife. Maybe my fingernails. I feel tears coming. Perfect. Because that's what guys like me do. They cry. They weep alone in their rooms over a girl who won't go on a date with them. Jack looks down at me. He's not smirking anymore. Now he just feels sorry for me. "Fuck you!" I tell him, and slam my fist against my headboard.

I bite my lip. I refuse to say ouch. I wait for the big heaving sobs. *Go on and cry,* I tell myself, only I hear it in Trevor's voice. *Go on and cry like a fucking baby. Why you gotta always fuck everything up?*

The tears don't come. Maybe I'm dehydrated. Maybe it's a sign.

Peter Wilkenson was in the Monty Python Appreciation Society. I remember now. I must have blocked it out. At freshman orientation he sat at the booth with the other geektools, a stack of untouched flyers in front of them, practically salivating on anyone who paused beside their table while contemplating the merits of joining Pep Society versus Student Government. There were lines for everything else, even the Sewing Club. But those guys sat alone, waiting patiently for the arrival of one of their own. Dingo was across the room, arguing with some guy at the Science booth about the merits of stem-cell research. Dingo was always arguing with someone. I sat alone, in one of those Day-Glo orange cafeteria chairs, and wished I had somewhere else to go.

I could have gone over. They could have been my friends. But I'd rather crawl through swamps of nobody-ness for the next four years if they were my only some-body option. It's one thing to be a loser, it's another thing entirely to take pride in it.

Nobody ever made fun of Peter Wilkenson, despite the Monty Python club. He didn't get shoved into lockers. He was just there. Backdrop. Nothing you'd notice, like bad scenery for a student production. He didn't have a brother like Trevor. He wasn't walking the hallways in a shadow.

When Peter came back from rehab, he was all anyone could talk about. It wasn't like he morphed into hotness all of a sudden, though he did look better than before. Something was different about his face. It was the way he walked down the hall. I heard everything because guys like me get that privilege. Who the hell cares what I hear? I'd have nobody to tell.

For weeks, Peter Wilkenson was a celebrity. He was

more discussed and analyzed than any of those asstards on *The Hills*. He was bigger than *American Idol*.

Who is that guy? Do you remember him? I think he might have been in one of my classes. My girlfriend won't stop talking about that fucker. What happened to him? What's his fucking deal? . . . Nah, I'm not gonna ask him. I could whup his ass, but it ain't worth it. Heard the guy is crazy. Heard he smoked crack. Seriously. Heard his dealer is still after him. Heard he's on probation. Heard he carries a gun for protection. Heard he fucked Melissa Denaughty in the janitor's closet. . . . Yeah. I know. She's a total uptight bitch. She wouldn't even let Coleman Rogers touch her tits through her shirt. He fucked her. He fucking creamed in the head cheerleader. Busted her cherry and dumped her the next day. It messed with her head. I heard someone heard that she was, like, hysterically bawling in the handicapped stall, and, like, saying his name over and over. "Peter. Oh, Peter. Peter."

If a Monty Python appreciator can do it, so can I. There are no tears, and there won't be. This isn't football. I'm not going to be a quitter this time.

I will become a meth addict, or I will kill myself trying.

With renewed energy I make my way to the kitchen. I still feel like straight-up shit, but at least I can walk again. It occurs to me that I am thirsty. In fact, I've never been so thirsty in my life. My throat is the Mojave. I could drink my own piss.

I scan the fridge for something else. The Dr Pepper

cans are all gone. There's only powdered creamer. It'll have to be from the tap. Taking a glass out of the cabinet will take too long. I dip my head under the faucet. I don't care if it's hard water. I don't care if it's full of chemicals or poison or catfish feces. It's the best water I've ever tasted. My head starts to clear. It drips down my face and onto my vomit-stained shirt. This nasty, lukewarm tap water is better than sex. Not that I've ever had sex.

When I'm done, I see the note stuck to the fridge with a CLASSEN KNIGHTS magnet.

Honey,

I'll be home late. Stay hydrated. There's a carton of juice in the cabinet. Call me if your temperature rises.

Love,
Mom

PS Please don't eat my supplies, Doug. There's bologna in the fridge.

It find the juice behind a dish of unidentified leftovers. It's the no-pulp kind, which is perfect because I hate when those orange strings get stuck in my teeth. I take the Tropicana and a coffee mug and head back to my room. No time like the present. Now or never. The only cure for a hangover. Hair of the dog, and all that.

This time I put in less crystals. I set the glass on the desk. I think about cleaning up the vomit but decide a real drug addict wouldn't do this. Besides, it adds ambience. I need to immerse myself in the filth, roll around in it like a pig. I stare at the mug. I pace. I pick the crust out of my eyes. I crack my knuckles. I go and take a shower.

"Fuck this," I say halfway through soaping up my balls. I push back the curtain, step through the dried vomit, don't even grab a towel. I stomp, dripping wet, back to my room. I pick up the mug of orange juice.

"You and me," I tell it, and slam the bitter liquid in a few gulps. Then I go and get a towel because I'm getting the floor all wet.

It doesn't take long. I know what is happening. I've done the research. My heart is pumping the amphetamines through my arteries. The chemicals have passed my brain barriers and are releasing neurotransmitters. The blood vessels beneath my skin are constricting, my temperature is rising, my lungs expanding, rising and falling like great monarch wings, greedily engulfing copious amounts of air.

I feel perfectly calm. I don't feel that crazy. It's not what I expected. I might be breathing a little faster, but not much else.

It's just a plant, after all. At the base of everything. A yellowish green desert shrub that looks like broom bristles. Ma huang, ephedra, a Chinese stem used for five thousand years for colds and breathing problems.

Extracted by a Japanese chemist, made into a new compound by a German scientist. Taken by British troops during World War II. Taken in the twenties to cure asthma. Taken by athletes in the forties to enhance stamina. Used by housewives to keep skinny. *Hollywood gin. The Jenny Crank diet.* It's not just me. Selznick took it when producing *Gone With the Wind.* He didn't have time for petty human weaknesses like sleep or food. *As God is my witness, we'll never go hungry again.* Kerouac and his bennies. They had jobs to do. It is a long tradition. Artistic enhancement. Personal elevation. I can't find my jeans. I want the stained ones. I find every pair but the stained ones. I'm carrying on a great legacy. Burroughs. Of course he accidentally shot his wife in the head, but that wasn't the drugs, just bad aim. Charlie Parker, twisting the scale in rebellious ways, making sounds the world had never heard. I find the jeans and put them on. I slick back my hair. In the glow of the people's lamp, my eyes are wet, crystalline. Windows to the soul. No, something better than that, something nobody has ever heard before, notes that Parker never thought to string together. I'm not sure if it worked. I feel too calm. Too centered. I know I've got to get out of here. Just for a while. It's just a plant. Aloe to heal a cut. Dried oregano in spaghetti sauce. It's natural.

I write a note and stick it to my door.

Mom—

Feel a lot better. Took some NyQuil, you know what that stuff does to me. Gonna pass out till morning. Just

*sleep it off. Probably be fine for school tomorrow. Don't
worry. I ate.*

Xoxoxoxo
Doug

I marvel at my note-writing gifts. Why hasn't anyone
written a novel in notes? Or have they? I should do that.
Just notes from mother to son. Notes on doors. Notes on
pads and Post-its, written on mirrors with lipstick, written in neon chalk on the sidewalk. A life in notes. *Lolita* in
text messages. I should do that. I should write it down so I
don't forget. Jack always carried a notebook in the pocket
of his jeans. I don't have a notebook that small. I'll have to
get one. First, though, I need to get out of here.

I climb out the bedroom window.

The neighborhood is quiet. It must be late. It's October,
it's probably cold out, but I'm roasting. My belly is radiating thermal energy. I take off my shirt, so I'm just in my
wifebeater. *Guido shirts,* Dingo calls them, reminding me
that because he is one-eighth Italian he is allowed to use
ethnic slurs pertaining to his own people. He also claims
direct familial ties to the Mafia. Of course, this all started
after he Netflixed season one of the *Sopranos.*

I start to jog down the sidewalk. The moon is smirking at me through the leaves. I can see through windows. I
can see into family rooms. What the fuck is a family room,
anyway? The family room is purgatory. Mundane conver-

sations about petty lives during commercial breaks: *Did you buy the Oreos? Did you set the coffeemaker? The oil change. The report due on Tuesday. The dishes are dirty. Wallpaper.* It sickens me. It's a monstrosity. Predestination. Family rooms are Calvinistic. Families passing bowls of microwave popcorn, watching the season finale of *Wife Swap,* A-OK with limited atonement. *Lug nuts. The answering machine. The litter box. Mammograms. Putting Grandma in a home. Dad in Mexico with a schizo heiress. Cutting coupons. Vacation days. The tax return.* I run faster than I ever have before. I could be in the Olympics, I'm that fast. I tear down the sidewalk. I leave a trail of smoke behind me. I could run out of my skin. Peewee football had nothing on this. I'm a sprinter in the final lap. I slice through suburbia like a model airplane. I am aerodynamic.

Then my breath is gone. I understand why they say that now. I stop outside the 7-Eleven trying to find it, find my breath, my hands on each of my knees. I am covered in a film of gleaming sweat. I ran a good four miles. I feel good. I could run even farther. I lean against the pay phone. They are blaring John Denver through the loudspeakers. The theory is that easy listening keeps the gang members away. John hits a high note, and I get a stiffy. I hope it's just a coincidence, and I don't have some deep-seated erotic connection to bad seventies music.

Next to me, an old black man sits on the stoop eating a hot dog slathered in yellow mustard. The mustard is so bright it hurts my eyes. Food should not be that color. It isn't right. The mustard is everything that is wrong with

America. The mustard is the capitalist system at its most deranged. The mustard is the physical manifest of our synthetic human consciousness. I know, with certainty, that I am an undiscovered genius. I should invent something. Something no one has ever thought of. Something everyone needs. My invention will better humanity. It'll be more celebrated than the microchip. Steve Jobs would bow down to my brilliant mind. My invention will make the world a better place. It would help everyone, even this grizzled old man shoving this bright yellow hot dog down his throat outside the 7-Eleven. It will belong to all of us. They will sell it on the Home Shopping Network for three easy installments of $19.95. I need to figure out what it is. I need to write it down before I forget.

I feel my calves twitch and know it will have to wait.

I'm not sure where I'm headed, but I have a feeling I better hurry or I'm going to be late.

I don't know where I'm going till I'm standing right outside. Infinity. The club Laurilee told me about. When I was a kid, it was a Baptist congregation. At some point it closed, and the windows were boarded up for years, the bell removed from the steeple. Weeds grew up around the foundation. The paint chipped. People said it was haunted. I heard some kids got caught squatting there. I heard it was a crack house, an opium den, an underground swingers' club, an S&M dungeon. No one cared much until someone in the Vietnamese Mafia bought the property and the CLUB INFINITY sign went up. For a few days, there were protesters. They thought it was sacrilegious, making a house of God into a nightclub. It was even on the news. Dingo and I skipped out on our usual Taco Bell for the one across the street from the scene. We ate bean burritos and Dingo added *Hell yeah*s after each protest chant.

"Only a louse drinks in Jesus' house!"

Hell yeah!

The next day it was over. The protesters went somewhere better, probably to shoot an abortion doctor at the Planned Parenthood down the street, and the local network found a more interesting story to cover, like some guy on the north side who taught his cat how to roller-skate. Club Infinity was more popular than ever. Still is. Laurilee goes there.

I've never been to a club in my life. Cliques stand outside, huddled together, smoking. Guys wear baggy jeans belted below their boxer-shorted asses. I wonder what future generations will think when they look at pictures. I think of the tight seventies pants the guys wear on *Nick at Nite* reruns, how retarded it looks having your balls on polyester display. I wonder which is worse. Maybe we are just the same. They did drugs in the seventies. Early variations of meth. It was acceptable. It was fine. No one is the worse for it. Well, except for all those people who got AIDS when they had doped-up unprotected sex.

The girls all look like the ones who work at Hot Topic in the mall. They are cheap imitations of Laurilee. I scan the crowd, but I can't find her. I know I'd see her right away. I'd smell her like a bloodhound. I'd know her lips from another state. These chicks are the cheap Wal-Mart knockoff of her, Mr. Pibb to her Dr Pepper. Now that these infants have infiltrated the place, she's probably moved somewhere else, somewhere undiscovered, with that Daniel neck dragon. I need to get a tattoo. A tattoo would prove something. But first I need to get in the building.

An hour or two ago I would have stood awkwardly at the side, out of place, staring into the weeds, invisible to these people. They would be too cool. They'd scare me with their confidence. But in the last couple of hours something has changed. Or maybe it wasn't hours. Maybe it was fifteen minutes, and it just feels like longer. The most important quarter of an hour of my life. My vision has changed. I had Lasik on my soul. I can see the truth in every phlegm ball these guys hack into the dirt, in every high-pitched, flirty giggle of these paper-girls wearing short skirts. I can see the Oklahoma dripping off every one of them. They are tiny, minuscule neurons in this vacuum state. I'm destined for something much bigger. I'll know things they are incapable of knowing. I'm not sure what those things are right now, but when I remember, it will be mind-blowingly earth-shattering.

I push through the crowd with a newfound confidence. I show my useless driver's permit to the security guy, shell out twenty bucks, and get an under-eighteen stamp on my hand.

And just like that, I'm on the inside.

. . .

The Doug that gets pushed into lockers avoids crowds of teenagers. He takes the back hallways and the long route to classes. Sometimes he'll go without lunch so he won't have to brave the cafeteria line. That Doug tries to convince himself he's paranoid when he hears someone say *loser* under their breath, even though, more often than not, he knows they are talking about him. *Faggot, loser, asshole. Get out of my way. What the fuck are you looking at?* But this Doug, the one in Club Infinity, doesn't give a fuck what anyone thinks. And, apparently, this Doug has no problem with crowds.

I push through the mass of throbbing bodies. My skin rubs against the slick flesh of strangers. I can feel their blood pulsing through their clothes. I touch the bare back of a girl as I pass her. Her goose bumps rise under my palm. I want to dance, even though I haven't danced since my uncle's wedding when I was ten. I'd thought I was cool up there under the portable disco lights, doing my best imitation of a Backstreet Boys video, until Trevor told me that even the bass player in the band was rolling his eyes at me. *Don't ever dance again,* he'd said. Then he disappeared to make out with one of the bridesmaids. She had big tits and I think she was our third cousin. In retrospect, incest is much more embarrassing than bad ten-year-old dancing, but I still hid at a corner table chewing ice cubes for the rest of the night.

Trevor was wrong. I can dance. I am a great dancer.

It was in me all the time. My body is doing crazy things. People are smiling and nodding at me. I punch the air with my fist, I clench my teeth. I am hard-core. I am so fucking sexy I make my own dick hard.

A few feet away, a girl with long hair is dancing by herself. Her eyes are half-closed and she chews on her bottom lip. Something about her expression reminds me of Laurilee. She might be pretty, or she might not be. I'm not sure and don't care. I dance over to her, and then we are dancing together. She lets me rub my dick against her ass. I gyrate against her like I'm in a rap video. I'm a rap star, and she's some oiled-up chick in a yellow bikini. I could fuck her. It would be easy. I run my hands across her bare, protruding stomach. I squeeze her belly with my hand. It feels like what Play-Doh would feel like if Play-Doh was softer and made you horny. She swings her hair around, and some of it gets in my mouth. For just a moment, I suck on a clump. I know that hair is nothing but an outgrowth of dead cells from one hundred thousand follicles on your scalp. Even so, hers tastes great.

At some point she whispers something in my ear and grins. I have no idea what she says, so I choose to believe it is something about how awesome I am and give her a knowing smile. Then she grips my arm and pulls me through the crowd. She leans against the wall and pants a little bit. We are standing still, but my body still feels like it is moving. She lights a cigarette and inhales. She hands it to me. I can taste her lipstick on the end. My veins are circuits conducting electricity. She smiles at me. Her face is round like a cherub's. Her teeth are very white.

"Are you on X?" she asks.

"No." I laugh.

"I am. I mean, I don't usually dance like that with random cute guys."

"You think I'm cute?" I say, moving in close to her.

She rolls her eyes. "You know you are."

I think that she must be right. Maybe I've been cute the whole time. Like those ugly guys in high school who get discovered on the street and put in magazines. No, I'm getting ahead of myself. But this Doug Schaffer doesn't think too hard. He just does stuff. He pushes her against the wall of that dirty old church because he is the kind of guy who can do that. I am James Dean in *Rebel Without a Cause,* only not so overdramatic. I am misunderstood. Dangerous. Cute.

"Ouch," she says. I have burned her hand with my cigarette. Still, she's grinning.

I wipe the ashes off and lift her hand to my mouth. I lick it. She tastes salty, like the water in Lake Texoma, only not polluted. "Better?"

"Yes." She giggles.

"What's your name?"

"Angela."

"Angel."

"Angela," she corrects me, and giggles again.

"Yup, just what I said. You're Angel. I knew it all along. Just look at you." I know, somewhere deep in the recesses of my brain, that this is a moron thing to say. It is cheesy and generic. It is what some random dude in a club says to some random chick when he wants to hit her up and he doesn't have a creative synapse in his body. For the first time in my life, I am that guy. Just some guy coming on to some girl in a club.

It is the most amazing feeling in the whole fucking world.

At some point we are in a car. Some guy with green hair is driving. Next to him is another kid with one of those asymmetrical haircuts that are innately illogical, a human sheepdog. His eyeliner has smeared, so he looks like he's been punched in his one visible eye. Angela's hand is intertwined with mine. It is clammy. She is playing with the hair on my arms, pushing it in one direction and then another. "Did you ever do Grow a Garden? When you were a kid?"

"No," I say. "We just went to the supermarket."

She gives a high-pitched giggle. "No, silly. Like this. First plant the seeds." Before I can stop her, she pinches my arm from wrist to elbow. It hurts. Not that I would actually stop her. I'm still trying to convince myself that this living human female actually exists, let alone that she is touching me of her own free will. "Then you cover it with dirt," she says, and rubs the top of my arm roughly back and forth.

"Ouch," I say, but don't mean it. I'm imagining she is doing it to my dick.

"Shhh. Then the sun comes out and warms the garden." She tickles my arm up and down. "And then the garden blooms!" She pulls back and grins at me like she's done something extraordinary.

"Neat."

"No, look at your arm!" She points to where my arm hair has matted into little clumps. "That's the garden! Get it?" She's beaming.

"So, I guess X makes everything, like, really fascinating."

"Man, she's always like that," says green-haired guy from the front seat, and laughs.

"I like games," she says with finality.

"Like, board games?"

"Sure. All kinds." Then she gives that high-pitched giggle again. I don't want her to talk anymore. I like her better when she is quiet. I fight the urge to smash my hand over her soft, little cupid mouth. It is time for something else to happen.

"So are you Emo?" I ask the eyeliner guy.

"I don't like categories," he tells me.

"If you had to pick one, though, would you pick Emo?" My voice is louder than I remember.

"I don't know how to answer that, man. Besides, no one says that term anymore, man."

Angela makes a gurgling sound in the back of her throat. I think it's a happy sound.

"Then what do they say?" I sound confident, like a prosecutor on *Law & Order*.

"I don't know, man. No one likes to be labeled," says the green-haired guy.

"You can't, like, put words to a state of being," says the eyeliner guy. "Listen. I don't really want to talk about it." He looks like he is about to cry, and it really pisses me off. *Act like a man,* I want to tell him. Angela gurgles again.

"So, by being Emo, I'm sorry, in an unlabeled state of being that makes you wear eyeliner and be pissed off, what does that, like, entail? Are you sad?" I can't believe I'm being such a chode. But the words just seem to keep coming, like from another mouth, another Doug Schaffer who is cute and pushes hot girls against walls.

"We all have pain, man. Let's leave it at that."

"But your pain is, like, worse? Is that why you wear black?"

"You wear black," he says.

"Yeah, but it isn't, like, a statement."

He ignores me. He begins to roll a cigarette. Something soft is between my fingers. My hand, as though disengaged from the rest of my body, has migrated upward. I am rubbing Angela's earlobe between two fingers. I'm the kind of guy who does that. Just squeezes a girl's earlobe. She is cooing. The eyeliner guy pouts as he measures out tobacco.

"Is that an Emo thing? Rolling your own cigarettes?"

Apparently, beside being the kind of guy who likes to be an asshole for no reason, I'm also the kind of guy who can't let something go.

Emo turns to me and sneers, pushing out his bottom lip like a little boy. "Don't try and define me, dude. Just let me be who I am, okay?" he whines.

"Where do you buy your eyeliner?"

The green-haired guy laughs. Angela coos again. I pinch her earlobe hard.

"Who the fuck are you anyway?" asks Emo. "Who is this guy, Angela?"

I feel the sudden urge to kick his ass. It's because of his hair. I hate his hair. He can't see out of one side of his face. I've never kicked someone's ass in my life. I wouldn't even know how to do it. But part of me wants to give it a try.

"Be quiet, Reggie," says Angela. "He's my friend."

"Your name is *Reggie*?" I say, and laugh. For some reason, this is the funniest thing I've ever heard. I laugh till I almost choke, and Angela laughs with me. This time her laugh is real, not just a giggle. Our laughter sounds really nice together. Tinkling wind chimes in Tijuana. She grins at me like I'm important. I want to chew on her round cheeks. I pull her up into my lap. She doesn't fight me. She'll do anything I say.

"This is bullshit." Emo glares at me from the front seat. "It's so easy for guys like you."

"Guys like me? What kind of guy am I?"

He turns from me and lights his sloppily constructed

cigarette. "Just like every other guy in the world. Just . . . regular. Just totally happy to be in your little comfortable little . . . womb of comfort."

"Are you a poet too?" I ask.

"Your ordinary life."

"You think I'm ordinary?"

"Yes," he spits at me. I try to wrap my brain around this.

"Cool," I say finally.

"It wasn't a compliment."

"Shut the fuck up now, Reggie. I'm sick of your voice." I sound mean. I sound like the kind of guy who would scare the shit out of the kind of guy I used to be a few hours ago. I am Reggie's Ronan Applegate. He does what I say because I have the capability to smash his face in and make him cry. It would be easy. Next to me, Angela has taken out a Sugar Daddy pop. She is sucking on it with concentration, stretching out the hard taffy with the roof of her mouth. I feel my dick stretch with each suck. It is almost unfathomable, all the things I am capable of making happen.

"Stop at the next place you see," I tell the green-haired guy. "I want a slushie."

We are on the northwest side of the city. I buy a slushie at the Kum and Go. "Kum and Go," I say, laughing, as I mix six different flavors into a Big Thirsty cup, which I haven't had the guts to do since I was eight years old.

Angela clings to me. In the convenience-store light, I can see her clearer. She looks about twelve, or maybe it is the way she is dressed. Her hair is pulled back in blue ribbons. She is wearing Mary Janes and still sucking on her Sugar Daddy, pulling it longer and longer with the roof of her mouth. I want to ask her how old she is. Then again, I'm not sure I want to know. *Old enough to bleed, old enough to breed.* That's what Dingo would say. *If she's got hair, you can mow that lawn.*

Outside, a group of Vietnamese boys with stiff-spiked hair pose around a convertible like they are on a calendar shoot. After the war they came here. Which war? I can't think. Not the great-grandparents one. Not the one with the people in ovens. The one after that. Vietnam. Of course. My brain is all mixed up. My brain is a six-flavor brown slushie. Soldiers who brought their Vietnamese brides back to Oklahoma. *Things they can do with their pretty little mouths. Ha ha ha.* Bring them to Oklahoma with the in-laws, the siblings, the second and third cousins. Now the neighborhood is infiltrated with *pho* restaurants and nail salons. The street sign on Twenty-third and Classen says LITTLE SAIGON. No one messes with the Vietnamese gang boys. They may be pretty waifs, but it's a known fact they carry Uzis in their trunks. They are scary as fuck. Usually, I would avoid eye contact. Now I nod at them. I nod upward. That's how the badasses do it in the movies. The downward nod shows vulnerability. The upward nod says, *I know I can take you, but let's be friends instead.*

The alpha pretty boy does the upward nod back at me. I see his eyes scan over Angela. I smirk. I pull her closer with my hand. I realize the hand is on her ass. I'm proud. I'm the kid who brought the coolest shit to show-and-tell.

We are at a party in a worn-down neighborhood I've never seen. Angela gives me a jumbo plastic cup of beer. I've never liked the taste of beer, but I make myself drink it anyway. If I can do the upward nod, I can chug a beer. I suck it down quick and hold it out to her. She races off to get me another one.

I meet Roger, who works at the DMV and mixes industrial-swamp-trance music. I tell him my theory about the DMV's covert ties to the Iranian terrorist infra-structure, which blows his mind, even though I'm making it up. I meet Tara, who has twenty-four piercings and is considering a twenty-fifth on her clit, only she is con-flicted because she heard it might take away her ability to orgasm. "Go for it," I tell her. "That's just a myth. Those nerves are incapable of desensitization. In fact, it will both heighten and augment your arousal."

"Really?" she says.

"Completely." I know it's true. I heard it somewhere. In fact, I'm pretty much an expert on everything. I had no idea I knew so much. I'm practically a guru. I sit next to a big Native American guy who has his arm wrapped around a small blond girl. She might or might not be a midget. I tell them my theory on how to initiate peace in the Middle East. I didn't even know I had a theory about the Middle East, but this one is great. I can't believe no one came up with it sooner. They nod. They think I'm fascinating. In front of us, a girl in a black cape dances by herself. She is graceful, her thin, pale body folding into itself and stretching to the ceiling, arms making wide arcs above her head. The arcs are glowing. Or maybe she is holding glow sticks. It doesn't matter. Nothing matters in the whole, wide world.

Angela is sitting on my lap. She is so small like that, curled up into me. She makes me feel big. Enormous. I want to be even bigger. I wonder if I should start lifting weights. She is playing with my hand. I think I'm really drunk, or maybe it is the meth, or maybe it is just my dick. Angela is tracing the lines in my palm. I am telling her my life story. I think she asked, or maybe she didn't. My life story is captivating, even though I keep getting hung up on the tiniest details. She doesn't seem to mind. In fact, she is enthralled.

"So, after dinosaurs, I started getting into snakes, 'cause that's the natural progression, really, and I figured dinosaurs were only for kids. But the thing is, and I think you'll agree with me here, I only liked the venomous ones. They were way cooler. I could name most of them too. I might even remember. Wait. Copperhead. Cottonmouth. Water moccasin, Asian cobra, diamondback rattle, timber rattle, black mamba, dusky pygmy, I mean, I could go on. I was a pretty obsessive kid. The Asian cobra.

He can spit venom when he's angry. The king cobra. Now, he's not dangerous, but he's special because he's big. His head, listen to this, this is fucking crazy, his head can grow as big as a man's hand."

"You're really smart," says Angela.

"Yeah. I know. Not to sound egotistical or anything. I'm not, like, a brainiac or anything. I mean, my grades aren't great. The thing about grades, they aren't an indicator of—"

"I dropped out of high school," she says, and gives that earsplitting giggle. If we are going to continue to nurture this relationship into a flourishing flower, she's going to have to stop doing that.

"Oh, yeah?" Part of me is relieved she isn't twelve. Part of me is a little disappointed. Part of me wonders if that means I'm a pedophile.

"I hated it. My mom doesn't care that I dropped out, though."

"What about, like, the government?"

"I'm getting homeschooled. My mom thinks high school is a bad influence anyway." I look around the room. In the corner, two guys with matching hipster mullets are sharing a bottle of tequila. The blond who may or may not be a dwarf is shoving her tongue down the Native American guy's throat. Emo is rolling another cigarette. Or maybe it's a joint.

"But your mom doesn't mind that you're here?"

Angela makes that sound again. "She thinks I'm on a church group retreat!"

"She believes that?"

"Sure. Besides, my youth pastor will cover for me. Tina. She's the big old dyke and she's in love with me. She'll do whatever I say. I mean, my mom thinks I'm the perfect daughter. I am. I read the Bible every day. That's not even an assignment. I do it to make her happy."

"The Bible?"

"Sure, silly. I've got it practically memorized."

"No way. I don't believe you."

"I do! I swear! Want to hear some?"

"I'm not sure—"

She untangles herself from my grip and stands facing me. She clasps her hands in front of her. "Give me a subject."

"What kind of subject?"

"Anything, silly." Behind her, the black-cape girl has moved on to an impromptu floor routine. She rolls around and writhes. She twitches her pelvis like she is getting fucked by a ghost. For some reason, I think of Casper. She's getting fucked by Casper the ghost. No one pays much attention. Someone, in another room, has started playing the drums, even though they don't know how. No one seems to mind.

"How about Jesus?" I say. I was never much on religion. I mean, I like getting shit on Christmas. But it seems kind of crazy to me that all these people believe in some big guy who lives in the clouds and watches us and has opinions. Believing in Jesus just seems strange. Like believing that Sesame Street is a real place and Oscar the

Grouch is a real dude and not a green furball with a guy's hand up his ass. Besides, if he was real, this big gray guy sitting up in the sky and making shit happen, why would he make guys like Ronan? Why would he give morons so much power?

"Well?" She's watching me.

"Well what?"

"What about Jesus? I mean, that's kind of a big topic."

I try to think of something. My brain is a spinning top. A kaleidoscope. "How he loves us. How he loves the little children."

"I could do that with my eyes closed. Gimme something harder."

"How he wants us to be good?"

She sighs and blows her bangs out of her eyes. "Too easy." She looks so cute standing there. Her skirt is very short. I wonder what her panties look like. I wonder if she's wearing any at all.

"How about sex?"

"What about sex?" she says innocently.

"Dirty sex," I say because the filter between my brain and my mouth evaporated several beers ago. Besides, I'm the kind of guy who can say anything he wants. A big guy. I wonder if I should buy a Soloflex machine. No, just some weights. Free weights are hard-core. That's what they use in prison. She looks at the wall above my head, as though it is a congregation. She smiles an innocent, little smile. I imagine my dick in her innocent, little mouth.

"'For she is not my wife, and I am not her husband.

And let her put away her harlotry from her face. And her adultery from between her breasts.'" I'm hard, even before Angela says *breasts.* "'Or I will strip her naked and expose her as on the day when she was born. I will make her like a wilderness . . .'" She sounds like one of those girls in the phone-sex commercials. I never knew the Bible was so hot. Maybe I'm missing out on something. Maybe Jesus isn't so bad after all.

Without thinking, I reach out and grip the back of her thighs under her skirt. "Come here."

She does not move. She does not look at me. She stares at the wall above me like this is a test in Sunday school. "'Make her like desert land and slay her with thirst . . .'"

"I'm gonna slay you with thirst," I mutter. My hands move, as though disattached from my body, upward. I squeeze her ass under her skirt.

"'Also I will have no compassion on her children, because they are children of harlotry. For their mother . . .'"

"Stop now." I pull her toward me, till she is straddling me across the dirty green couch, her knees on either side of me. Like that, I start to kiss her neck. Her skin tastes like it should be marked fragile.

"'For she said, "I will go after my lovers, who give me my bread and water."'"

I think about what Jack would do. I bite her. She moans.

"'My wool and my flax, my oil and my drink—'"

I bite her again. Harder. Not hard enough to make her bleed, but hard enough to make her pay attention. She moans again. I think she likes it. Or maybe she doesn't. It doesn't matter.

"'Therefore, behold, I will hedge up . . .'" she says, her voice faltering. "Wait. I can't remember now. You made me forget." She giggles for the fifty-millionth time that night.

"No more giggling."

She starts to do it again, then catches herself. "It just comes out! I can't—"

"It's time to stop talking." Then I kiss her. I kiss her hard.

When I imagined my first real kiss, I had expectations. It's easy to have expectations about something you don't think will ever happen. I thought it would be romantic, like a movie kiss. There'd be fireworks. Not literal fireworks. Then again, sometimes they were literal in my fantasy, because it was a fantasy, and they were blasting up behind Laurilee and me the instant our lips touched for the first time. We were in the glow of a sunset. On a beach. On an island. In Fiji. Laurilee was wearing a lei. Or a negligee. And we said things no one would ever say, total clichéd bullshit, embarrassing shit you aren't supposed to say. But it was okay because we felt it. We meant every word. *You are the one. You are it. I want to be with you forever.* Besides, you can do whatever you want in a stupid, infantile first-kiss fantasy. The sex fantasies are altogether different.

But none of my fantasies prepared me for this.

This is the real thing, and it has nothing to do with expectations of emotional completion and a two-meeting-as-one, you-complete-me, la-la, happily-ever-after load of bull-honky crap.

This isn't Laurilee. This is some fucked-up Christian chick who looks twelve years old. And I was right. She isn't wearing underwear.

I had no idea my tongue would do that. I had no idea my tongue knew *how* to do that. I guess it isn't something you teach. We all know it. We've known it since we greedily suckled our first titty. *Oh, God, don't think about my mother's breasts.* Think about Angela, her hand resting on the thigh of my jeans, just a half inch away from my dick. Just a millimeter. A hand that isn't my own. On my dick. The possibility is exhilarating.

And I don't give a damn about her. That's the best part.

I glance over her shoulder, and Reggie the Emo is watching us intently as he smokes. I narrow my eyes at him, but he doesn't turn away. Maybe he can learn something from my technique. I had no idea I'd be so good at this.

Kerouac said, *All life is a foreign country.* This girl in my lap, whose name I can barely remember, is unexplored territory. I am a settler, the first of my kind. This is my land. I own it. I want to touch every part of it. I run my hand over her shirt. Just thin fabric separates my hands from live human female nipples. She squirms. My dick is trapped in a denim torture chamber. I kiss her harder. I'm afraid I might eat her. That was something I never expected. That kissing was so close to cannibalism.

I am about to suggest we go somewhere else. I'd settle

for anywhere at this point. Behind a Dumpster. Inside an abandoned oil drum. We are both panting. She pulls back. Red spots are on her cheeks. "That was kind of crazy," she says. "Maybe we should slow down."

"That is how a girl can get herself raped." I can't believe I said it. We stare at each other. I'm afraid she'll do something. That she'll slap me. Even worse, that she'll get up and leave me there, my dick hard and aching. She can't. I haven't even been under her shirt yet. "I think I'm in love with you," I say quickly.

"Really?" she squeaks, and grins at me. She starts to giggle. I give her a look, and she bites her lip to stop herself.

"Yeah," I say, and dive back into her. This was something else I never expected: that I could be such a great liar.

At some point she untangles from me. I reach for her like a toddler that had his sippy cup taken away. Only this sippy cup was full of crack, and this toddler is an addict. "Where are you going?" I say.

"To pee."

"Hurry." I look around. I try to calm myself down. The room has emptied out. Emo is still there, smoking cigarettes and furiously scrawling in a journal. The dancing girl has exhausted herself. She sits cross-legged in the ravages of the party, moving her arms in a sweeping motion in front of her, as though she is conducting a symphony of crushed beer cans and cigarette butts. I am alone. My throat is raw from talking. My jaw aches from kissing. The back of my neck has begun to throb, and my chapped bottom lip has cracked. I have a cut on my lip. If that girl, Angela, has a cut in her lip, she could give me AIDS. Wait, you can't get AIDS from kissing, can you? But what about open sores? I try to remember what the coach said in Sex Education, but all I can remember are analogies to passes and home runs and taking the defensive end, and I have forgotten what sexual acts he was talking about.

I have a horrible feeling. I've done something wrong. The meth. The meth must be wearing off. Some guy sits next to me. He's got dreadlocks and a tie-dyed shirt. He could be Bob Marley, except he's white and has acne and this is Oklahoma.

"Havin' fun?"

"Yeah," I say, willing Angela to come back.

"You friends with Donnie?"

"No."

"Who you know here?"

"Donnie. Sure. Donnie."

"I love Donnie. Donnie is a cool guy, huh, mon?" he slurs. I try to ignore that this Caucasian dude with zits just called me *mon*. "I'm gonna be really fucked up at work tomorrow."

"Yeah? What do you do?"

"I fry donuts. At the Save-A-Lot." I nod. I think I see something move across his head, like lice or a flea. I hope they make him wear a hairnet.

"Cool," I say. I wonder why the fuck it takes women so long in the bathroom. What are they doing in there? She said she had to pee. I could do that in under twenty seconds. I don't think having to sit and wipe would really add on that much time. Something else is going on. Something no guy knows about. There's a secret society in the bathroom. A cabal. Sacrifices to the toilet god, offerings. I need her to hurry. My dick is throbbing. Or maybe I have AIDS.

"I hate working the morning shift. I mean, I gotta be there at six. I'm gonna be so fucked-up, man. Hey, can you give me a ride?"

"I don't think so."

"You know anyone who can? I gotta be there soon, man."

I turn to him. "Why? What time is it?"

"Like, five forty-five, mon."

"Are you fucking kidding me?" I bum-rush the window and lift the heavy flannel sheet attached with duct tape. A sharp beam of sunlight burns my eyes.

We run to the nearest main street. I pull Angela behind me. She thinks we are playing a game. She laughs as we run. She laughed as I pulled her from room to room in search of Reggie, who, now that I actually want to see his jacked-up eyeliner face, has somehow disappeared with our only possible mode of transportation. Now she laughs as we almost get run over by a guy in a sedan. The driver is wearing a tie. He looks at us with disdain. "I got to get a cab," I tell her.

"Around here? No way. You'll have to call one."

"You know the number?"

"I think it's 777-TAXI. No, wait, maybe 888-TAXI. Or is it C-A-B? No, that only has three letters." She giggles.

"I need to find a pay phone. C'mon." I pull her down the street to a Laundromat. It hasn't opened yet, and the tiny Asian lady inside eyes us warily. I pick up the pay phone. The receiver is sticky. Cum. Spit. Residual crack residue. I dig in my pockets.

"I need a quarter."

"I don't have one," Angela says, digging in her teddy-bear-shaped backpack.

"Fuck. Fuck, fuck, fuck. My mom is probably gonna call the police." I bang on the window of the Laundro-mat. The lady pretends she can't hear me. I bang harder. "I just need a quarter!" I yell through the bars.

"Wait," says Angela.

I turn around. She is holding out a BlackBerry in her tiny hand, an expensive one that can send messages and show movies and probably even take a shit for you. I grab it out of her hand. I fight the urge to call her a dumb bitch. "Thanks," I say, and force a smile through my cracked lip.

"Well, well, well," says Dingo when he pulls up to the curb in his mom's minivan. "And who is this lovely lady?"

His hair is standing up like a rooster, and he's got some dried drool in the corner of his mouth.

"Angela," I say.

"Well, hello, Angela," he says in a voice he probably considers sexy. She giggles. This is the most positive response Dingo has ever got from a live woman. He leans farther out of the window. "Does anyone ever call you Angel?"

"We got to go," I tell him.

He ignores me. "Where can I take you, pretty lady?"

"That's okay," she says. "I've got to go back and find Reggie."

"Are you sure?" I say, feigning like I give a damn what she and her BlackBerry do with the rest of the morning. I am already in the passenger seat.

"Yeah. He's got the car. He'll get worried if I don't come back."

"Okay, well, I guess I should probably get home anyway." She looks really cute all of a sudden, standing there on the sidewalk of Western Avenue. Half an hour ago, I had my tongue in her mouth. It kind of blows my mind. She might be a dingy, skankish bitch, but I really want to do it again. I try to think of something smooth to say, leaning over a pajama-wearing Dingo in a minivan. A few hours ago, I could have made this work. "So, I guess that we can. Um—"

"You want my number?" she says.

"Sure!" says Dingo. "I mean, hold on, I'll get him a piece of paper." He pulls a Post-it off one of those pads with an attached pen that you stick to the dashboard. The top is inscribed MOTHER OF A CLASSEN HONOR STUDENT. Angela says her number and I write it down. We stare at each other awkwardly with Dingo between us.

"So. I guess I'll see you around?" she says.

I try to think of the perfect thing to say. I grin at her. I make my voice husky and say, "I'm always around. Good night, Angela."

She grins as Dingo pulls the van out onto the street.

"*Superman Returns*. Superman's last line to Lois. Nice choice."

"Thanks," I say.

For a moment, we are silent, grappling with our own thoughts. Then Dingo opens his mouth and begins to howl. "What in Jesus Christ on a fucking crutch's name are you doing out at seven a.m. with that little filly? What the fuck is going on? Are you drunk? Who the fuck are you, man? Where the fuck is Doug Schaffer?" He slams the steering wheel excitedly with his hand, weaving through cars without his turn signal.

"Faster, dude. You got to get me home. My mom is going to phone in an Amber Alert."

"How did you meet her? Did you bang her? What the fuck is happening?"

"Long story. No. Almost. Just drive. I'll tell you everything later."

"You better call me next time, man." He chuckles to himself as he makes an illegal U-turn onto the I-40 ramp.

"Okay, okay, just get me home quick."

"Unbelievable," he says, merging into morning traffic.

It's rush hour, but this isn't New York City. More like rush minute, and people do their best to avoid him. A few give weak honks that sound almost polite as he cuts them off. "Un-ba-fuckin'-lievable! Doug Schaffer, out with a hot little bitch? Doug Schaffer, Classen's most inconsequential, microscopic peon, drunk on a weeknight with a hot little chickie? What is the world coming to? Why didn't you call me?"

"Nice pants," I say, motioning to his pajama bottoms. They are covered in tiny smiley-faced trains that are saying *choo choo*.

"My nana got 'em, okay?" he says, sneering. "You know she's senile. Don't change the subject. Just tell me. Did you get your dick wet or not?"

"Wettish. Later. I'll tell you everything. Just drive now, okay? And hurry."

He mutters to himself, and I lean back in my seat and take a deep breath.

In a few miles I will be home and have to deal with my mother. I push the thought far into the recesses of my brain, back into the place I put dirty laundry and Trevor. For this one moment, I just let the night flood back over me—Infinity, dancing, a party in a house I don't know, my tongue in another mouth. I let it flow over me, like I am sinking into a bathtub of hot water, mounds of Mr. Bubble rising around me, my flesh melting down into all the things I never dreamed were possible for a guy like me.

I feel my whole body grinning.

. . .

A few minutes later Dingo starts talking again. He won't shut up about *how fucking un-ba-fuckin-credible this shit is* and how he *had no idea a total pathetic noob* like me *was capable of such great things* and why didn't I *bother to call him?* When he finally drops me off at the end of my block, I jump out of the car. "Wait, man," he says. "Just tell me this. Just tell me one thing, okay?"

"Fine. Just hurry." Across the street, Mrs. Lockmeyer heads down the driveway in a pink robe to get her paper. I duck so she doesn't see me.

"Did you see her—"

"Shut up for a second," I hiss at him. "Tell me when she goes back in the house!"

The Lockmeyers are known as *that nice Jewish family.* I used to be obsessed with them, especially after Trevor told me their little boy had a tail. I pulled down his pants once, when we were six and he was bending over in the sandbox, just to see. I was kind of sad when there was nothing but ass crack beneath his Power Rangers Underoos. He hasn't talked to me since and still looks at me in fourth-period Economics like I'm after him to be my prison bitch.

"Did you see her thingy?"

"Is she gone?" I ask.

"Yeah, man. Yeah. Is it shaved?" I pop up from where I am crouched.

"I didn't see it."

"Did you touch it?"

"I don't have time for this."

"Did you do anything?" he asks. I smirk. "Tell me, man. What did you do?"

"Later. I got to go."

"Just one detail." He looks at me with awe. This is what real men do. They brag to their friends. They don't wash their hands for the rest of the day. They keep the smell of their conquest on their fingers. Dingo, in his choo-choo-train pajama pants, is looking at me like I am a real man. An actual stud. I can't help myself.

"Well, I'll say this . . ." He looks at me expectantly. "She's Christian."

"So?"

"So she's *real* fucked-up in the head. You know what I mean."

"I guess," he says, looking disappointed.

"And she wasn't wearing panties."

Dingo eyes widen. "Nice," he says, almost to himself. "Nice."

I am as stealthy as James Bond opening the front door. The lock barely clicks. I throw my Converse behind the umbrella rack. I sneak down the hallway to my room like I am prowling through a Vietnamese minefield, slithering around the side table as though it will erupt. I am almost to home base. I am inches from the doorknob of my room.

"Doug?" says my mom from the kitchen. I jump, almost knocking down a vase.

"Yeah?" I say, my voice cracking like it did when I was fourteen.

"You up?"

"Yup." Across from me, Trevor grins at me from his engorged senior portrait. He's wearing his jersey and has his arm wrapped around the football like they are on a date. He's laughing at me.

My mom stands at the end of the hallway in her bathrobe, a solitary curler hanging by her left ear. This is it. I'm busted. I feel my face flush. I didn't think it would happen this quickly. My dick only got wettish.

"How are you feeling?" she asks, her eyes narrowed.

"I feel a lot better. Must have been one of those twenty-four-hour things. I was just going to take a shower. Get ready for school." I wonder what I look like to her, in my dirty clothes, reeking of beer, cigarettes, and Christian slut. There is a long pause. We stare at each other.

Then she sighs. "I have so much to do, I can hardly keep my mind together."

"Make a list?" I squeak. "Like, on Post-its?"

She pulls out the dangling curler. "I'm going to be home late tonight. Homeland came through with the Hostess stuff. We've got a ton of packages to make."

"Okay."

"Can you feed yourself?"

"No problem."

She stares at me, and I brace myself. She sees. This is

it. The confrontation. I'm almost sorry it had to end this quickly. Last night was fun. I wanted to do it again.

"Dougie, something just occurred to me."

"The cookies?" I say, hearing my voice squeak. "I'll ask Roger today. I won't forget this time, I promise."

"No, honey. I couldn't sleep last night, thinking about all the stuff I had to do—"

"Did you take one of your pills?" I ask, searching frantically for a distraction.

"I need to refill my prescription. But that's not the point." She steps closer to me. I try to back up, afraid she can smell the sin on me. She touches my cheek. "We haven't really talked in a long time, have we?"

"We talk all the—"

"It's my fault. There's just so much to do with OMSOT and work and—"

"Seriously, Mom. It's okay."

She smiles. "You always were very independent, Doug. You get that from me. I just want you to know I'm here, okay? If you need anything. If you want to talk about anything, I'm here. I'm never too busy for you, Eeyore."

"I know that," I say, wincing at the name. He'd been my favorite character in the Pooh books. I liked his ears.

"I'm serious about that trip during your spring break. I could get a Friday off work. We don't have to do Six Flags. We could go to the lake for a couple of days. Anything you want."

My chest wells up with guilt. I really do love her. It's not her fault that the world sucks the big one. It's not her fault I'm such a weird configuration of genes. If only it had been another sperm, I'd be something completely more satisfactory. Instead, she got a fucked-up cocktail of DNA that can't play sports or make the honor roll.

I force a smile. "That sounds really great, Mom."

She smiles. "Okay. Wow. I better get ready or I'll be late."

"Me too," I say, backing up toward my bedroom.

She wrinkles her forehead. "Doug?"

"Yes?"

"It really isn't sanitary to sleep in your clothes."

The bathroom is covered in dried puke. Luckily, Mom would never come in here. She's avoided my bathroom since I turned thirteen, probably afraid she'll find the walls and floors splattered in ambiguous teenage-boy secretions. I throw off my clothes and turn the shower as hot as it will go without giving me visible burns. I stand there, letting the water smack against my face and the steam rise around me. She had no idea. I may be a weird loser geek, my grades may suck, but I'm dependable. I'm not the kind of kid to sneak out. I'm a disappointment, but not the rebellious, break-the-rules kind of disappointment. I'm just an average, everyday kind of underachiever disappointment. Part of me is hurt. She didn't even notice. Then I think about Angela. She called me cute. She let me put my tongue in her mouth. I was a different person last night, and she liked that dude, and she could have been Laurilee. She was practice, and I did okay. I passed. I more than passed. If she were the SATs, I would have broken two thousand. Angela was community college, and pretty soon I'll be ready for Yale.

Angela wasn't wearing panties. I didn't actually touch it, but I could have. It would have been easy. Solar heat was practically radiating from her pussy. Or maybe it was the meth that made me think that. Or maybe it wasn't. Maybe she was all worked up for me, Doug Schaffer. It was my hands that did that. My tongue. I had no idea that women were like that. Like intricate machines. Push this button, she moans, turn a knob, she drips. I could have spent hours with her stretched out in front of me, learning the circuitry of her motherboard. I am Montgomery Scott, she is my starship, and she could have been Laurilee. Laurilee could have straddled me across that couch. The image makes my chest ache in a good way. I think about Angela with Laurilee's face and jack off, the shower steam rising up around me, my skin falling off like an abandoned shell. I come so hard I have to brace myself on the shower rod, and I don't even feel guilty.

I want more. Of everything.

I put in more crystals this time. The orange juice is hot from sitting in my room all day. It's probably gone bad. I don't even care. At least it's the no-pulp kind.

• • •

Dingo and I sit next to each other in Advanced Chemistry. I've been moved out of all my honors classes except this one. I've maintained a steady A in here because Dingo lets me copy his homework and test answers. He doesn't mind. It makes him feel important. Instead of one A, he's getting two. Captain Richards doesn't notice anyway. He's morbidly obese and wears a lab coat even though we've never actually done an experiment. He isn't even a captain of anything. He's been teaching here for twenty years, and they say he killed over twenty people in Vietnam. Rumor is that when the bomb went off downtown in '95, Captain Richards had a vet flashback and ordered everyone to get under desks before the rice monkeys got them. In class we work on equations and he supposedly screens scientific films on his portable DVD player to show us in future classes, though he's never actually shown one and we all know he's watching reruns of *The Andy Griffith Show*. Once, during an especially unbearable first period, I randomly opened one of the doors under our unused lab table. The cabinet was full of bones. I stole a pelvis. I don't know why, I just did it. Now it's somewhere under my bed.

"What the fuck happened?" says Dingo as I finish copying his homework for Captain to collect when class ends. I don't feel anything yet. The crystals aren't working. I feel like the same invisible loser I do every day, taking the long way to avoid a morning Ronan ass-whupping. It's like last night never happened.

"I told you. I snuck out the window. I got home before Mom even woke up."

"But why did you sneak out?"

"I don't know."

Around us social hour continues. Two girls giggle over lesbian Lindsay Lohan in *US Weekly*, another plucks her eyebrows in front of a compact mirror. It's pretty gross. I wonder why she can't do that at home. In the corner, Elroy Densfield and Chuck Broyer are chewing tobacco and spitting it in the wastepaper basket. Cap Richards chuckles to himself over some whacked-out adventure in Mayberry.

"That isn't an answer, man. I mean, you aren't that kind of guy."

"It was an impulse."

"You aren't, like, impulsive. I mean, you're the kind of guy who practically schedules when he's going to take a dump—"

"Shut up." Six forty-five every morning. I can do it in ten minutes, which leaves me just enough time to shower, get dressed, grab a Pop-Tart, and catch the bus to school. Then 8:30–9:30 p.m., when I get home from my cookie shift. On rare occasions, if it is an emergency, I'll use the guys' bathroom in Dillard's. It's right behind Homewares and is usually empty. I don't think this makes me weird. I figure all guys prefer to shit in their own bathroom.

"Just explain it to me, okay? I'm your best friend since elementary. I thought I knew you. Then I get this call, and you're on Western with some hot little bitch salivating all over you and the whole situation fucks with the natural order of things. I mean, what am I supposed to think about this? How exactly do I process this information? Should I be worried? I mean, it's cool, you can do whatever you want, you know I'm all about intrinsic finality, though a true bud would have taken the forty-five seconds to pick up a phone and *invite me,* but the thing about this whole incident that I find worrisome, I mean, I was thinking about it when I got home, and the thing is . . . *it isn't you.* I mean, maybe you're bipolar or something. Sometimes it shows up in your teens. My mom saw it on *Oprah.* If you were bipolar, dude, that would be an issue. That would really fuck things up for me."

"I'm not bipolar."

"Manic-depressive? ADHD?"

"No!"

"I mean, they got drugs for that shit, man. They got drugs for everything. You don't need to be, like, ashamed—"

"I just did it, okay?" I hiss. I'm already pissed off, and Dingo is making it worse. That's the thing about Dingo. He never understood social cues. Friend is angry: leave friend alone. How hard is that? I should make Roger give him human relations lessons. "There isn't a reason for anything. Things just happen sometimes, right? Isn't that what you taught me? Aren't you the philosophy expert?"

"This isn't philosophy, man. That's more, like, postmodern."

"What the fuck is *postmodern*?"

"You can't describe it. If you could, it wouldn't be post-modern. Postmodern is you and a hot-ass ho on Western at six a.m. after having gone out on, like, a school night. I mean, what if you're having a nervous breakdown? Do I need to tell someone? Do you need, like, help?"

"No. I'm fine. Just one of those things, okay?" He stares at me. I tap my pencil and ignore him. I wiggle my toes in my shoes.

Twenty minutes till class is over. Over an hour since I took the crystal and nothing has happened. I am still the loser in the corner. No one looks at me with awe and respect. It's like last night never existed. I'm the invisible jackass in the back of Advanced Chemistry, watching my life tick away on the school-board-issued clock. I took one chance, and it didn't matter. I'm back where I was. Not existing.

"Just tell me one thing, okay?" says Dingo. He stares at me, his bottom lip sticking out and his eyebrows drawn together. I know that look. He is worried about me. He cares about me, as much as he is capable of caring about something other than his virtual girlfriends and the newest *Grand Theft Auto*. Dingo's world is a reliable place. It has reason. And I have taken the snow globe of his existence and shaken the fuck out of it. "Why did you do it?"

"I'm just sick of everything. I just want something interesting to happen."

"Yeah. I get that, man. I do, I mean, it's cool and all. But the thing is . . . maybe you shouldn't do it again, okay? I was thinking about it, and, like, you don't even know that girl. You don't know those people. They could be, like, Waco-ites or a Manson gang or something worse. I don't want you to, like, die. They could be satanists. Jehovah's. You can't go running around like some sort of crazed asshole. You aren't Sid Vicious, man." He sighs. "Besides, don't blow your wad on a bunch of Okie losers. Just wait. We just got to wait it out, man." His eyes have glazed over. He isn't talking about me anymore. He's see-ing his future. He is Bill Gates, minus the charity work. He is on his yacht in the Caribbean. He is fucking two girls at once. On a waterbed. A waterbed on the ocean, just because he can. They probably aren't even real girls he's imagining. They are probably animated Second Life chicks. He is real, live, flesh-and-blood Dingo having fan-tasy intercourse with cartoons while I, the guy he thinks is a pathetic chode, had a real, living, breathing pantyless girl straddling my lap a few hours ago. And now I am back here right where I started, in Oklahoma City, in the junk-yard of humanity, a speck of nothing in the nothingest state in the whole damn union, and Dingo has the balls to judge me. And he's still talking. "Wait it out till we gradu-ate and get out of this futile crapfest of a state. Just a few years. We just have to wait—"

"No! I'm sick of waiting!" I must be loud because the magazine girls turn and stare at me, giving me that look that only teenage girls can pull off, like I am not worth the energy it took to shift their heads in my direction.

"What?" I ask them. "What?"

They look at each other, then back at me, their upper

lips curled like they just got a whiff of something rotten.

"Excuse me?" says one of them. I think her name is Channella. She's on the pom-pom squad, and she's considered beautiful. There's a rumor she got a nose job, as if that makes her face a little less intimidating to everyone else. She wasn't always perfect, they can tell themselves. She is rich. She is going to be a debutante. She'll wear a white dress and walk down a long staircase while everyone watches her with worship. She is an adoration sponge. She is staring at me as though I am dirt. Lower than dirt. I am sedimentary layer and fossil. She will walk across me for the rest of my life. I am one of a thousand Dougs who have never registered on her radar, and now we stare at each other. She is wearing too much mascara. It looks like daddy longlegs are growing out of her eye sockets.

"Did you want to ask me something?" I hiss at her.

"Um, not really," she says flippantly, and turns away. And like that it is over. We will never speak again. She'll glance at me and giggle when Ronan throws me against a locker, but other than that I will disappear, like a camouflage lizard, taking on the dingy gray of our lockers and the dirty oatmeal color of our cafeteria floor.

"Hey," I say to her. I don't know why I speak. I just do.

She turns back around and glares at me. Her look says it all: *You dare talk to me?* We stare at each other, and I see it all. She'll graduate in a few years, go to OU, pledge the best sorority, marry a plastic surgeon, live in Nichols Hills, have Mexicans put up lavish Christmas lights each October, bang out a few kids, and they will grow up to look at guys like me with the same expression. To everything there is a season. Turn fucking turn turn.

She rolls her eyes and turns back around. "Loser," she says to her friend in that way that bitchy teenage girls have mastered, loud enough for me to hear, but quiet enough to be considered within the realms of proper etiquette. Suddenly I realize the truth: the Channellas of the world serve no purpose other than to make the rest of us hate ourselves. They strut around with their attitude and their untouchable breasts. They pick at their cafeteria food, and they never get a faulty lock on their locker, and every time they laugh, thirty people think it is at their expense. Channella is everything wrong with society, and Channella can suck my dick. Something snaps in my head. Maybe it's that I haven't slept in over twenty-four hours. Maybe it's the unnatural pink of her lipstick. Maybe the crystals have started working.

"Hey, Channella," I say, my voice sounding faraway and poisonous, her name sounding as ridiculous as it really is. "Is it true?"

"Is what true?" she hisses.

"That you got a nose job? That your natural, real nose is, like, completely different?"

"What did you say?" she screeches, her voice rising to a decibel level only a pom-pom girl is capable of making, her face turning bright red. The rest of the class turns to watch, except Captain Richards, who is way too absorbed in Mayberry. He doesn't care what we do. I could hang myself from the fluorescent light, swing to death in front of his Table of Chemical Elements, and he'd be grunting with satisfaction as Opie learns an important life lesson. The educational system is a joke. It is as pointless as Channella, who is standing up now, staring at me with lifeless mannequin eyes. "Do you know. Who. You are talking to?" she says.

"Do you know. Who. *You* are talking to?" I say right back at her. She looks confused. I can practically see the circuits in her brains sparking into overdrive. I feel Dingo tense next to me. All eyes are on us: Pom-Pom Princess and Loser Outcast. Pom-Pom Princess is upset. Loser Outcast is the cause. This doesn't happen every day. The world spins on its axis, we weave our way through our lives, and certain elements never come into contact. The results would be unnatural, explosive, corrosive, and dangerous. This isn't an eighties teen flick, where Pom-Pom Princess and Outcast Loser can come to some sort of understanding. This is the real world, and I've fucked with the laws of nature and synergy and God.

"Who do you think you are?" she says again. I see Elroy Densfield and Chuck Broyer begin to rise, their bottom lips gaping with chew like blowfish.

"Did you call me a loser?" I asked her.

"Yeah? So what?"

"Then I guess it's okay if I call you a *bitch*."

Next to me, Dingo gasps.

"What did you call me?"

"A. Bitch."

Elroy and Chuck are working their way between desks. They are coming for me. The class is silent. I stand, throw my backpack over my shoulder.

She steps close enough for me to smell the artificial orange of her wad of Bubble Yum. "Listen, I don't know who you are, but you better watch—"

"Doug Schaffer," I spit at her. "Doug S-C-H-A-F-F-E-R. You want me to write it down for you?"

"Hey, slow down," says Dingo, next to me. "Come on, man, this is unnecessary—"

Then Elroy is in my face, defending a chick who wouldn't give his farmboy ass the time of day. His face is the color of a red hot. He towers over me. He pulls his arm back. He is going to hit me. My fist moves without warning my brain first, independent of the rest of my body. It's all in slow motion. My fist swings, making a satisfying smacking sound against his face. It is the best sound I ever heard. It is better than Santa's sleigh bells and a fire alarm during a midterm. I want a recording of that smack, and I want to play it on a loop for eternity. He reaches for his face. He touches his nose, then looks at his hand, and the blood is bright red on his stubby fingers. I look down at my own miraculous red knuckles. "Ow," he says in a little-boy whine. He pauses, then lurches for me. He has caveman eyes. Chuck pulls him back, and Channella shrieks, and someone is looking for a Kleenex to stop the blood, and Cap Richards has hauled his morbidly obese body to a standing position and is asking what the hell is going on. Everyone is excited and talking at once.

This is the best thing to happen since Ellie Trachenberg's shirt popped open during her modern-dance routine at the talent show. That loser Doug Schaffer punched Elroy Densfield during Advanced Chemistry. Yeah, that guy. The one that never talks. The stuff of urban legends.

And somehow I get to the door without anyone noticing, and out in the hall. I stand there for a millisecond, wondering who I am and whether I have morphed into the Incredible Hulk. Then I look at my own familiar hands, which aren't green, and laugh. Behind the door, somewhere deep in the chaos and shouting of Classen Period One Advanced Chemistry, I hear Dingo say, "It's not his fault. Seriously. I think he's bipolar."

And then I know it's time to run.

CHAPTER FIVE

"Put your hand in your pocket," says Angela, under her breath, when I open the door. We both gaze down at my knuckles, caked with Elroy's dried blood. I'm breathing heavily. I ran the three miles to her house.

Angela is different in the daylight. She looks even younger now, not even out of her preteens. Maybe it is because she isn't wearing makeup. She's wearing jeans and a pink T-shirt with a crown and SOMEDAY MY PRINCE WILL COME across her little boobs. Underneath, in smaller letters, it says JESUS SAID HE WILL COME AGAIN AND RECEIVE US UNTO HIMSELF. Her chest is smaller than I remember its being. I'm still shaking, and my breath is coming out in ragged huffs. The house wasn't hard to find. Angela lives in the lower-middle-class white neighborhood that borders the lower-class white-trash neighborhood that borders the lower-middle-class black neighborhood that borders the crack dens off twenty-third Street. This is Oklahoma. Everything is in the obvious place.

"Keep your hand in your pocket. My mom hates blood. You have to meet her first. Follow me."

The couches are covered in plastic. Everything smells too clean, like a hospital or doctor's office.

Jesus is everywhere.

He watches me from every wall. He's surrounded by multicultural little children and baby sheep. He's comforting a filthy, homeless-looking dude who smiles up at him rapturously, probably hoping Jesus is about to give him a Whopper or a fifth of vodka. In another Jesus appears to be coaching a kids' soccer team. He's got the ball under his arm, and the little boys look up at him with big smiles, like he's going to lead them to a national championship. No one seems to even notice that Jesus is walking around with a ball of shiny light shooting out of his head. I mean, if some dude in white robes was coaching my kid's team, I'd probably have some serious questions.

Maybe I'm seeing things. Maybe this is all my imagination. I think back on my research. Meth makes you imagine bugs crawling under your skin. Snakes. Not weird Jesus hallucinations.

"Are you okay?" says a voice, startling me. Angela is standing below me with a smirk.

"I like the art."

"You should see the rest of the house," she says softly, only it doesn't sound bitter or ironic. "It's a collection. C'mon. Follow me." I fight the urge to run out the door. It would be so easy. But I have no idea where to go, so I follow her down the hall.

In the kitchen, a mousy woman is wiping down a counter with spray cleaner. When she sees us, she stops midswipe and stares at us. "This is Doug, Mommy," says Angela, her voice babyish and low. "The one I told you about."

"Hi, Doug. I'm Angela's mom." Everything she says is measured, as though it has great weight and importance. "I'm just doing some housekeeping."

"Hi," I croak.

She sets down the spray cleaner and walks to me. She puts her palm on my head. It feels like a warm hat. Still clutching the wet paper towel in her other fist, she drops her chin, and so does Angela. "Lord, please take care of Doug, especially now, in his time of need. In Christ's name."

"In Christ's name," says Angela.

"Thanks," I say. "In. Uh. In Christ's name."

Angela's mom smiles at me with concern. But something's missing. Her eyes are creepy. She's like that bad seventies movie Dingo and I saw on late-night TNT about perfect housewives who turn out to be machines manufactured by a Disney genius. "This is so unrealistic," Dingo had said, his voice snide. "I mean, I could make a better female automaton." For the next two hours he'd elaborated on the various possibilities while I played Xbox.

Angela's mom-bot steps back. "Well, I know you two need to talk. I've got so much to do." Then, like that, she's back scrubbing down her already spotless counter.

"Okay, Mommy . . . follow me," says Angela.

We walk down the hall to her room. Crosses are everywhere. On one wall is a framed box with an imitation crown of thorns. Two spikes are displayed on either side. I watch Angela's ass swing back and forth as she walks in front of me. I think she's doing it on purpose. She's swinging in his name.

Angela shuts the door behind her. I've never been in a teenage girl's room before. A pair of pale blue panties is on the floor. I think it is the thong kind. It must feel like dental floss up your ass, but it looks fucking hot. I feel suddenly shy. I can't look at her, and I don't want to look at the panties, so I look down at the green shag carpet.

"Let me see your hand."

I lift it up. She holds it up in her tiny one and moves close. We stare down at the dried blood. She had on nail polish last night. I think it was black. Now her nails are bare, chewed all the way down to the quick, the cuticles scabby.

"I got in a fight." I like the way it sounds, so I say it again, my voice gruffer. "I got into a fight."

"I told my mom I met you when my youth group was witnessing at the mall. I told her you struggle with thoughts of suicide and I'm helping to bring you to the Savior."

"I got in a fight," I repeat, my voice sounding like it belongs to someone else. She looks up at me. Her eyes are glinting. We are both greedy for something.

"I'm a drug addict," I tell her, and it sounds fucking awesome coming out of my mouth.

"Oh," she says. Then, in slow motion, her pink tongue slides out of her mouth. The pointy tip licks my bloody knuckle. She grins up at me. This girl is sick. She is fucked in the head.

"Take off your T-shirt," I tell her.

Her bedspread is covered in a daisy pattern. We are only wearing our underwear. I am on top of her, rubbing my hard dick against her Play-Doh belly. My hands are on her tiny breasts. Her nipples are hard. I made them hard. She giggles and looks at the ceiling. When I kiss her, she kisses back. She presses her lips against mine so hard it hurts. I can do anything I want to her because I am a drug addict. I am a man. I run through a lifetime of pornos and dirty magazines in my head. I remember positions that have only been described to me, like urban legends: *the wheelbarrow, splitting the bamboo, the piledriver. Dirty Sanchezes, Hot Lunches, Rusty Trombones.*

I don't know if I'm doing this right. Now I'm questioning myself. Like clicking back and forth between two shows you want to watch. Doug the drug-addict stud and

Doug the clumsy virgin who doesn't know where to put his hands. I feel myself going soft.

I imagine this is Laurilee beneath me, with her sharp teeth and stick-out ears. Her plaid jumper. Laurilee cocking her head as she listens to me and her throaty, tinkling laugh. "Laugh," I tell Angela. She giggles, like we are playing a game. "Don't giggle. Laugh. Laugh really low for me." I do it for her, and she imitates me. I close my eyes, and Angela laughs, and I am hard again. I keep my eyes closed. My hands know what to do. *Would Laurilee like this?* I wonder as I lick up the side of Angela's neck. The taste of skin. She moans. *Would Laurilee like this?* I wonder as I run my hands down Angela's thighs, squeezing them at the meatiest part. Thinking of beef. The parts of a cow you can eat. Angela's knees are round and puckered like a child's. Her legs don't have the angles of Laurilee's, so I move upward. I let my finger creep along the elastic edge of her panties. She doesn't giggle anymore. She isn't making any noise at all. She has gone quiet. I look up at her. She stares at the ceiling, her face blank. I think she is smiling, but it isn't really a happy smile.

Above her head is a poster of Jesus. He isn't on the cross or anything, he just stares off into the distance knowingly. His hair is brown and shiny, like in a TV commercial for shampoo. This is a sexy Jesus. He could be the lead singer of some indie band. I roll over on my side so I don't have to look at him. Angela is still staring at the ceiling. I look at her. A female face. A stranger's face. Not pretty or ugly, just a regular girl's face staring up at the ceiling, blank, like she has gone to another place. She is somewhere else, and I'm not sure if I want her to come back.

My dick is pulsing. I take her tiny, limp hand in mine. She looks at me, as though she doesn't recognize my face. Then she smiles at me. "Hi," I say, then I slide her hand down into my boxer shorts. She doesn't object. It isn't what I expected, this moment, the first time since I was a baby that someone touched my dick besides me. She smiles and moves her hand up and down quickly. She's done this before.

On my own, my jerk-off record is about twelve seconds. She stares at me while she moves her hand. For a small girl, she has a firefighter grip. She looks at me while she does it, grinning slightly, her eyes as round and glassy as a one of those creepy Precious Moments dolls my aunt Lila collects. She knows what she's doing. I look up at the ceiling. Jesus looks back. He looks kind of turned-on himself. I don't want to look at her, but looking away is rude. She's a crazy-Christian ho-bag nympho, but I don't want to hurt her feelings.

I stop her hand with mine midpump. "I think you're really cool," I tell her. She smiles at me. I take her hand off my dick. She nestles against me, her head resting on my chest. We are *cuddling*. I don't want to *cuddle*.

So I put my hand on the top of her head and push her downward.

I don't know how long it takes. It couldn't be long. But for that fraction of eternity, I am plunging through space.

The flesh is melting off my body. There is nothing in the universe except my cock and her mouth. Warm. Insane. Putting your fingers in a wall outlet. Getting shocked, only in a good way. It occurs to me, the instant before I detonate, *So this is why everyone makes such a big deal about it.*

She stands at her dresser in her panties. She drinks from a half-empty bottle of Mountain Dew. She didn't make a face after she swallowed, which I take as a good sign. Maybe I don't taste that bad. Some guys do, I've heard. Dingo says that eating celery makes you taste better, but he talks a lot of shit. I don't really eat celery, but had I known this was even a remote possibility, I would have eaten ten stalks at every meal in preparation. When I was a kid, my mom used to put peanut butter inside celery sticks. She'd line up raisins on the top and call it ants on a log, which I remember thinking was pretty fucking cool.

I scan the room for my jeans. I feel Angela staring at me. I reach for my boxer shorts on the floor, feeling myself blush at my exposed dick, which is totally retarded and irrational since two minutes ago it was in her mouth. I try to think of something to say. Is *thanks* appropriate? *Good job?* Do I high-five her? I try to remember all the blow jobs I've seen in movies, but I can't remember what comes afterward. I put on my jeans and button the fly. The dried blood is still on my hand.

The school has probably already called to inform my mother that I punched Elroy and have gone MIA. She probably got the call at her secretary's cubicle. I've seen her office a few times, during boring holiday parties. Next to my mother's desk is a picture of Trevor in his football uniform. There is one of me on my fifteenth birthday, smiling grudgingly at the camera. My mom holds up a red velvet cake. She got it in her head I like red velvet cake. She makes them on every birthday. I never had the heart to tell her they taste like a sugar-flavored dish sponge. There are no pictures from when we were really young. It's as though time stopped when my father took off to Mexico.

I imagine my mother sorting papers into in and out boxes when the principal calls. "Doogan and Associates," she says. ". . . Yes. Yes, this is Doug Schaffer's mother. Is everything all right?" When I get home, she'll be waiting for me at the kitchen table. I'll tell her everything and she'll start to cry and that will be that. The jig will be up. End of show. Curtain. Ob-la-di, ob-la-dah.

"Hey," says Angela. I had forgotten she was there. She has put on her bra. She doesn't really need a bra.

"Hey."

"Are you really a drug addict?"

"Yes," I say, my voice solemn and rough. This is how drug addicts sound.

"What kind of drug?"

"Meth."

She leans against her desk. She has a Hello Kitty night-light. I never understood Hello Kitty. It's a cat, I guess, but it has no mouth or fur and its eyes kind of freak me out. A little like Angela.

"I did that once," she says nonchalantly. "Meth."

"It isn't a toy. It's serious business."

"You got any?" she asks innocently.

"Not much." The packet is almost empty.

"You got it here?"

"Yes."

Her eyes widen. She nods. I feel like a stud. "Let's do some," she says.

I think about my mom waiting at the house. Things will move quickly. I'll tell her I'm a drug addict and storm out. That will give her enough time to organize the intervention. Then I'll throw a fit when Laurilee isn't there. I tell her that I'll only consider rehab if Laurilee shows up. Someone will go to the mall. "It's an emergency," they'll tell her. Denise will cover Trinkets while she's gone. It will all happen so fast. I'll go to rehab, make some friends, lift weights. I'll come back a rock star. The future is all planned out. The future is exciting. This is what some people must feel like when they get a fat packet in the mail from their first-choice college. Only much, much better.

It can wait a few hours.

We crush up the rest of the meth on her science textbook. It's one of those Christian ones that probably talks about the fallacy of evolution and that global warming is made up by the government. I know because sometimes I watch the Christian channel if nothing else is on. My favorite show is that guy with the white, floppy hair who smacks people on the head for Jesus. And Kirk Cameron, who was some heartthrob in the seventies and now harasses people on the street for Christ.

Angela has done this before, or she's a good actress. She crushes the rest of the rock with a playing card and uses a protractor to make four neat lines. I guess Jesus doesn't have a problem with geometry. She bites her bottom lip in concentration. "Can I go first?" she asks. She has rolled up a dollar bill.

"Are you sure about this? I mean, I don't want to get you hooked."

"I'm not a child, Doug." Then she giggles, leans down, and whoosh, the line disappears. She rubs her finger where the line has been, then rubs her upper gums, which are the same pink as one of those gumballs you get for a quarter outside the IGA. I've seen druggies do this in movies. It looks really cool. I nod at her. The downward nod. We are in this together.

She hands me the dollar bill. I don't care if a million hands have touched it before. I put it up my nose, take a deep breath, lean down, and snort.

Your daughter just sucked my dick, I think as Angela tells her mom we are going to some Christian youth-group function. She's a good liar. I almost believe her myself. I stand there looking down at the kitchen tile, trying not to look like someone who just snorted meth off a science textbook. "It's an emergency meeting, Mommy. For Doug.

He's ready to face the truth. He needs his flock right now, Mommy." I'm nodding. Not one speck of dust is on the floor. Not a fleck or a crumb. As soon as we leave, she will probably go over where we have been standing with a rag and bleach and wash away our sins.

In the station wagon, Angela puts the radio up loud. "I love the Jonas Brothers," she squeals as she drives toward the Northwest Expressway. She sings along loudly. "They're Christians, did you know that?" She holds the steering wheel in one hand while putting on lipstick in the rearview mirror. "My mom doesn't let me listen to worldly music at home, but the Jonas Brothers are okay. She thinks they are adorable. They've got purity rings and everything. Hey, get that shirt out of my backpack, okay?" I feel weird digging in her backpack, like it is a private place that no man should go. I try not to look until I feel something soft. I hand her some sort of tight black thing with holes and safety pins. "'Time for me to fly, time for me to soar . . . Time for me to open up my heart and knock on heaven's door,'" she croons while throwing her T-shirt in the backseat and slithering into the new one. The car weaves a little bit.

"'The cops are gonna stop us," I tell her, wondering if the meth paranoia is setting in.

"Even if they did, I wouldn't get a ticket."

I believe her. "Are you fucked up?"

"Sure am, mister."

"Where we going?" I ask.

"Where do you wanna go?"

We are somewhere in downtown Oklahoma City. It's probably afternoon, or maybe it's still morning. The streets are vacant.

"Oooh, look at all the animals," she says.

"You must be really fucked-up."

"No, they're so cute!" I follow her gaze. She has stopped the car. We are at the back end of the bombing memorial, which seems to take up half of downtown. The animals are stuffed. This is the fence where people leave crap. They come from all over the world to leave crap. Candles and notes and wreathes with fake flowers. Yellow ribbons, bags of candy, rosaries. This has been here for as long as I remember. I try to avoid it. In middle school we went every year on a field tip. "God, not the memorial again," kids would say, and roll their eyes. A few people mill around the fence, looking at stuff. The memorial used to be a lot more popular.

"I love the animals," says Angela, still gazing at the fence. They are everywhere. There are frogs and bears. There are rabbits with big, floppy ears wearing jump-suits in American-flag patterns. Some are shoved between wires, others are hung limply by their necks or from ribbons and strings. It's like a mass animal suicide.

"Get me the monkey," she says.

"What monkey?"

"That one." She points to a sad-looking one low on the fence. "He's lonely."

"I can't."

"Why not?"

"Someone left it there," I say, thinking of the kids who were in the preschool, the tiny chairs that represent each one. "You can't take a dead kid's monkey."

"They'd want me to have it."

"No," I tell her sternly.

She clenches her teeth and stares at me. "You're not my dad," she hisses. Then, like that, the door is open and she is streaking across the street, barefoot. She grabs the monkey. A few people turn to look at her, confused. For a moment she stands there on the sidewalk, the monkey clutched to her chest, and grins at me. Only it's kind of a sneer. Then she is back in the car and we are pulling onto the I-40 ramp. The monkey is on her lap. He looks happy to be off the fence. She strokes his head absentmindedly.

"Ouch," she says. "I think I stepped on a pebble."

"Better put on some shoes."

We are fucked-up. At some point, we decide to go see the real animals at Arbuckle Wilderness. If I get a blow job, I can handle an ostrich. Then at some point I realize we are going in the opposite direction. I don't know how that happened. I've taken this highway a gazillion times. When we finally get it right, it is getting dark. "It'll be closed," whines Angela. "We'll have to sneak in." Then I flash on the ostrich attacking me in the car and am not sure I want to go after all.

"Hey," I say. "Pull off. Right there. Scenic Turnout." She screeches off the road. The Scenic Turnout hasn't changed. It's the same Scenic Turnout it's always been since I was a kid, a gate overlooking a pasture with a few lazy cows standing around. The sun is setting, so the field is dark with shadows. You can't see much, so it's almost pretty.

"Ever been cow-tipping?" asks Angela. It's a trick question, like *Do I look fat in this?* She'll do it. She'll run out there in a second. She'll probably take the monkey. I may be a meth addict, but she's a crazy bitch. Unrestrained, like they say after car wrecks when the driver wasn't wearing a seat belt. I don't want to chase her through cow patties in some sad-ass field between the Oklahoma and Texas border. She smiles at me. I need to distract her. I pull her tiny body close to me and kiss her hard. I make a decision, or don't make it. Maybe my dick makes it. Maybe it's the sun setting over this sad pasture that inspires me. Maybe, for just a second, I think I'm Clyde and she's Bonnie. I'm Sid to her Nancy. We are wild and free and untamable.

I fuck her, right there on the dirt, the sun setting orange over us, a few cows mooing, the traffic of the I-40 whizzing below us. I fumble to find the right hole. It takes forever. She lies there, passive. I don't have a condom, but she says she's on the pill. She's Christian, so I'm sure she hasn't got any diseases. I'm not worried. About anything. Except that there is no point of entry. Where is my dick supposed to go? It's frustrating and confusing as fuck. If I don't figure it out soon, I will splooge all over her.

"Can you help me?" I ask finally, embarrassed at the sound of my own frustration. She sighs and guides me inside, like it's a big-ass bother. I cum almost instantly. I'm not even halfway in there. But it counts. I think it counts.

I pull out of her and lie on my back beside her. There is dirt on the tip of my nose.

"Sorry," I tell her, though I'm not. I just lost my virginity. I punched someone. I got a blow job. What else can I do? I just want a little more time. A few hours. A few days. A month, maybe. I've never seen an alligator. I've never been to a strip club.

"Have you ever heard of Jack Kerouac?" I say.

We are going On the Road, Angela and I. I'm her Neal Cassady, she's my Marylou. Neal had lots of women, hundreds, thousands. Angela is fine for right now. She is adequate. We are going to Mexico, Angela and I. I'm driving. We are going to Mexico in a station wagon. My father is in Mexico, but it doesn't matter. It's a big place, and we wouldn't recognize each other anyway. Mexico just seems right. This wasn't part of the plan. The plan has changed. Plans change. Jack didn't make plans. America was his empty canvas. I wonder how to find Route 66. It's dark now. Late. I stop to pee off the road. I like the air on my dick. I try to draw a star, but there isn't enough pee. I get a large coffee at a gas station. I get a pack of cigarettes. I chain-smoke them, one by one. I wonder which way is Tijuana. I'd like to see a donkey show, just to say I did. I'm not exactly sure what a donkey show is, but I'd like to see one anyway. I'm driving and driving. I wonder how much longer the drugs will last. I wonder if I can get more in Mexico. I'm sure I can in Tijuana. They sell them at stands like tacos. I wonder if Angela has an ATM card. My money is almost gone. I know I can get more drugs in Mexico. You can do anything in Mexico.

Jack wrote a poem about Mexico. I try to remember it, to recite it to Angela. She stares out the window. It was something about being done playing American, having a good quiet life. *Having thirty-five cents and the Mexican girls making eyes at you.*

And maybe I will find my dad. Who knows? Maybe we'll run into each other at a street market, and he'll be amazed at who I've become, independent and traveling the world. He'll look like shit, haggard and broke and run down by life. We'll do shots of tequila at a bar. He'll realize the truth, that I never needed him in the first place. He'll get sloppy drunk and cry about all the years he lost, the son he could have had, the mistakes he can't take back. I might comfort him. Or I might not. I might punch him first, then comfort him.

"We can go to San Miguel," I tell her. "That's where Neal Cassady died. On a railroad track. Kerouac wasn't there, he was with his mother probably, this was later, y'know, a lot of them were dead. Kerouac might have been dead, I'm not sure. But they all went to Mexico, at some point or another." I ramble on and on, not really listening to myself anymore, with visions of street markets and cheap Corona and the Virgin of Guadalupe. Long-deserted beaches, four-cent burritos. I've never been out of the country. I'll even drink the water. That's how you get immune. You actually drink it. Mind over matter. I can do anything.

Somewhere near the Tanger Outlet outside the Texas border, where my mom used to force us on a yearly trek for discounted school clothes, Angela begins to sputter. She hasn't spoken in a long time, but I haven't noticed. I'd forgotten she was there. I look over and she is crying. She's sobbing like a little girl does, with snot bubbling up in her nose, clutching that dumbass stuffed animal to her chest and periodically wiping her nose on his head. It's kind of repugnant. I pull over on the highway. A truck honks at me for not using my turn signal.

"Are you okay?" My throat hurts from all the cigarettes.

"I don't want you to be mad at me."

"I won't be mad."

"I can't go to Mexico." It hangs there in the air. She sniffles. "My mom will be worried about me." We stare at each other for a long time. I try to remember who she is and how I met her.

"Are you sure?"

"I don't even have a passport," she says.

I hadn't even thought of a passport. I would have had to sneak over, like an illegal alien, only going in the opposite direction. Then she starts to sob even more, big obnoxious heaving sobs, and she's so ugly like that. I just want her to shut up. I wonder if I should push her out of the car and keep going. I actually think about it for a second. She could hitch back to OKC wasteland with her backpack and her monkey.

"Okay," I say with a sigh. "Okay. Stop crying. I'll take you home."

She has stopped crying and is cheerful again. I get her McNuggets at one of those gas-stations-slash-McDonald's. She dips them in honey-mustard sauce. She makes a call on her cell. I hate her phone and I hate her. Her voice gets all whispery and flirty between bites of congealed chicken lips and assholes.

"Just cover for me, 'kay? . . . I know, I know. I miss you too. . . . Tomorrow. After my school session. . . . Just tell her I fell asleep at your house. Tell her you were praying for Doug with me. . . . No one. Just some guy I met. . . . I know. I know it's a sin. Forgive me? . . . Yeah. Me too. . . . Soon, okay?"

"Who was that?" I ask when she hangs up. We are outside Norman. We are almost there.

"Eleanor. My youth group leader," she says, chewing. "I should have gotten the sweet-and-sour instead."

"Why does she cover for you?"

"She's in love with me." Then Angela does it. She giggles. It's like a lion clawing a blackboard. It makes my teeth hurt, that sound. It's like the worst realm of hell, more painful than burning in fire, hearing Angela giggle at that moment. Angela, eating her McNuggets, ruining my plan, acting like a crazy ho *in his name*.

"You fuck her?"

"What?" says Angela, the sound fading into the back of her throat.

"I mean, do you kiss her? That lady. Eleanor. Do you let her finger you?"

"Why are you . . . that's none of your business."

"So you do, then? You must, since you didn't say no. I'm just wondering, that's all. I mean, it's kinda weird, the whole thing. She's a youth pastor and she'll cover for you? I mean, she must want something in return, right?"

"Shut up, Doug."

"I'm just curious." I see downtown OKC in the distance. During Christmas one of the skyscrapers designates specific office lights to burn throughout the night, making a huge fluorescent cross you can probably see counties away. "Just tell me this: do you let her eat you out?"

"Shut the fuck up," Angela hisses.

"I just wonder if Jesus minds. I mean, what would Jesus do? Would he let Eleanor eat him out?"

"Don't. Mention. Him. Again."

"Who?"

"I freaking mean it."

"Don't mention Jesus? Why? I mean, I thought you were all about him. He's on your bedroom ceiling—"

"Shut up!"

"JesusJesusJesusJesus—"

"I hate you!" she screams, then pinches my arm. She uses her nails.

"Bitch!" I say, almost swerving off the road.

She leans back in the seat. "Take me home," she says, her voice very small.

In the driveway of her house, we stare at each other. "Are you getting out?" I ask her.

"It's my mother's car," she says icily. I realize she is right and feel like a complete retard. I get out, walk around, and hand her the keys. She has changed back into her regular clothes and wiped off her lipstick. Her eyes are red in the glow of the interior light. She gets out and closes the car door. I guess I feel guilty.

"Want me to walk you—"

"No." She has her backpack over her shoulder.

"Okay."

"Okay." She doesn't look at me. She walks to the front door.

"Angela?"

She is on the porch. She turns to me. She waits.

"I'm going to go away now. For a long time, probably." She doesn't say anything. "I'm going to rehab. Probably tomorrow. So I won't see you again. Not for a while, at least." A moment passes, and the *bitch* melts from her face. She just looks sad. "So. Well. Thanks. I mean . . . it was fun, right?" She stares at me. "I mean . . . well, it was kinda fun, wasn't it?"

"I'll pray for you," she says quietly. Then she goes into the house, shutting the door behind her. The last thing I see is the monkey, tucked under her left arm, staring at me with his beady black eyes and a sneer.

I stand there for a moment, alone on the dark lawn, waiting for something.

I turn around and walk away.

It occurs to me I never asked her about her father. If she knows him. Or if, like me, he's somewhere far away. So far away it's almost like he doesn't exist.

I stand outside the door of our house. I am sweaty, even in the chill. It's still October. I think. I am covered in the dirt of Scenic Turnout. My Converse sneakers are caked in mud. It seems so long ago that I scrawled on the white soles in permanent marker. I thought I was being rebellious. The New Doug thinks of that Old Doug doodling on his feet and wants to puke in embarrassment. The New Doug, meth addict on the porch of his suburban home, about to embark upon the newest chapter of his life, wants to take that Old Doug and shake him and tell him to *man up and grow some balls, you fucking pussy.* He was a child, a stupid, infantile wimp who spent his whole life ducking bullies. Creeping around so he wouldn't make noise. Old Doug was afraid of shadows. He slid against walls in the dark. He fell through sidewalk cracks. A vagina was a foreign country. A tongue was only for food. That kid's mantra was duck and run.

Of course Laurilee didn't want me. I wouldn't want the Old Doug either.

But this guy, the one about to go into his mother's house with greasy hair and filthy clothes and a raw knuckle, well, he's different. He got his dick wet. He's kind of a stud.

I don't have my key. I ring the doorbell. I take a deep breath. I wonder if I should stand up straight, or would a drug addict hunch over? Then I realize it doesn't matter what a drug addict *would do* anymore. I *am* a drug addict.

The door flies open, slamming the wall. "Doug!" says my mother, lunging for me and gripping me in a bear hug that knocks all the air out of me and probably crushes a couple of ribs. She is still wearing her work clothes.

"Doug, honey, where have you been?" she says, her tears getting my neck wet. She is stuck to me like one of those scaredy-cat toys you suction to your windshield. "Oh, God, honey, I've been looking everywhere," she says, sobbing into my shoulder.

I had no idea it would be this big a deal. It's pretty damn satisfying. She is muttering into the crook of my shoulder, saying my name, laughing and crying at the same time like a nuthouse psycho. I love this moment. I want it to go on for half an hour.

I grip her shoulders in my manly hands. I unstick her from me and hold her at arm's length. She is shaking. Her mascara has been running and her eyes are bloodshot.

Behind her stands one of the OMSOT bitches with her mouth gaping open. Other voices are coming from inside the house. People have already gathered. They probably filed a report, and now they are making posters of my face to attach to mailboxes and stop signs. I'm practically famous.

This is how a chick must feel on her wedding day.

"Mom." My voice sounds like a man's. "Mom. It's going to be okay."

"Honey! Doug, honey—" Her eyes look kind of crazy.

"Mom. Calm down. I'm going to be okay, all right?" In silence we stare at each other. It's like the climax of a cheesy movie and I'm the star.

My mother takes a deep breath. "Doug. Trevor has been injured. He's coming home, Doug." She beams at me. "Your brother is coming home."

The house is swarming with middle-aged ladies. There is clanking in the kitchen and the smell of food. Two women are making a banner on the coffee table. I can see the word TREVOR in capital letters. Red, white, and blue. Fucking ingenious. One of the hyenas is vacuuming. She stops the machine when she sees me. Everything stops. Everyone stares at me.

"What the fuck is going on?" I scream.

"Sit down, honey," says my mom, pushing me toward living room.

"Not there," says the vacuum hyena. "He's covered in dirt! I just vacuumed the couch!"

Someone pulls up a foldout chair, and someone else pushes me down in it. The television is clicked off and everything is dead quiet. The room is hazy around me, like it is filled with smoke. Maybe it is. Maybe this is just a meth thing. A dream sequence. My mother kneels in front of me. She takes my hand. She composes herself. All the women are gathered around, staring down at me, their faces like gigantic caricatures of concern.

"Trevor was injured, honey."

"Is he dead?" I squeak.

"No, honey. No." For a split second I'm disappointed. "There was an accident. He's disabled. He lost two fingers. The last two on his hand. It wasn't combat, okay? Thank God. It was during a routine maintenance check. There as a malfunction with the tank and—"

That's when I yell. "Bullshit! This is fucking bullshit!"

"Honey. Listen. It's going to be okay. They treated him at the platoon level and then took him to the field hospital. He's been there three days. They couldn't find the fingers to put them back on. Retransplantation, that's what they call it. So he's disabled, honey. Now he's coming home. Just for a few days. Then they'll take him to Walter Reed for rehabilitation. I know this is a lot to take in, Dougie. It's going to be okay."

I feel the women watching me, waiting for a reaction. I look at them. I scan across their dumb faces. "This is fucking bullshit!"

I'm not the star of a movie. If anything, this is a straight-to-video flick, and I've only got a cameo.

"Please, Dougie," says my mom, looking up at me with pleading eyes. "Please say something."

"This is fucking—"

"No, say something real. I know you're in shock. Just say something real."

"Which hand?"

"What?" asks my mom.

"Which hand got messed up?"

"The left one."

"But he's right-handed," I say, hearing the whine in my voice.

"I know, I know, thank God," says my mother.

"Thank God," the hyena chorus murmurs, nodding their massive heads.

"Trevor is coming home because he *lost his pinkie*?" I ask.

"And his ring finger," says my mother solemnly.

That's when I start to laugh. I laugh hysterically. I laugh until my eyes water. This is a crazy noise, like no other sound I've ever made or will probably ever again make.

"He's in shock," says someone. "Get him some water!"

"I'll get a cold washcloth," says someone else. The bodies swarm around me. Like flies love shit. I stare down at my kneeling mother. Her eyes are bright. She smiles at me.

"Trevor is a hero, Doug," she says, awe in her voice. "Your brother is a hero."

They forget about me within milliseconds. *There is so much to do,* they cackle. *His flight comes in at 8:00* A.M. *Are his clothes clean? Should we change the sheets on his bed? The refrigerator. We got the Nilla wafers. He likes them.* They gather around my mother in a tight nucleus. They follow her from room to room. I slip away without anyone noticing.

I lock my door. I put on Johnny Cash. I turn it up loud. I look for something to break. Nothing is valuable enough, so I just throw shit around for a while. Sweep all the crap off my desk onto the floor. Kick piles of dirty laundry. I punch the wall as hard as I can. I don't make a hole, just a tiny dent, and you have to look really close to see it.

I need to destroy something.

I run down the hall to Trevor's room. The hyenas are in a frenzy a room over. I hear them barking orders at each other, clanging shit around.

I haven't been in his room in years. It is spotless because of the OMSOTers, but otherwise it looks just how he left it when he went to college. It is a shrine to his perfection. Attached to his dresser are ribbons. The most important ones are displayed at school, in the glass case in Senior Hall. These are the second-tier ribbons. They go all the way back to elementary school. *Perfect Attendance. Sportsmanship. Peewee Football Most Valuable Player, Best Attitude, First in Relay, First in Sixty-Yard Sprint, Most Charming, Most Likely to Succeed.* I stare at them. I flick one with my finger, and it sways back and forth.

Then I rip down every single one.

Back in my room, I use a scissors to cut them all up into confetti. Maybe I'll throw it on him at the airport. *Welcome home, asstard,* I'll say.

I wake up to my mother knocking. "Doug, get up! Doug! Unlock the door! We have to go pick up your brother!"

"Okay!" I yell. "Okay, okay!" I sit up. I don't remember falling asleep. My stomach hurts like I have to take a shit, which is impossible since I haven't eaten in days. I am naked. Scraps of ribbon are pasted to my sweaty skin. I try to wipe them off, but they are stuck there. I start to hyperventilate. *Calm down,* I tell myself, *calm down.*

This must be the beginning of withdrawal.

That's when I decide that I've come too far to quit. This isn't over. Trevor ruins everything, but he won't ruin this.

I'll have to find a way to restock. I'll go back to Mitch. Just because my asshole war-hero brother is coming back doesn't mean I have to give up my own promising future.

This isn't over. I've worked too hard for it. I've earned it.

CHAPTER SIX

On the way to the airport, Mom gives me a speech about dealing with veterans that one of the hyenas obviously downloaded from some internet site for her.

"It will take time for him to adjust," she says. "He needs to be reminded that he is still needed by us. We don't want to overschedule him with activities before he goes to rehabilitation. We won't let all his friends visit at once. He doesn't need overstimulation. We have to watch for any signs of PTSD. That's post-dramatic stress disorder."

"You mean post-*traumatic* stress disorder?"

"Yes, Doug. That's just what I said. Bad dreams. Flash-backs. Feelings of distress. Nausea, sweating, muscle tension." I wonder if I have post-traumatic stress disorder. The car feels too hot, and the windows seem to be closing in on me. I wonder if there is a special form of PTSD for the siblings of asshole veterans upon their return to the States. My mom is wearing too much makeup and keeps applying more in the rearview mirror. "Just be normal," she says, her voice high-pitched. "Just act like everything is fine. Normal."

"You want me to pretend he was on spring break?"

"No, Doug," hisses my mom. "Don't pretend anything. Just act like you always do." She smiles at me. "Isn't this exciting?" she asks, her voice giddy.

At Arrivals, my mother lunges for Trevor. I stare at the back of his uniform. His left hand is bandaged. I'm kind of disappointed. I was hoping to see the stumps. My mom babbles incoherently, her voice muffled by his chest. Trevor laughs. "Hi, Mom," he says into the top of her head. Others have forgotten that they are waiting for their loved ones. They watch the scene with satisfied smiles, pulling their children closer to them, God-blessing America and our injured fighting men, drunk on the patriotism. It's a fucking Norman Rockwell moment.

The Trevor-adoring masses are nothing new. They've always been there. Gathered about him after football games, giggling girls staring at him through the Banana Republic window during Christmas shopping, kids honking outside the house for him on Saturday night like popular kids do in teen movies. When the phone rings, you know it is for Trevor. Starving children in third-world countries probably pray to his image for rice, he probably controls the fucking weather with his sweat glands. I stare down at my dirty Converse. My mom is making a huge scene, like he's been away at war or something, which I guess he has.

At her order, I'm wearing the Gap khaki pants she bought me two years ago for special occasions. This is the first time I've ever worn them. It took me thirty minutes to find them in the back of my closet, tags still attached. They are falling off me, and I have to pull in two belt holes to make them stay up. My hands are shaking. I know my heart is pumping faster than it should. My teeth ache from grinding in my sleep. I feel like I just went through a couple of rounds for the WWE, only it wasn't staged. I'm going through withdrawal, but it doesn't matter, because Stumpy the Hero is home in all his glory and the world may resume spinning on its Trevor axis as usual.

When she finally lets go, Trevor turns to me. "Hey. How you doing, Cheeks?"

"Fine," I say without looking at him. He hasn't called me Cheeks since I was eight years old and going through a chubby phase, all of which seemed centered around my face. I'd forgotten about the nickname. I didn't like it then and I don't like it now. He steps forward and hugs me with his good arm. I don't remember the last time he hugged me. Maybe Christmas a few years back? Or was that just one of those manly, vaguely painful good-bye smacks on the back? Even with just one arm, he grips me tight. I feel my body tighten. I can't believe we came out of the same vagina.

Awkwardly, I put a limp arm around him. My mom sniffles at this heartstring-tugging moment. Finally, he steps back. I look at him. I almost gasp but force myself to swallow instead. He looks different. His hair has been buzzed, and he's scrawnier than I remember. His cheekbones are sharper and his chin is pointier. But the weirdest part is his skin. Trevor has always had color. His cheeks were always ruddy, even in winter, like he'd been out on a beach somewhere playing volleyball. Now his face is the color of day-old grits. His lips have lost their redness and are translucent, chapped lines pulled into a tight smile. He looks like he's got a tapeworm.

I read somewhere that beauty is determined by the symmetry of your face. It always seemed unfair that guys like Trevor can fuck anyone they want because the halves of their face are identical, while the rest of us are destined to be only passable because one eye is a fraction of an inch higher than the other. I feel a moment of satisfaction, seeing him like that, scrawny and unremarkable. Then I feel bad about it because he was injured fighting for our country. Still, it kind of rocks a little bit that my hot brother looks like total shit.

"I know I look like crap," says Trevor. "You don't have to look so happy about it."

"I wasn't looking—"

"Whatever, Cheeks. I was just kidding." With a big grin he mock-punches me in the jaw, like we are buddies.

It's something guys only do in the movies. His eyes dart around. "We should get out of here."

"Okay," I say.

He stares at me for a second, like I'm a stranger. "Damn, you got skinny."

You should talk, I want to say. "Yeah," I mutter.

"Nice fucking pants," he says, looking at my khakis. He kind of chuckles, then his eyes dart around again. "We need to get out of here. Everyone is looking at us."

Aren't you used to that? I almost ask. *Isn't that, like, your thing?*

I turn to Mom. I've always thought the phrase *lit up with joy* was stupid, but it's like someone shoved a burning thousand-watt lightbulb down her throat. She looks so happy. I force myself to smile at her. I glance at Trevor. He's smiling at her too, only his grin is as fake as mine.

"I wish I'd brought my camera," says my mother.

We sit around the dinner table. We never eat at the table, let alone together. There's a tablecloth. I didn't know we even had one. My mom put out the good china, then replaced it right before we went to the airport with regular plates, somehow finding three that match. *Normal,* she'd muttered to herself. *Make him comfortable. Little baby Trevor.* There is enough food for a family of twenty, a really disturbing configuration of Trevor's favorites and the stuff we have on holidays and special occasions. Frog's-eye salad, steak, hash-brown casserole, a layered Jell-O mold Mom hasn't made since we were kids and takes six hours of preparation. I wonder which hyena followed the recipe, and if it will taste right. Mom flits around, adjusting plates and filling glasses.

"Wow," says Trevor. "Mom. This looks amazing." He's already put his duffel bag in his room. He's still wearing his fatigues, which is so lame. How long does it take to throw on a pair of jeans? I cringe, waiting for him to mention his missing ribbons. He hasn't said a word about them, or anything else, including the WELCOME HOME, TREVOR sign on the wall or the vacuumed couch or the bowl of Milk Duds on the living room table. Trevor is the only person I know who likes Milk Duds. In the wide array of candy options, I think they fucking suck. They take way too long to chew and get stuck in the back of your teeth. Candy shouldn't be so much work.

My mom makes him a plate and sets it in front of him. She runs her hand over his buzzed head. "Honey, I'm so glad you're home."

"Yeah, me too," he says. She stares at him. He looks uncomfortable. I don't remember Trevor ever looking uncomfortable before. He makes a big show of lifting up his fork and taking a bite of macaroni salad. His bandaged gimp hand rests on the table beside him. I try not to look at it.

"Yum," he says.

My mom smiles at him. "How do you feel?"

"Fine. Good."

"Are you jet-lagged?"

"Nah, I'm okay. Sit down, Mom. Eat."

She smiles at him, then looks at his heaping plate. Without pause, like someone flicked a switch in her brain, her grin drops and she starts to sob. "Oh, God, what's wrong with me?"

"It's okay, Mom," says Trevor.

"Oh, honey, I'm so sorry. Trevor, I'm so, so sorry."

"What are you sorry about?"

"I made you a steak!" she shrieks.

"I like steak—"

"You can't cut a steak. What was I thinking?"

"Mom, relax—"

"I don't know how I could have . . . I mean, you're injured, and here I am, right away, reminding you that—"

"Mom, sit down. It's going to be fine." My mom is blubbering. So much for normalcy. "You can cut the steak for me, okay?"

"But you're *disabled*!" she shrieks.

"Mom, it's just a couple of fingers. It's gonna be okay. You need to calm down." He turns to me. His face is red, his jaw tight. "What's wrong with her?" he hisses.

"I don't know." I dig out a big lump of red, white, and blue Jell-O and mash it into a gross, grayish mass.

"Get her a drink or something," he says. "Get her something strong. Whiskey."

"We don't have any whiskey. We don't even have beer." My mom is sitting now, crying, blowing her nose and blubbering into a cloth napkin, which she'll just have to wash, which makes me wonder why they make them in the first place. We usually use paper towels.

"Do something!" spits Trevor. "I really can't deal with this right now."

"What do you want me to do?"

"Calm her down!" he says, clenching his nongimpy hand into a fist on the fancy tablecloth.

"Mom," I say. "Calm down." I take a big bite of gray Jell-O, which completely sucks because the hyena had no idea what she was doing. Mom keeps crying, muttering to herself about a handicapped sticker for the car and all the things she forgot to do.

"She's freaking out!" says Trevor.

"Yeah, well, she's just tired. She stayed up all night getting ready for you." I motion to the sign over his head. He looks at it vaguely, as though he is seeing it for the first time and doesn't know what it is referencing. There is a clanking noise. We both turn to my mother, who is hunched over his plate, frantically cutting the steak into tiny pieces while she sobs, her tears and snot falling all over the meat and scoop of macaroni.

"Welcome home," I say, and take a long gulp of milk.

Trevor somehow convinces our mom that he isn't hungry. "You need to take a nap," he tells her. His voice is calm and controlled, like the old Trevor. He leads her to the bedroom. I follow them. He takes off her shoes with his one hand, makes her get in the bed. "Get my backpack," he says to me, agitated. Trevor rarely loses his cool. It isn't in his genetic makeup. I'm having a blast.

"Why?" I say calmly, taking another gulp of milk at the bedroom door.

"Just fucking do it, Cheeks," he hisses through his teeth.

"Oh, okay," I say as though it is a huge burden.

My mom has her hand up to his forehead. Her mascara is all over her face. "Oh, honey," she says to Trevor. "I can't believe you're home."

When I get back, he pulls out a bottle of pills. "Bring me that milk," he says. He takes out a pill and breaks it in half. "Open your mouth," he tells my mom. She does, like a child. He puts the pill in her mouth, holds the glass up to her lips. She drinks, still staring at him adoringly. "Close your eyes. Take a deep breath. Too much excitement, Mom. You need to rest."

"She's got sleeping pills," I tell him.

"Well, these are stronger," he says without looking at me.

"Trevor," she says, "I'm just going to rest my eyes. Just for a minute."

"Good job, dude," I say, making my voice loud.

"Shut the fuck up," rasps Trevor, glaring at me.

"Whatever," I say, shrugging my shoulders.

I go into the living room and stretch across the couch, making sure to put my dirty shoes all over the cushions. I turn on *America's Funniest Home Videos*. I watch some kid fall off a plastic horse on a carousel. I watch some guy get hit in the nuts with a football. Someone is always getting hit in the nuts on this show. Wow, there must be a million ways to get hit in the nuts. It's hilarious. I laugh and laugh.

"She's asleep," says Trevor fifteen minutes later, flicking off the television just as they are about to announce the winner.

"I was watching that." It was down to the retarded cat attacking its own reflection in a car mirror, the football-nuts guy, and some little girl saying something adorable while swinging around a gushing garden hose. Now I'll never know.

"What the hell is wrong with her?" he asks. He stares at me, his lips pinched together. He's got huge dark circles under his eyes.

I pop a Milk Dud in my mouth and chew vigorously. "She's been worried about you. I mean, you get a call your son is injured, and I guess it's pretty upsetting. Duh. What'd you give her?"

"Something from the hospital. She won't wake up for a long time."

"How long?" I ask.

"Tomorrow."

Perfect, I think. Plenty of time to score. I figured I wouldn't get away until the next morning. I figured I'd be forced to participate in family-bonding time, play Pictionary, listen to Trevor's stories of heroically maiming camel jockeys.

Trevor is pacing back and forth. I go to the kitchen and find Mom's purse. I hesitate before reaching inside. Purses are as foreign as vaginas. Vaginas aren't as scary now that I've had my dick in one, but I still feel the same way about purses. I cringe and do it anyway, thrusting my hand in the alien universe of female disorder. Eventually, I find the keys. I take forty bucks out of her wallet for good measure. She probably won't notice in the Trevor-induced choke hold that's suffocating the house.

I'm about to walk out the front door when Trevor says, "Stop."

"What?" I say without turning.

"Where are you going?"

"None of your business, Sergeant."

"I'm not kidding around, Cheeks. Where are you going?" I turn to look at him. Even having lost weight and with a gimp arm he looks intimidating.

"I'm going out. O. U. T. Out."

"Where?"

"Fuck you," I say, and step out the door.

"Hey. You better stop, Cheeks." I look at him. He's got on his stern-father face. He's been back a few hours and he's already telling me what to do. The thing is, he's not my father and never has been. He has no idea who he's dealing with. I'm not a little kid anymore. I do drugs and have sex at Scenic Turnouts.

"Whatever," I say, and keep going.

Then he's on me. He's pulled me back in the living room and slammed the door. He has me in a headlock with his good arm. I squirm to get out, but I know it's pointless. He used to do this when I was a kid. "Smell my armpit," he'd say, while I writhed around and whimpered. "Act like a man. Do it. Smell my armpit or I won't let you go."

If was smart, I would just have played dead. That's what hognose snakes do when faced with a predator. Just flip over on their backs with their mouths hanging open. Sometimes they even release a drop of blood from their jaw, making the charade complete. But it would have been worse, being called a pussy boy or wimp. I try to jerk myself out of his grip, even though I know, logically, I won't get away. I've never been able to get away.

This time is no different, except that it isn't a game for him. He's hurting me, and I'm fighting back, try to jab him with my elbow, using every ounce of strength I have to worm out of his grip. "Fuck you!" I keep saying, trying to wrench away. I hate him. I hate that he's still stronger than me. I feel like a worthless six-year-old.

"Stop fighting," he says.

"Fuck you motherfucking, cocksucking—" Then he has me facedown, holding my arm down, straddling my back. I try to speak, but my mouth is pushed down on the floor. I can taste the rug fibers against my tongue. At least Mom just vacuumed. I swing around my free arm and punch at air. I'm not going anywhere.

"I hate you," I say, though garbled. I have literally become his carpet-munching bitch.

"Don't make this harder," he says gruffly. "I know

what's going on, Cheeks. I'm not living in some la-di-da dreamy world like Mom." He loosens his grip so I can lift my head.

"Let me go, dicktard! You can't tell me what to do! You don't have any—"

"Tell me what you're on, Doug."

It's like a cold snap through my nervous system. *How does he know?* "What the hell are you talking about, ass-wipe? Are you, like, having some sort of post-traumatic flashback or something? Should I call the—"

"What. Drugs. Are. You. On. Doug." His voice is gruff. "I knew the minute I saw you that something was up. Have you seen yourself lately? You look like a bum."

"Like you should talk, you fingerless fuck—"

"Stop!" he says, pushing the back of my head so my face smushes harder against the rug.

I'm afraid of him. I wonder if he really is having some sort of Iraq flashback, and pretty soon he'll decide I'm an insurgent and snap my neck. I try to make my voice calm.

"I'm not on drugs."

"Liar," he hisses. Then he stands and pulls me by my armpit to my feet. "Go to the car."

"I don't have to—"

He goes for the headlock again. Hot tears are rolling down my face, and I'm hating myself even more. I hate my tear ducts. I hate him for being born.

"Okay," I whimper like a five-year-old boy. "Okay, okay."

• • •

I unlock the car door.

"You'll have to drive," he says.

"I only have a learner's permit," I say, even though I almost drove to Mexico with Angela. "Remember? You sold your car. I didn't have a reason to get a license." He can bully me around, but I won't make it easy.

"Get in the driver's seat and drive."

"I told you I don't have the proper fucking ID. You want me to get arrested? You drive, if you want to go somewhere so—"

"I can't. I'm missing two fingers." He wins.

We get inside. The car makes a weird sound when I start it up. "When did she have it tuned up? Has she checked the oil?"

"I don't know," I say, pulling out of the driveway. "I don't care. I don't know and I don't care." I like how this sounds, like a little song. I stop there, in the middle of the street, and hum it to myself.

"Go."

"Where?" I say.

"Wherever you get your drugs."

"I told you I don't—"

"Don't talk anymore. Just drive. Take me to whatever douche bag thinks it's okay to sell a kid drugs. And don't tell me it's just pot. I know it isn't pot."

We stare at each other. I remember, suddenly, having a stare-down contest on a road trip when we were little. It was so long ago. The memory pops up, just like that, like how fat floats to the top when my mom used to make us chicken soup. Two kids, in the backseat of that old Ford. Was Dad there? Where were we going? Trevor and I sit across from each other. The car interior is baby blue. There is a rip in the leather. Trevor and I stuff things in that rip. Little balls of paper, pennies, green Skittles. Neither of us will eat the green ones. I'm not sure why. Something about their being made of boogers. We are having a staring contest. He has a cowlick. I might be in a car seat. He wrinkles his nose, sticks out his bottom lip. He pinches his lips together and puffs out his face like a blowfish. He crosses his eyes. I wish I could cross my eyes. It's a showdown. Who can go the longest without laughing? If you laugh, you lose. I'm always the first to laugh, but it doesn't matter.

Neither of us are laughing now. "Cheeks. Oh, Cheeks. Don't you get it? You don't have a choice in this situation. So don't make this hard on yourself, okay? Just drive."

I'm trapped in a car with a possibly delusional vet and no way to get out. No choices, no place to go. It's like a metaphor for my whole life.

He takes out a pack of Parliaments and puts one in his mouth. He tries to light the end, but my window is open, and the flame keeps going out. I watch him shield the lighter with his bandaged hand. "Fuck," he says.

I swipe the lighter from him. "You're gonna set your

bandage on fire." I roll up the window and light his cigarette. I light one for myself. "You don't smoke," I say, handing it to him.

"Neither do you." We both inhale deeply.

"You said you'd never smoke," I say. "You said only wusses need that kind of crutch."

"Yeah, well, I talked a lot of bullshit, didn't I, Cheeks?" I don't say anything. I'm not crying anymore, but my face is burning. "Are we almost there?"

"Yeah." There is no way out. "But I need to tell you something. This guy. He's kind of fucked-up. I mean, he's not exactly, um, wired right."

"Yeah, I figured. He's a drug dealer."

"I mean, the thing is, he's—"

"Just drive, Cheeks. I'll meet him for myself."

We are standing outside Mitch's door. The lawn is still overgrown, the mailbox still hanging at a weird angle. I feel like I was just here yesterday. At the same time, it feels like light-years ago, eons, centuries, I've been to a land far away, I've been on the *Methship Enterprise*.

When I knock, no one answers. I knock again. Trevor pushes me out of the way and knocks hard and loud with his good hand. It's the kind of knock you can't ignore. I look over my shoulder at the condos on either side, but they are dark. Where is everyone? Maybe it's Saturday night. When did I punch that guy? Was it a Tuesday or a Wednesday? What time is it?

"What the fuck?" says a voice from inside, and the door opens a slit. An eyeball stares out at me. There is a long pause. "Little Schaffer?" says Mitch.

"Yeah."

"Did you see anyone out there?"

"Like who?"

"Patrol? Cops? Neighborhood Association?"

"No. No one. It's dead out here."

"Hold on." Mitch closes the door. I hear him undo a lock, then he undoes another. And another. He opens the door and stares at me. He smells like roadkill. I don't remember him smelling that bad. I want to cover my nose and mouth, but I don't want to hurt his feelings.

"Whatcha doin' here, Little Schaffer? Come back for some more boom shakalaka?"

I turn to Trevor, and so does Mitch. His eyes get wide and his mouth drops open like a cartoon character. I hear the sound effect in my head. *Boooooooo-iiiiiing!*

"What the fuck?" he says, and whooshes back in the house like in that bad eighties movie Dingo and I saw where the basement door has a big demon mouth that sucks people into hell.

"No," says Trevor, stopping the door from closing with his good hand. He may have lost weight and fingers, but he's still strong as fuck. Just another reason to hate him.

"Are you a cop?" asks Mitch, practically crying.

"Am I dressed like a cop?" Mitch stares at Trevor's fatigues through the half-open door. He seems confused. He struggles to close the door, but against Trevor he's got the strength of a buzzing gnat circling the head of an elephant. Mitch is breathing heavily. His whole body convulses with each intake of air. He looks in the house, then out in the yard, then back in the house. There's nowhere to go.

"It's me, Mitch. Your old friend," says Trevor, his voice smooth and insistent. "Trevor. Your bud. Let us in, Mitch. C'mon. Just let us in. Now."

"Trevor? Trevor? Fuck." Mitch gives up struggling and steps backward into the house. We follow him and Trevor closes the door behind us.

"God, it's fucking dark. Turn on a light, Mitch," says Trevor.

"Lock the door," chokes Mitch. Trevor clicks the lock. "The other ones."

"I got it, I got it. Just turn on a fucking light, man."

Mitch flicks the switch on a lamp. He looks even scarier than the last time I saw him. It's like he bought a cheap polyester Drug Dealer Halloween costume off the rack at Wal-Mart. He stares at Trevor. "Dude, I know you! I fucking know you!" he says, his voice giddy.

"Yeah," says Trevor.

"You're Trevor, man! Dude! What the hell? Man, I didn't know it was you! That uniform threw me off, man. Fuck!" Mitch goes over and puts out his hand. Trevor pauses, then puts his good one in Mitch's. They shake like real men do in the movies, despite that one only has one good hand and the other looks like Skeletor. They drop hands and look at each other.

"Long fucking time, man," says Mitch.

"Yup. When was the last time I saw you?"

"Dude, I have no fucking idea. Years, man. Graduation, man. Wow. Trevor Schaffer, Trevor the man, right here in my living room. Damn. How ya doin', man?"

"Fine. Hey, I don't want this to come out of nowhere, okay? That wouldn't be fair to you." Trevor sighs. "I'm going to have to kick your ass, okay?"

"What?"

"I'm going to hit you." Trevor sighs, pulls back his good arm, and punches Mitch dead in the nose. It makes one of those cracking noises like you hear on TV shows, and blood spurts all over the place.

Mitch falls backward, clutching his face. He looks up at Trevor, who is standing above him. "I think you broke it!"

"Yeah, I probably did."

"Why'd you do that, man? What the fuck? What'd I ever do to you, man?" He's wriggling around on the floor, turning his head from side to side. He reminds me of one of those dogs that scratch their asses by dragging them across the floor with their hind legs pointed upward. The blood is gushing down both cheeks and in the corners of his mouth. He's crying. "What'd I ever do to you?"

"You gave my brother drugs. What kind of drugs where they, Doug?"

"Meth," I say quietly, my voice shaking.

"You gave a kid meth?" Trevor booms. I can practically hear his blood pressure rising. He stands over Mitch, his good arm pulled back. I've never seen him look that angry. "Are you fucking psychotic?"

"No way, man!" says Mitch, sitting up. "That's a fucking lie, man! I didn't give him shit!"

I suck in my breath.

"Doug told me you gave him meth and I believe my brother. That's a messed-up thing to do, man, getting a fifteen-year-old hooked on drugs."

"Sixteen," I squeak.

"Getting a sixteen-year-old hooked on drugs." Mitch has wriggled toward the wall. "Sorry, Cheeks," Trevor says without ever taking his eyes off Mitch. "I never sent you a birthday card. Slipped my mind."

"It's okay."

"Come over here, okay?" Trevor says to me without taking his eyes off the lump of flesh in front of him. I step forward so I am standing next to him, looking down at the bloody, wriggling fungus that is Mitchell Dwight Thompson III.

"Why would you give a fift—sixteen-year-old drugs? You don't need the money, Mitch. Unless you snorted up that whole trust fund already."

"I didn't give him meth," says Mitch quietly.

Trevor pulls back his good arm again, like it's time for round two. I squeeze my eyes shut. This isn't like *Rocky*, where Stallone gets punched and spews blood all over and it's pretty gross, but in your heart you know the blood is nothing but corn syrup and food coloring. This is way more blood than my baby sucker punch in Advanced

Chemistry. This is real, and it's everywhere. I didn't know so much stuff could come out of a human nose.

"It wasn't meth, okay?" shrieks Mitch, his voice sounding a little like Channella's, shielding his face. "It was the same thing I give all the other kids, just a bunch of leftover crap, okay? It's about as strong as a handful of No-Doz. My friend makes it up for me, okay? It's a fucking scam. I wouldn't give a little kid meth, okay? I'm not, like, immoral." He looks up at us, his nose cocked at a weird angle. "I don't have a trust fund anymore, okay? It's all fucking gone. I have to pay my electric bill. I need the money. I wouldn't give a kid meth, though. I swear to fucking God I wouldn't."

It takes me a few seconds to understand. I look at Trevor, then back at Mitch. I see it all there on his face.

He's telling the truth.

I feel like someone sucker punched me in the stomach. I stumble backward. The room is turning around me. I find the wall and brace myself against it. *Like a handful of No-Doz.* It wasn't real. This whole thing. My whole life. It was all a lie. It was pretend. Everything. Everything I thought and did. Was all made up.

"Fucking liar. You're a fucking liar, you pathetic addict sack of shit. You're a motherfucking liar. *Say it. Say you made it up.*"

He looks at me like he's mute.

"I'm not fucking kidding you, you motherfucking liar! You're fucking lying. You're trying to save your own ass by telling your fucking junky asshole lies, you're a fucking liar!"

Now I'm crying. I'm spurting tears all over the world.

"You're a fucking piece of shit liar and you better fucking say it! *I'm a liar.* Say it, you fucking dick asshole. *Say it, Mitch.*"

He looks up at me with his scared junky eyes. "I'm lying," he whispers.

That's when I know he's telling the truth.

Something takes over my body. Like that, I'm on him, kicking him in the ribs like the sack of shit he really is. Blood is on the tip of my Converse, right where I drew a star. I'm on top of him, punching him in the face and getting his blood all over me. I am screaming *cocksucker-asshole-dick-fuck-cock-fuck-motherfucking-asshole-I-hate-you-motherfucking-bastard*. I am a caveman. And somewhere in all this, as Mitch sobs and begs me to stop, and my fists move independently of my mind, and the endorphins rush through my body, and I am ripe and dangerous and unstoppable—something occurs to me. *It wasn't the meth after all. It was in me all the time. I am a man.* And I know the man in me might actually kill him.

But then Trevor is pulling me off. I keep punching the air, my knuckles covered in Mitch blood, baring my teeth at him like a rabid animal. "Okay, okay," says Trevor, his voice measured and cool in my ear. "Okay, calm down. You fucked him up good, Doug. You can stop now. You already fucked him up good enough." I bend over, my hands on my knees, and try to find some air to breathe. Tears are falling down my face, but I don't feel sad. I feel alive.

. . .

We stand over Mitch, who has his arms crossed over his chest. He is groaning. "That fucking hurt!"

"You'll be okay," says Trevor.

Mitch looks up at us. "I hate you fucking Schaffers. You fucking Schaffers. Neanderthals. That's what you are."

Trevor looks at me. We are both smiling. We have big, goofy grins.

"Damn, I didn't know you had it in you, Cheeks. Wow. I had no idea you could fuck someone up like that. You jihad-ed all over his ass. I might have to call you Jihad now."

"Ow," says Mitch. "It hurts!"

Trevor has never looked at me like he does right now. He looks at me like he's proud, and I bask in it.

"Nice job, Jihad."

"Thanks." I am still smiling.

"I need to go to the hospital," sobs Mitch.

Trevor leans over and squints at him. "Yeah, man. You should probably go to the emergency room. Your nose is broken for sure. And Jihad here probably cracked a couple of ribs."

"That was a fucked-up thing to do," says Mitch in a whine.

"You deserved it," says Trevor. "Listen. I'll call the ambulance. But first you have to tell me where you keep the stuff. The real stuff. And don't fuck with me. Don't try to give me some of that crap you pull on the kids, or I will hurt you worse. We both will."

He said *we*. I feel something flush my body. Satisfaction. Power. *We both will.*

Mitch groans, then whimpers, then winces. "The nightstand by my bed," he says in a wheezy sob. "Taped underneath. Just don't hurt me anymore."

"You wouldn't fuck with me, would you, Mitch? That would be a really bad idea."

"No. No. Please. I need help. It ouches so bad."

"Ouches so bad? You are such a fag, Mitch," says Trevor, striding to the hallway. He looks at me. "Just wait here for a minute, okay, Jihad?"

A few minutes later we are about to walk out the door.

"What about me?" says Mitch.

"I'll call the hospital from a pay phone. Tell them some guys broke in and messed you up. They'll believe you. It's a fucking pigsty in here."

"Not the hospital! I don't want them to tell the cops!"

"I don't think you got much choice, man." Trevor found a dirty rag somewhere. He drops it on Mitch's face. "Here. Apply pressure until they get here."

"It hurts so bad."

"Don't be a pussy," says Trevor. "It's not as bad as that time you dislocated your shoulder."

"My shoulder?"

"Last game of the season. Against Shawnee. And they had to pop it back into place so you could play the last quarter."

"Shit, I forgot about that!" says Mitch, and laughs. It's a high-pitched wheezing sound, one of those recorders they make you play in elementary school so they won't have to buy real instruments. "That was a good fucking pass, huh?"

"Yeah," says Trevor. "That was a great fucking pass, actually. That was a great fucking game." Trevor's hand squeezes my shoulder as he leads me to the door.

"That was the night I fucked Tina Latchkey," says Mitch, almost to himself, holding the bloody rag up to his nose. "Out on Beau Dresden's farm. Even with my shoulder messed up. Beau had a kegger there, after the game, 'member? There was a bonfire. That huge-ass pile of beer cans we'd been building since junior year. I fucked her, right in the back of Beau's pickup. She had to do most of the work, because of my shoulder. I just laid there and took it." He laughs, then winces. "God. I really hated that dumb bitch." He sighs. "Still. Good times."

"I remember," says Trevor. "I'll call the hospital, okay? We have to leave now."

"Those were good times, weren't they, man?"

"Yeah." Trevor opens the door and leads me out into the overgrown lawn. "They were."

"Good times, good times," says Mitch from behind us. He'll probably keep saying it, even after the door closes.

Trevor is driving, even with the gimp hand. For a long time we don't speak. "Put on your seat belt," he tells me.

I don't move. I think I'm still in shock. He leans over and fastens it across me at a stoplight. Then he starts talking. I don't really listen. It doesn't matter because he isn't really talking to me anyway.

"That little asshole, I had to punch that fucker, really, I had no choice. Sad kid. Really smart, could have done something with his life. But you. Damn. I didn't know you had it in you. I could have pulled you off sooner, but it was great, watching you go at the little pansy. Y'know why he got kicked out of OU, right? He tells people it was his grades, but that's crap. Not with his family connections. They fund that school. They got plaques all over the campus. One call to the president, and he isn't failing Great Philosophers anymore. It wasn't his grades." We are on the I-35, passing Frontier City, Oklahoma's sad excuse for a theme park. Thousands of hard gobs of chewed gum stuck to the inside of the Log Ride tunnel. A place you can dress up in a heinous cowboy costume worn by a zillion other sweaty people and get your picture taken with a fake rifle. A machine pulls taffy for $10.

A few years ago, there was a new roller coaster, one of those indoor ones where you can't see shit. The Dark Tycoon. No one seemed to notice that the Orange Crush, that old Day-Glo roller coaster on the other side of the park, the one we'd all grown up with, had magically evaporated. They'd just moved it across the park, built a big barn around it, and given it a new name. For some reason, thinking about this makes me want to cry. My head hurts. Trevor is still talking.

"Rape. He raped a girl." My mouth is moving, words are coming out, but I have no idea what I'm saying or why.

"Raped a girl? He said that? He wishes. His parents would have gotten him the best lawyer in town. Nah, he didn't rape anyone. He was in Kappa, right? With all those guys whose parents make over a mil a year, and he got caught fucking a pledge in his room. They kicked him out. They said it was because fucking a pledge was against frat regulations, but the truth was, no one wanted an ass-bandit representing their fraternity. His parents were humiliated. I mean, anything would have been better than having a homosexual son. Even being a heroin addict. His dad was pissed. Up for reelection. He wasn't supposed to get his trust fund for a few years, but they signed it over anyway. Asked him to disappear. But I guess it's gone now. The money. Spent it on drugs, that little butt pirate. Not that I have a problem with gay guys, I mean, you wouldn't believe the number of fags in the army. Good guys. Tough fuckers. You know they got your back. But that little homo, fuck, he's something else entirely." Trevor's voice is shaky as he drives one-handed. He swerves off the highway onto the northwest side of the city. He hits all green lights. We are in familiar territory now. Kum and Go. Walgreens. Salvation Army. Cock O The Walk.

That's when I get the nerve to ask him, "Why did you take his drugs? Are you going to throw them away?"

He sighs. "No, Jihad. I'm not." We don't say anything for a few blocks. Then he says, "My hand is starting to hurt. I only had three pills left from the hospital. I was saving them. And I gave Mom one. I took the others, but that was a long time ago."

It couldn't have been more than an hour and a half, but I don't feel like arguing. "What kind of pills were they?"

"OxyContin."

"Oh. OxyContin. That's strong shit." Those are the ones that get celebrities sent to rehab. I like how it sounds. Oxy-cotton. It sounds soft and sweet. It sounds like one of those sugary dough concoctions you'd buy at the State Fair.

"I got three bottles in the medical camp from this nurse, Cindy. Fugly chick from Ohio, but really sweet. She swiped them for me. All I had to do was flirt. I let her give me a hand job under the sheets and told her I'd write."

"OxyContin."

"Yeah. I filled the painkiller prescription the doc gave me on layover in Atlanta. Only a few pills. Took a cab to Walgreens and got back to make the flight in twenty-two minutes. The stuff isn't nearly as good."

"And now it's all gone?"

"Can't fill it again till next month. I don't know where to get some. I can probably go to the army hospital to-morrow, but I need something now." His hand is shaking cigarette ash all over his fatigues.

Suddenly, everything makes sense.

"See, Doug, we have more in common than you thought. Except that your stuff wasn't real. Still. Damn. That was pretty impressive, how you fucked up Mitch. You've really grown up since I last—"

"Meth is different." I am suddenly scared for him. I still think he's an asshole, but this isn't No-Doz. "It's not like pills. I researched it. It's really dangerous. It can—"

"I know all about meth."

"It's serious business. It isn't pill popping."

"I've done it, okay?" He makes a horrible face all of a sudden, like he's trying to shit an armadillo out of his ass. It's a scary face, like he's being tortured by that clown in *Saw*, asked to remove his own kidney with a box cutter or something.

"Are you all right?"

"No, okay? I'm in some fucking pain right now!" he says, and it is almost a scream. It hurts my own throat to hear it. I back myself against the car door. I've never seen him like that. This isn't Trevor. Trevor doesn't lose control of his emotions. Trevor doesn't feel rage. This is a brother I don't know. He looks desperate. He might even cry. He stares at me, squeezed against the door, like he just remembered who I am. His face softens.

"Sorry. Sorry," he says, his voice calm. "Here's the thing, Doug. The thing is—" He sighs. "The thing is, I feel like I'm going to die."

"Where are we going?" I say finally, my voice small.

"I'm taking you home."

It's like he punched me instead of Mitch. "No!" I slam the dashboard with my fist. "No fucking way! I'm not going home!"

"Yeah, you are."

"No, I'm not!" I sound like a twelve-year-old who got grounded. *Like a handful of No-Doz*. It wasn't real. It was all in my head. It was like tuning in to a sitcom and everyone is sitting around the table talking, and you keep waiting for the story to start, then, boom, the screen goes fuzzy and the music plays and it's a fucking flashback episode.

"I'm doing it with you," I growl.

"Hell no," says Trevor calmly.

"I'm doing it with you. The real stuff."

Trevor pulls over at a 7-Eleven and parks. He knows it's a road hazard to have a confrontation while driving. Always the responsible driver, Trevor. Even when he's got crack or horse tranquilizers in his pocket. We sit there in silence. Even with the windows closed, I can hear the easy listening blaring through the loudspeakers to keep the bums away. It's that asstard with the pubes on his head that plays that gay-looking sax-slash-flute thing. It isn't even a real instrument.

"You don't want to do this stuff," says Trevor, lighting a cigarette. His hand isn't shaking anymore. He seems calm. "You saw Mitch. You wanna turn into that?"

"Do you?"

"Fuck no. This is it. The last time."

"Yeah, right. That's what the drug addicts say on television. 'I swear to God, this is it. Last time, I promise.' You think I'm an idiot? You think this is a Lifetime movie?"

"No, I'm serious. I'm going to the army hospital tomorrow morning. I'm telling them I'm . . . whatever.

Addicted. This is it. The last time. I've had this planned, Cheeks. It's over. Just something to get me through till tomorrow."

"Why don't you go right now, then? To the army hospital. I'll drive you." My voice is seething. I've read that word, *seethe,* in so many books, but this is the first time I've actually done it. "I'll drive you right now."

"It doesn't work like that," says Trevor through clenched teeth. He's getting angry.

"Then how does it work?"

"I'm in a lot of pain, you little fucker."

"They'll give you stuff for that. For the withdrawal. I mean, not as much as you're used to taking. It'll still hurt a shitload, but they'll give you something. That's part of the recovery process. You don't know anything. I read all about it."

"I'm taking you home."

"I'm going with you." It can't end like this.

"No way," says Trevor.

"I'll call the cops on you if you don't take me."

"And tell them what?"

"I don't know. Something. That you forced me to go score drugs with you. That you're an addict. Mom'll love that. When she wakes up. The cops in the living room, taking my—whatever you call it. Statement."

Trevor puts his head in the crook of his arm on the steering wheel. "You watch too much *Law and Order.* I know you wouldn't do that to me." I don't say anything because he's right. I wouldn't do that, and we both know it. I bite my bottom lip hard enough that I taste blood. I look at the tip of my shoe, where Mitch's blood has dried.

"Please." I hear the desperation in my own voice. I have to do it for real. Just once. I have to do it for real or it was all for nothing. A cardboard backdrop at a school dance. A knockoff Rolex that breaks in two days. The remake of a Clint Eastwood film starring some guy from *High School Musical*. I need this. I can't quit knowing I was the generic version of who I could have been.

"Listen. This is the last time. Like you said." I look at him in what I imagine is a meaningful way. "I want to do it with you." I try to sound adult. I will be rational. I will rationally convince my dickward brother to get me fucked-up on drugs. It can be done. I'm smarter than him. "One time won't hurt me. I'll be with you. I'll be safe."

"This isn't a good—"

"C'mon, Trevor. Then I'll take you to the army hospital in the morning. You shouldn't go alone anyway. I mean, really, I'm doing this for you. As a favor."

"Doug—"

"Besides, one time won't get me addicted. I know that. I did research. That's just, like, government propaganda. Please. I took you to Mitch, didn't I?"

Trevor looks up at me. I wonder what he sees. I feel like I'm six years old, begging for a new action figure at Toys 'R' Us. I want this more than anything in the entire world. I will bargain, beg, throw myself down in the aisles and kick my legs until I get this.

"Please," I say. "Just say yes. Yes. I know you're in pain.

Say yes and we'll go. Ten minutes and you'll feel better. Say yes."

Trevor stares at me, his forehead wrinkling. Then he stares out at Classen Boulevard, like he's looking for something, like it isn't the same Classen Boulevard it was when we were kids and the same Classen Boulevard it will be when we are old and need walkers. Oklahoma never changes. They'll put in a Starbucks, tear down a ghetto mall for an office building, add a lane to the highway, expanding the bombing memorial—but this little mediocre street in this mediocre city in this mediocre state will forever be cemented in concrete, a time capsule of adequate. And I'll be here too. Trevor starts the engine. I know we are headed home, and I hate him.

"Just do this one fucking thing for me. It's the only thing I've ever asked you to do, Trevor. I know you don't give, like, a flying fuck about me, but this is all I ask of you. The one fucking thing I ask of you in your entire life."

"Did you just say *flying fuck*?" asks Trevor, smiling.

"Fuck you." He smiles at me, and I want to smack him.

"Cheeks. Listen to me. Carefully. If we do this, you have to promise me one thing."

I turn to him. I can't believe it. I want to kiss him, even though I'm not gay and it would be incestuous and I still think he's an asstard. "Anything."

"You'll get me to that hospital tomorrow. No matter what. No matter what I say. You'll make sure I get there. You'll tell them I need help. I got to fix this. For Mom. This has got to end."

"I promise. I swear."

"Okay. Okay." He pulls out onto Classen. "Besides, I decided I was gonna take you twenty minutes ago, anyway. It was just fun to hear you whimper like a little girl."

I don't believe him, but I don't care. I'm going to get fucked-up on drugs, and I'm really, really happy.

We go to a hotel in Nichols Hills. Back in the day, it was the nicest hotel in the city. Now, since high-end chains have sprouted on the highway, it's the place where rich old oil heirs take their mistresses to be incognito. Trevor parks the car way in the back near a deserted parking garage.

"C'mon," he says.

"This place is expensive," I say, mostly to myself.

"We aren't going to do this in some shitty motel you rent by the hour, okay? We aren't white trash."

The lobby is dim, with worn-out Persian carpets and a big chandelier. No one is around. It must be late.

"Stay here." Trevor pushes me down in an armchair. "I'll be right back."

I watch him walk into the lobby. The half-asleep middle-aged woman behind the counter sees him and hops to attention like she got a jump start. They talk quietly. She laughs like a teenager. I guess chicks like fatigues.

"C'mon," says Trevor a few minutes later. He is standing over me. He doesn't look happy. "Let's go. Now."

. . .

He got a penthouse. It's seen better days, but it's still a penthouse, with the living room and balcony. A separate door leads to a bedroom.

"Wow," I say. "Fuck. How much did this cost?"

"Standard rate. I told her I just got back from Iraq. Told her you were my son, we were going on a road trip to bond."

"Gross."

He locks the door. He goes to the bed and takes off his boots.

"Your feet stink," I tell him. I fight the urge to act like a total idiot and jump on the bed and hack loogies off the balcony and open all the dresser doors to see if there is some free shit to take home with me. Casually, I open the minifridge. I take out one of those little bottles of Jack Daniel's that probably cost thirty bucks. I open it and suck it down. It burns my throat in a good way. I don't even make a face.

Trevor makes sure the laces are inside his boots and sets them neatly side by side. He looks at me, with my empty minibottle. "Bring me one. Bring a couple, actually."

The real meth looks about the same as the fake stuff did. The crystals are in the middle of the coffee table, pushed into a pile. Trevor has closed all the curtains, rechecked the locked door. We sit across from each other. We smoke. We look at the crystals.

I can tell Trevor doesn't know where to start, but won't ask for my help. "So," he says. "So. How you want to do this?"

"I thought you'd done it before."

"Yeah. We snorted it. But I wasn't the one who crushed it. I guess we could do that, right? Snort it?"

It all comes back to me. *Injecting, shooting, parachuting, booty bumping, slamming, bikers' coffee.*

I was such a child.

"We could drink it," I tell him. "It'll take about fifteen minutes to work. Or we could snort it. That'll be faster. Three to five minutes."

"How do you know all that?"

"I just know shit," I tell him casually.

He smiles. "You always were the smart one. Almost a genius, that's what Mom and I would say. Let's crush it."

"Really?"

"Yeah," he says.

"You are the one who got good grades."

"You know grades don't indicate bullshit, Cheeks. Yeah, I could pass a test. Write a paper. But you got something else. You know that already." He never takes his eyes off the crystals.

"I know that?"

"Yeah. You do. But don't start fishing for compliments, Cheeks."

"You got a pocketknife?"

"Yeah. Army-issued."

"Crush it, then. As finely as you can. That causes the least irritation to your nasal passages."

"I'll go first," says Trevor. There are two lines of powder. He leans down and snorts the first through a rolled bill, like how they do in drug movies, only they use hundreds and this is only a dollar. He screws up his face and pinches the bridge of his nose. I wait for him to keel over and start twitching and foaming at the mouth, but then his face relaxes. All the tension is gone. He looks at me. I am kneeling beside him, watching. He turns to me. "You sure about this?"

"Yeah," I say, because I am.

He holds out the bill to me. "Careful. It stings really bad for a second."

I take the bill.

"You need any help?"

"No. It isn't rocket science. I got it." I lean down. I feel the imprint of his big, warm, nongimpy hand in the middle of my back as I snort.

"I don't feel anything," he says. He is lying across the couch. He needs to clip his toenails. They look like claws.

"Nothing?"

"No. How about you?"

"A little something, maybe." I light a cigarette. My hand is shaking. I light one for him.

"Thanks. Fuck. My hand really hurts."

"Just wait."

"If that asshole screwed me over, I will go back there and fucking kill him."

"How will you kill him?" I blow smoke at the ceiling. I wonder if this is a nonsmoking room. I hope it is. It makes me feel badass. I am Sid Vicious at the Chelsea Hotel.

"I'll stab him, I guess. They confiscate all your weapons when they send you home. All I got is the pocketknife."

"You're gonna kill him with a pocketknife?"

"Sure. Don't forget, I was at war."

Something occurs to me, and I sit up suddenly. "Did you, like, kill anyone over there?"

"Yeah," says Trevor, his voice monotone. I feel my body go numb. Then he starts laughing. "Psyched you out!"

For some reason, his laugh reminds me of something from a long time ago. Eating Count Chocula. Watching cartoons. Saturday morning. It's a big sound. It fills the room. I start to laugh too. I don't know why. We are both laughing now.

"Hey," says Trevor, snorting, tears at the corner of his eyes. "Do you feel anything?"

"Yeah. I think I do."

"It's good, isn't it?"

I nod because it is.

It's like all my circuits and wires are conducting electricity. I try to remember what is happening in my body. Cytoplasmic extensions. Nerve fibers. Gray matter. Effectors. I can't put it all together in my head. It's basic shit you learn in high school science. The American Educational System has failed me. I'll I can think is *whoosh*.

"Neurotransmitters," I say, remembering. I am standing. I am excited.

"What are you talking about?"

"That's how our neurons send messages to each other. Through our synapses. There are all kinds of neurotransmitters. But there's this one, dopamine. He's the one we like. He makes us feel good. Like when you, I don't know, eat something that tastes really good, like a steak, or you ride a roller coaster, it's the dopamine that gets released. Meth releases dopamine. Lots and lots of it. That's why it feels so good. It's, like, basic human anatomy. You, like, learn it freshman year."

Trevor nods. "I do feel good."

"Dopamine. God. It's good shit. Shit. I fucking love my neurotransmitters."

"Neurotransmitters." Trevor is standing now. I've been moving around. I'm holding a pillow from the couch. I don't remember picking it up.

"My hand doesn't even hurt," says Trevor. "I can't even feel it."

"Yeah."

"Let's do more."

"Yeah. Good idea."

He measures out two lines. It takes him too long. I

crack my knuckles while he does it. I crack my neck. I'm thinking of other things to crack.

"Stop it, asshole," he says. "I'm concentrating. Wait. There."

We snort two more lines. We are both smiling. "God, it's hot in here. Where's the air conditioner?" Trevor circles the room with his eyes. "Where the fuck is it, Cheeks?"

Then we are both looking for it, going from room to room. We are running our hands along the walls. I look under the bed, even.

"Here!" says Trevor, like he found the treasure in the cereal box before I did, which is what always happened when we were kids. The monitor is right by the door.

"You found it!" He found it. He's awesome.

He clicks it on. "I wish we had noise. It's too fucking quiet."

So I scream, as loud as I can.

He doesn't even flinch. He smiles at me. "I meant music."

"Want me to sing?"

"Hell no. You can't sing for shit."

"Neither can you," I say.

"Yeah. Well, we got that in common."

"I can dance, though."

"I'll bet you dance like a gay man."

"Fuck you. I'll show you." I find some music on the TV. I find one of those radio channels. It's something old-school. Boyz II Men. "Watch." I stand in the middle of the room.

Then I dance, like I did in the club that night with Angela. It feels great. I even throw in a couple of retro break-dance moves I've seen in the movies. I do the centipede. I pound my fists in the air, kick over the desk chair. I'm about to start throwing shit.

"Okay, okay!" says Trevor, gripping my shoulder with his good hand. "Okay, rock star. Don't trash the room. I don't have that much money." He goes over and cuts another line. "That was pretty good, Jihad." I have my hands on my knees, sweaty and huffing for air. "I didn't know you could do that."

"Yeah. You always said I couldn't dance for shit."

"I never said that."

"You did."

"Well, I was wrong. I'd clap, but it'll hurt." We both look at his bandaged hand. No one speaks. He laughs, leans down, and snorts. He holds out the dollar to me. "Dopamine," he says as I lean over. "Is that what you called it?"

"Yeah."

"Like riding a roller coaster."

"Yeah. Or sprinting a mile. Or having sex."

"How would you know?" He hands me a minibottle of Bacardi.

"Ha! I've had it!" He raises his eyebrows and downs his bottle. I do the same.

"No fucking way," he says.

"Yeah! I totally had sex!"

"Okay, Cheeks, whatever you say."

"I did."

"Whatever." Then he makes a face I know. The Trevor face.

"I did!" I say, angry. "I fucking did!" I throw the empty minibottle against the wall. It smashes. "I did. I fucked a girl. You don't know shit about me! I fucking fucked her pussy, okay? Is that so fucking hard to believe, asshole? That a girl would fuck me?"

"Hey," says Trevor softly. "Hey."

"And I was fucking awesome!" I say, even though I know that part is a lie.

"Hey. I believe you, Doug. I do. I believe you." His voice is softer.

"And she blew me!" My voice is not my own.

"I believe you, okay? I do."

"Her name is Laurilee. No. Wait. It's not. It's Angela." We stare at each other. Some song is playing. It's familiar. It heard it a long time ago. A time I can't quite remember.

"So," says Trevor. "Wow. You lost it early, dude. Way before I did."

"Yeah?"

"I was seventeen."

"Really?" I say, surprised. "I thought you'd have been, like, I don't know, fighting off the bitches in, like, the sandbox or something."

"So. Did you like it?"

"I think so. Yeah. I think so."

"You think so?"

"I don't know."

"I thought you were awesome."

"No. I wasn't. I lied. I was terrible."

"Nah, I'm sure that's not true—"

"I sucked. I only lasted . . . fuck. Never mind."

"A three-second man?" says Trevor.

"I don't know."

"My first time, I didn't even make it all the way inside. I jizzed all over her belly."

"Really?"

"Yeah. You get better. It takes practice."

"I don't even like her. She was just, like, there."

"Yeah. If you like the girl, then, well, that's a totally different thing."

"Really?"

"Yeah. You'll see."

"You think I'll do it again?" I ask.

"Yeah. Of course."

"It wasn't just, like, a onetime, like, fluke or—"

"No way. You got a lot going for you. Seriously. You're a good-looking guy, and fucking smart. Really fucking sharp. I wish I was as smart as you. I could have been, y'know? If it wasn't for football. I could have applied myself, not just, I don't know, sailed by. Maybe I'd be good at something. Who knows? Maybe I'd be something important. A mathematician. Something that matters. Instead of . . . well, this."

I know what he's saying. I want to tell him it isn't too late. But I am a minute earlier in the conversation. We are on different frequencies. We are watching different commercial breaks. "You wish you were as smart as me?"

"Yeah. Of course. I thought you knew that. Okay. Stop fishing. Let's do another line."

"Okay."

"This is fun," I say. We are on the balcony. We smoke. We drink from minibottles. We look out on the empty parking lot. "Oklahoma is a shithole."

"Try the desert for six months. You'll love this fucking place."

"You were at war," I say, remembering.

"Yeah. And I'm back."

"Why?"

"Why what?"

"Did you go?"

"I don't know." He throws a spitball over the railing. Then I do. Mine is bigger, I think.

"It made no sense," I say. "Just like that, without telling anyone. I mean, don't get me wrong. Mom was superproud. It was just . . . weird. You were in college, like, getting good grades and shit. Playing football. Then you enlisted. It was weird."

He shoots another spitball. He looks at me. "Amy."

"Amy?"

"Amy. A girl. Her name is Amy. I did it for her."

"You went to war for a girl?"

"She's not just a girl. She's Amy. She's beautiful. She could have any guy she wants. Everyone wanted Amy.

All my frat brothers. Every guy on the street. She's, like, pure. I can't describe it. I'm not a poet like you. When she looks at you. She makes you feel like you are the only one in the room with her, and she is, like, honoring you with her time."

"She sounds like a bitch."

"She is," he says, sighing. "But I didn't know that then. And her daddy is an officer. He was in Vietnam. And her granddaddy was in WW Two. He's a hero. And her great-granddaddy was in WW One. And they have medals and ribbons all over their house."

"So?"

"So." He turns to me. He takes out a cigarette. I light it for him. He inhales deeply. He blows the smoke out at Oklahoma City. "I wanted her to love me. And she said she couldn't love a man who wouldn't fight for his country."

"You went to war . . . for a girl?"

"Yeah."

"You went to Iraq for—"

"Yeah, asshole. Just what I said. Yes. For a girl. 'Cause she made me fucking crazy. 'Cause she wouldn't even let me inside of her. And I wanted to be. I was all fucked in the head for her. I wanted to—it doesn't make any sense. I wanted to live insider her. It was like I was on drugs. Like now. But I wasn't on anything except her. Amy. She made me shake. And so I did it. I don't even remember. I was a little drunk. Eight A.M. There I am, sitting in the office, saying, 'I love my country. I want to fight for my country.'" His voice is loud now. "I went to the fucking desert for a stupid fucking chick who doesn't give a fuck about me and started fucking one of my frat brothers six weeks after I left. That's what I fucking did because I am a stupid motherfucking idiot and now I'm home, okay? And I'm fucking missing fingers. You understand?"

We don't speak for a long time.

"Laurilee," I say.

"What?"

"A girl. That's why I did the drugs. I mean, thought I did drugs . . . I didn't know they were fake. I thought I was, like . . . never mind. Laurilee. She's cool. She likes cool guys. I wasn't cool enough."

"So you did drugs for her?"

"Yeah."

"To be cool?"

"I guess."

He snorts. "That was a fucking stupid thing to do." He starts laughing. "What a dumbass thing to do, Cheeks."

"Fuck you!"

"I'm just saying. Doing drugs for some little ho is kind of—"

"She isn't a ho!" I screech. "Your girl is a ho! Amy is a fucking ho!"

"I agree." He sighs. His gray face looks really sad all of a sudden.

"Yeah, well, maybe I was stupid. But going to war for some chick is pretty fucking stupid too."

"Yeah. Yeah. We're both pretty fucking stupid."

"Yeah. Stupid."

"She wasn't even that great. Amy, I mean. I thought she was. Her voice is kind of annoying, actually. Really high, like a bird, what's that word? That noise birds make?"

"Chirping."

"And one boob was, like, twice as big as the other. Not that it should matter, but it was. And she likes purses. Like, obsessively. She, like, dreamed about them. Circled them in magazines. I bought her one. It cost a thousand dollars—"

"A thousand dollars?"

"And it was used. I got it on eBay. And she was pissed off. Because it wasn't new. I mean, she didn't outright say that, but I could tell. Bitch." He blows smoke. "I want that purse back. So. What about your girl? Laurel?"

"Laurilee. Laurilee is pretty . . . great." We look out at the city.

"Oklahoma is so damn ugly," I say. "I need to get out of here."

"I'm doing another line. Let's do another line."

I am organizing the minibar. Making sure we have enough rations. I have a system, with bullet points. It is an intricate cobweb. Empty bottles, full bottles, edibles with sugar, edibles with starch. Water. Then the system changes. Nutrients. Energy. Empty bottles by brand. Full bottles. I drink one and put it in the empty pile. I forget the system. I try to think of a new, improved, more logical one.

"What are you doing?" says Trevor. "Hey, are you hot?"

"No. Yes. Organizing."

"Stop that. It's annoying." I look up at him. His shirt is off. He's got scars and bruises all over his chest. "You're fucked up."

"Yeah." He runs his hand over his buzzed head. Again and again. It's mesmerizing.

Then I'm thinking about the bottles. The system. I try to stop thinking about the system, which makes me think about the system more. *Don't think about the bottles.* I look at his hand. "Does it hurt?"

"Not right now." He laughs.

Bottles. Rations. Nutrients. My brother, Trevor. His hand. "Can I see?"

"What?"

"Your hand."

"You don't want to see that. It's not awesome, anyway. Just stupid stumps."

"How'd it happen?"

"Want to do another line? There's plenty left." Empty bottles. Peanut crackers. M&M's. Skittles. Green Skittles in a separate pile. My brother, Trevor. Stumps.

He reaches out his good hand to pull me up.

I jump on the bed for half an hour. He flips channels on the TV. We both talk, but not really to each other. We tell each other secrets we won't remember. Secrets that aren't even secrets. We talk about the best kind of toilet paper. We talk about James Bond. I jump on the bed some more, and he tells me to stop because it is annoying.

• • •

We are lying on the bare mattress. I stripped the bed. We are staring at the ceiling. I am counting the bumps in the ceiling. There are thousands, millions. I divide the ceiling into divisions. Allotments. I'm working on the area nearest the smoke detector. I used to do this when I was a kid and the dentist was cleaning my teeth. Counting bumps. The bumps are reassuring. Trevor is with me. I am listening to Trevor. I am counting bumps at the same time. I am at 468.

"Jack off to porn magazines. Sit around. Lift weights. I went to Ash Wednesday service. Pretended I was a Catholic, just for the convoy and to kill a couple of hours. Get out of the tent. There is so much sand out there. That's all you see. I fucking hate sand. I never want to go to the beach again. Jack off to the same magazines. Sit around. The same assholes telling the same fucking stories. This girl they screwed, the time they kicked this guy's ass in a bar. All lies, probably. How much they hate the sand niggers. How much we miss McDonald's. You get stupid out there. There's so much sand, and it's hot. And you can't get away from the hot. It follows you everywhere. You get really stupid out there."

"Yeah." *Five hundred and thirty-two. Five hundred and thirty-three.*

"Beanie. This kid from Iowa. I think he was, like, mentally disabled. But he had all this stuff. Whiskey in shampoo bottles. A fake iPod full of acid. Acid in the desert, right? You just laugh and laugh. And then you go to your tent and cry into your pillow for a couple of hours. Lots of pot too. Every day. Wake and bake. The minute the alarm sounds in the morning." *Five hundred and eighty. Five hundred and eighty-one.* "The showers didn't work for two weeks. We were so gross, we stunk so bad, and it didn't matter because we just kept getting fucked-up. We were so bored. We made coffee with the tank."

"How?" *Six hundred and twelve. Six hundred and thirteen. Six hundred and fourteen.*

"Easy. You wedge the lid of a fifty-caliber ammo can between the grill doors on the exhaust, then you start the tank. Just to heat some water. It costs, like, a thousand dollars a minute to run that tank. It was great, knowing American taxes were paying to heat that water for our coffee. It was great coffee too. The best I ever had."

"I drink coffee." *Six hundred and twenty-seven.*

"I had a bumper sticker on my tank. 'Know when to say when. Don't drink and drive.' It's all a joke, you see, the whole thing. Just gotta waste more time. Find stupid things to do. Nobody cares. Nothing is happening anyway. They keep saying we will be doing simulations. Stay prepared. We're gonna see action. Get ready, they say, you're gonna be hella busy. Then nothing. You know what they say about the army? 'It's not just a job, it's the roundabout way of doing things.'"

"Were you scared?" *Seven hundred and ninety-two. Ninety-three.*

"Nah. Wait. Hold on. Listen to this. This is the best. Are you listening."

"Yes." *Eight hundred even.* A good place to stop. But not as good as a thousand. *Eight hundred and one.*

"So, there are atropine injectors in gas masks, did you know that? I shouldn't tell you this. I might get in trouble. I don't care. So the gas masks are hooked to your side, down your leg. And if these atropine injectors go off, it's like a shot of speed in your leg. Kinda like right now. Just this fucking crazy high—like set it off, boom, wham, and you're crazy high."

"What are those for?"

"To keep you going. If you're in the middle of action. So you won't be thinking about how you're just about to die."

Eight hundred and forty. Kamikazi pilots. Smurfing.

"So the upper-level assholes are supposed to change them every year, but they forget. Some of these are four years old. Five years old. So we'd set them off, tell the sergeant it was because they were old, they'd gone off on their own, it wasn't our fault, right? So we'd get fucked-up on speed. That was fun, until someone caught on and we got a lecture. See, it's like study hall, only in a desert and there's a war going on. And you never see that war, so you just gotta kill time. Jack off to the same magazines. Wake and bake. And the food fucking sucks. It sucks so bad, you can't imagine. It's like eating five-day-old turds somebody zapped in the microwave. Thank God for those packages Mom sent."

"Didn't you have, like, jobs?" *Eight hundred and fifty-four. Eight hundred and fifty-five.*

"Sure. Of course. Had to maintain the tank, then we had to run tests. Chores. I burned shit from the latrine a couple of times. Nobody wanted to do it, but I didn't mind. Something about fire in the desert is really cool. It's kind of amazing. Especially when you're messed up. And the weirdest thing is how it smells. Burnt shit. It kind of smells like bacon."

"Gross." I've lost count. I don't remember where I left off. I should start again. Don't start counting again. Don't start. I sit up and look at him. I try not to think about the bumps on the ceiling. Jack wouldn't have counted bumps.

"You ever heard of Jack Kerouac?" I say.

"Is he on TV?"

"He's this famous fucking writer. The beat generation. *On the Road.* I got a poster of him on my wall."

"I don't go in your room, Cheeks. Wait. I know this guy. Freshman English, right? Nothing happens, right? They drive around."

I'm standing now. "No, it isn't like that. It's more than that. He was driving, right, but having all these experiences, right? Seeing America how it really was, just driving Route 66, meeting all these people, seeing America, like, fuck the status quo, fuck sitting in an office, just keep moving, see where life takes you—"

"He sounds like a freak."

"He wasn't! You don't understand! He saw America for what it really was. He wasn't afraid to just—"

"I'll read it." Trevor is sitting up. He's grinning.

"No, you won't."

"I'll read it. I promise. I want to read it."

"He wrote it in three weeks. On speed. When he was like this. Like me. Right now. I should right a novel. On a typewriter. Right now."

"Go ahead. Maybe I'll help. I can still type. I only used two fingers to type in the first place." We both look at his hand. I'd forgotten about his hand. I want to say something. I don't know if I should. I say it anyway.

"How'd it happen?"

"What?"

"You know what."

"I don't want to talk about it." Then he's on the floor doing crunches. He's doing them fast, his arms crossed over his chest. I won't count them. *Don't count them. Sixteen, seventeen, eighteen.*

"You've been talking for hours," I say. *Twenty-three, twenty-four, twenty-five.*

"Not hours."

"And you won't tell me about your hand? That's fucked."

He sits up so there is nothing to count. He gets up and goes to the table. I follow him. He leans down and does another line. There isn't much left. I reach for the bill.

"No," he says, holding it behind him.

"C'mon."

"You've done enough, Cheeks. You're getting kind of weird. I'm cutting you off."

"You can't tell me what to do." I try to reach over his shoulder.

"You've done enough. Tell me about that guy. The one who drove around America." Now he's standing in front of me, blocking my path to the meth.

"You need to share." *Sharing is caring,* that's what they taught us in kindergarten. *Sharing is fucking caring.* I try to go around him to the table, but he blocks my path. "C'mon, asstard. Don't be a dick, Trevor." I try to dodge him, but he keeps blocking me.

He's laughing. "No wonder you quit peewee football. You can't do a fake-out for shit."

"Fuck you." I'm getting mad. I should have kept counting the bumps. I try to get around him. I try left and right. I'm sweating. He's laughing and he's got the Trevor face. Then I push him, but he's like a tree. I push him again.

"You won't get around me. Just sit down."

"You can't tell me what to do! You're not Dad!" I'm making sounds I've never made before. I try the left again, the right side. I pivot. He's always right there. I can't get past.

"Give it up, Cheeks. It ain't happening." He grins at me. I hate his lips. I hate his face.

"That's. Not. My fucking name!" I scream. Then, without thinking, I'm throwing punches at him. They don't land anywhere. They land in space. Then he's wrapped his arm around my neck and pulls me down and we are on the floor and I can't move. He's sitting on me, his legs are holding my arms to my sides. I'm in a Trevor prison. I hate him. I kick at nothing. I scream.

"Shut up. Shut the fuck up, Cheeks! I mean it, you fucker. Stop. Don't be a baby. They'll call the police. Want to go to prison, Cheeks? Want to get your ass raped? Shut the fuck up. Now. Shut. The. Fuck. Up."

"I fucking hate you! I've always fucking hated you! You're a fucking stupid fucking imbecile! You're a fucking caveman, plebeian-Neanderthal-retard, you stupid fucking asshole dick—" Then my face is smushed into the carpet and I can't speak. My lips are open. There is dirty carpet on my tongue. Again.

"You're right." His voice is calm. "About all those things. I am stupid. I am a caveman. You're right, Doug. You've always been right, okay? But now I've got two stumps on my hand and my football scholarship is done, and I'll probably be working at some fucking taco stand in the mall this time next year. So stop yelling. You win. You hear me? I am a useless piece of crap, and you're smart and got your whole future ahead of you. You're gonna go to college and cure cancer. Or write a fucking novel or something. So you're the winner. So stop yelling. Just stop."

He gets off me, and my rib cage expands. I think I'm crying. I sit up. I look at him. He's leaning over the table. He's snorting another line. "It's almost gone, anyway," he says, rubbing his nose. "Hardly anything left."

"You're . . . not that bad."

"Thanks."

"No, I mean it. You're not stupid."

"I am," he says, not looking at me. "I'm just like Dad."

"You're nothing like him. You didn't go to Mexico with some stupid bitch."

"I went to Iraq for one." He snorts a line and works on making another.

"And I took drugs for one, but I'm not like him either. You're not like him. You wouldn't leave your wife and kids."

"I might. If I had them. I might. Who knows?" He leans down again and snorts another line.

"Slow down."

"I can handle myself."

"You're not like him."

"You have no idea, Cheeks. I'm just like him. I'm weak like him. I'm a pussy like him."

"Bullshit. You went to war. I mean, maybe it was for a girl, but you went to war and pussies don't do that."

He laughs. It is the saddest sound I ever heard in my whole damn life. "Let me tell you about what a pussy I am, Doug." He leans down. "So. Listen to this. This is a great story, swear to God. So. Thing is. Hold on." He snorts, nudges under his nose, and makes a face. "Thing is, Cheeks, that I sliced off my own fingers. Because I couldn't take it out there. I sliced off my own fucking fingers." He's got out his knife. He's messing with the powder. "Fuck. This stuff is almost gone. Fuck."

"I don't believe you."

"It's almost gone, I swear. I'm not even sure I can make another line."

"No. No. About your hand. I don't believe you."

He doesn't look at me. I can taste my heart. Or maybe it is bile. I taste innards, and they are my own, and they taste horrible.

"Oh, fucking, yeah," he says, leaning back. "Oh fucking yeah." The room is smaller. His voice sounds like he's in the other end of a cavern.

I can't look at him. I don't know where to look. I am standing now, but the room is moving around me. "You wouldn't do that. No way." But my own voice defies me. Because he would do that. He did that. And I think I knew already.

"It's easy-peasy, bro," he says from somewhere else. Some other solar system. He's my brother and his name is Trevor. I try to stabilize myself on something. I can't find a surface. I think I'm going to puke.

"Like candy to a child, kid. Ain't nothin' to it. Cleaning the breech on the smooth-bore main gun. The 120. My job. I'm the tank loader, after all. I've done it so many times. Standard procedure. Regular test run. This time I didn't move my hand out of the springboard breech when I pulled the lever. That's it. *Shhh-whack!* No more fingers. Fingers here, fingers gone. Look down and the blood is spurting out of the stumps. Like in a horror film. Like *Saw*. Kinda funny, actually, when you think about it. So I start laughing. Then I pass out. Then I wake up in the field hospital. Easy. Just cut them right off like the guy does with the slicer in the deli. Like that thing . . . y'know that thing they use to chop off heads? Y'know what I'm talking about? That thing they used, back in castles, with the blade? I've been trying to remember the word for days . . ."

"Guillotine."

"Fuck! Guillotine! Yup, just like that."

"It was an accident," I say. I think I say.

"I was pretty lucky it was only two. I'd been prepared for more. At least four. So I guess I was lucky. Especially considering how stoned I was. Hey. Y'know what? I think I can make one more line with this stuff. Dopamine, huh? I love this shit. Fuck, I love this shit."

"Didn't they know?"

"There was an investigation, yeah. But, c'mon, Doug, look at me. Do I look psycho to you? One more line. Just enough to make one more. I just acted shocked. Horrified. And that wasn't hard. 'Cause the thing is, well, I sort of was. And in the end, they just chalked it up to a fluke. One of those horrible things that just happens. And especially bad, 'cause it was *me* that it happened to. And everyone *likes me*. Did you know that, Doug? I'm a likable guy."

"Yeah."

Then he grins at me. That old-Trevor, aw-shucks grin. But there is something off about it. It is crooked now. One side is higher than the other.

"I'm going to puke," I say.

"I'm going to finish this off."

I turn around and vomit all over the penthouse wall.

· · ·

I wipe my mouth with my arm. I'm dizzy. The room is spinning. If this were a movie, the camera would be going in circles around me, creating a sense of uneasiness. The room is going in circles around me, like a movie, a sense of uneasiness. Trevor is laughing, I think.

"We gotta get out of here."

"I ain't going nowhere," he says from somewhere. The couch.

"I can't breathe. We gotta get out of here."

"Go ahead, Cheeks. Get out of here." His voice is slurry, the words are melting into each other, hot-lava words, falling all over each other. Slicing through the air. Blades slicing through fingers.

"No, both of us," I say. "C'mon. This is fucking crazy. Let's go home." My brother amputated his own fingers. People don't do that. That's something they do in scary movies or internet snuff films. He's sick in the head. He's crazy. We have to get out of here before he cuts off something else. I stagger over to him. He's fucking with the drugs. There is hardly any left. There isn't any left. He's fucking with invisible specks. "Trevor."

He looks up at me. He grins.

"C'mon. I want to go home."

"Then go." Back to the drugs. "Go home, little boy, go on home." He almost sings it.

"Come with me."

"No fucking way." His words are rolling over each other. "Hell no. But you go. I'm fine. You go. I'm gonna stay here, right here. I like it here. Penthouse. I haven't been in a penthouse since Homecoming. Junior year. And there were twelve of us. Now there's me. I want it to myself, anyway. I've been in the desert. I want my big fat penthouse to myself. So go ahead."

"Come with me now, Trevor. I fucking mean it. I feel sick."

He looks up at me with the Trevor face. The most Trevor of all Trevor faces possible. Like a caricature of himself that some hack scribbled at the fairgrounds for twenty bucks. "Get the fuck out of here, then. You little fucking baby. I shouldn't have brought you in the first place."

"Shut up—"

"Go home, baby Doug, go on home. Go home, you little pussy. Weak. Weak. I can't look at your face anymore."

We stare at each other. His face is hard. He is someone I've never seen before. I stagger backward. I'm going to puke again.

"I just think—"

Then he's on his feet, right in my face. His skin is sweaty and red. His eyes are dark. He is the ugliest person I have ever seen. He cut off his own fingers. He's crazy. He smells crazy. He's got a pocketknife. "Leave," he hisses through his teeth. "Leave."

"I don't think I should—"

Then he's loud. He's getting his sour spit all over my face. Dangerous spit. "Get the fuck out of here, you little fucking pussy faggot baby. I mean it. You are a worthless piece of shit, you've always been a worthless piece of shit. I know it, you know, fuck, even Dad knew it. He probably left because of you. *Because you're so worthless.* You can't do anything right. You aren't normal. You're weird. You're a freak. A total fucking freak. I don't want to look at your face anymore. Just get the fuck out of here. Fuck. I mean it. Just go already."

We stand there, face-to-face.

He lunges for me. I scream and jump backward.

His face softens. He snorts to himself. "Weak." Then he sits down and goes back to his nonexistent drugs.

"Fuck you." It sounds like a mouse squeaking.

"Fuck you," he imitates in a high-pitched, little-girl voice. Then he snorts again. "Freak."

I'm fucking with the lock. Then the door is open and I'm running down the hall. I can't find an exit. An elevator. *The Shining.* There are stairs and I take them two at a time, six at a time. There's the lobby. Air. I run out into the parking lot. He sliced off his own fingers. Blood was spurting out of the stumps. I need to tell someone. I want my mommy. I want her so bad. I'm in the parking lot. I'm not wearing shoes. I'm not wearing a shirt. I want my mom.

I start to run.

Someone honks at me. They'll probably call the police.

I'm miles from home. I can run it.

I stop a block later.

The army hospital. I promised him. The army hospital.

But I hate him. He doesn't deserve my help. He said I was worthless.

I think of my dad. Running away. That's what he did.

I look at the moon, just for a second.

This is what a man does.

I know what an overdose looks like because I've seen them on TV. I'm calm. I've never felt calmer. *Trevor*, I say, and slap his face. His face is hot. He's shaking. I slap him again. His eyelids flutter. He isn't dead. Drool is coming out of the side of his mouth. I turn him on his side. I read this somewhere. Turn them on their side. He's heavy. He's got a six-pack. I wonder if this is genetic and if I could get one. I call 911. I am calm. *Overdose*, I tell them. *My brother. Meth. His name, Trevor. Doug. Schaffer. S-c-h-a-f-f-e-r. I don't know how much. I'm not sure how much.* I tell them the hotel. The room number. *Yes, he's breathing. Yes. Hurry.*

Stay awake, I tell him. I shake him. *Stay awake. Trevor. Listen to me. Mom is gonna be really pissed if you die. Fucking listen to me.* Eyelids flutter. Rock stars choke on their vomit. I put fingers down his throat. Feel around for something. I feel throat. He moans. He convulses. *If you die, I will never forgive you. Trevor. Listen to me. Remember when we used to watch cartoons? Remember that? Count Choc-*

ula. How come you always found the prizes in the box? Listen to me. You are a fucking asshole. You better not fucking die or I will fucking kill you.

Then the paramedics are in the room. So many people. I am pushed to the side. They are around him. Doing things with instruments. Poking him. Prodding him. All I see is fatigued legs. And they move. I think they flicker. Do it again. Move again. *Can you hear me?* they ask him. *What's your name? Can you say your name, son? Do you know where you are? Listen. Listen to me. You're going to be okay.* They fire questions at me. *What did he take?* Meth. *How much?* A lot. A bunch. I don't know. This much. Hours. Um. Four? Five? I'm his brother. Doug.

I'm calm. I'm very, very calm.

You better take care of him, I tell them. *He just got back from Iraq. He served his country. You better take care of him. Trevor Schaffer. He better not die. He's a hero.*

CHAPTER SEVEN

"So when exactly do you leave for CyberGeek Camp?" I ask.

"The flight is at ten tomorrow," says Dingo. He's packing his suitcase full of electronics.

"You going to take any clothes? I mean, like, at least put in some deodorant. What if you meet a chick? Wait a minute, I forgot, chicks don't go to CyberGeek Camp."

"There'll be girls there, asstard." He winds a black cord around his hand.

"Yeah. CyberGeek girls. Bet they'll be hot. What'll you talk to them about? 'Hey, baby, want to see me program some data?'" I make my voice really high. "'Oh,

Dingo, I really like your hard drive. Your hard drive makes me so wet.'"

"That is so fucking stupid. Get some new material. I thought you were going to be a writer," says Dingo, but he's laughing.

I'm sitting on his bed, eating scallops wrapped in bacon. Dingo's mom isn't one to half-ass a snack. "So how long will you be gone?"

"A month."

"Will there be weenie roasts and campfire songs?"

"You can say whatever you want, fucker." Dingo puts a disemboweled computer monitor in the suitcase. "You're just jealous. They only let in smart kids."

"You got me, dude. That's my dream. Go to college for the summer and take a class in *World of Warcraft*." Dingo makes a funny face. "Wait a minute. Are you fucking with me? They have a class in *World of Warcraft*?"

"It's an elective. So? They got everything. Programming in Java, Web Design Hybrid—"

"Okay, okay."

"You think it's funny now, but when I'm going to my private island right next to Oprah's on my private jet with three Playboy Bunnies and you're some starving artist or something, I'll be laughing then. And maybe, if you beg and plead, maybe I'll invite you for a weekend."

"Playboy Bunnies?"

"Did I stutter? Yeah, me and three bisexual Playboy Bunnies. And one of them is gonna be *African American*."

His computer beeps. He goes over and types something quick. "It's Penelope. She's really sad I'm leaving."

"I'm sure you'll be able to do Second Life at Cyber-Camp."

"Yeah." He turns to me. "That's the thing. I'm going to be really busy there. I got a programming empire to develop. So I broke up with her. She's really sad."

I don't know what to say. How do you comfort your best friend when he broke up with his virtual girlfriend?

"She's freaking out about it, actually. She wanted to fly me to Montana to meet her. She said her parents would buy the ticket."

I think it sounds pretty sketchy. "You haven't even seen her. And the cartoon version of her doesn't count."

"She sent me her picture." He clicks on the computer. A photo of a brown-haired girl in a bikini at the beach pops up. She's wearing a sun hat and grinning at the camera. She's not a model, but she's definitely okay. Better than okay.

"She's cute," I say.

"Yeah. She looks just like her avatar. She thinks I look just like mine too."

"You sent her a picture of you?"

"Yeah, dude. We even talked on the phone. She's wants to be a medical geneticist."

"That sounds, uh, fun. So why didn't you tell me about her?"

"I did. I talk about her all the time."

"Yeah, but, like, as a virtual person. Not a real chick in a bikini."

"Grow up, man. Virtual reality is real reality. The world is changing, and you better get on board. Don't deny it, man. Just 'cause something is old doesn't make it better. You don't think Picasso would have loved to Photoshop? I know, I know, you're into writer guys. Kerouac and his fucking scroll. But who says it's gotta be ink on paper? That's kinda small-minded, man." I roll my eyes and pop another scallop in my mouth. "You don't think Jack Kerouac would have been all about the internet? He would have, man. The *Road* would have been hypertext. He'd have loved it, man. You click a word, and an entire universe explodes under your hand. And you don't even have to pay to fill up a tank." Dings goes to the suitcase and tries to close it, but it won't zip. He tries again, and it doesn't work. He sits on the suitcase, then can't figure out where the zipper begins. I laugh at him. I guess genius doesn't always transfer to everyday stuff. "Fuck you," he says, grinning, then gives up. "I'll have to get my mom to do this." He sits on his desk chair, leans back, and stares at me. "But I guess it's too late for you to reconsider, huh? You're gonna do it, I guess. So. Tomorrow, huh? That's the big day?"

"Yup."

"Should be cool, I guess. I mean, not as cool as Cyber-Camp, but pretty cool. Still can't believe it, though. Fuck. Who'da thought?"

"Yeah." I chew the last scallop. "Hey, what time is it?"

"Noon."

"Fuck, I got to go. I got all sorts of stuff to do before I leave. I'll call you in a few days, okay? Find out how your empire is doing." I pick up my backpack.

"Okay. You're distracting me with your bullshit anyway." We are standing by his bedroom door.

"Don't dump Penelope just yet, okay?" I say. "You never know. She seems to really like you."

"Yeah, well. I'll think about it."

There is a pause. It isn't awkward exactly. You can't have awkward pauses when you've known somebody for your whole life. Dingo was with me when I shit myself during a soccer game in first grade. I couldn't stop crying. I was ashamed. *Only a baby poops themselves,* I kept thinking. "Stop crying," he told me. He took me to the bathroom and hid me in a stall. Handed me wet paper towels underneath. Together we buried my dirty Underoos in the dirt behind a bush on the playground during Free Time. The teacher paid no attention. She already thought we were weird anyway and had stopped trying to figure us out long ago. "Accidents happen," Dingo had said, which was something I figured he heard from his mom. But Dingo has always been there. I could shit myself now and he'd still be my friend. He'd never let me forget it, but he'd still be my friend.

"So," he says. "Wow. I guess I'll see you in August, huh?"

"Sure." I clear my throat. I've tried this six times, but he'll never let me finish. "Dingo, y'know, I know this has been a crazy—"

"Shut the fuck up."

"You gotta let me finish, man."

"You already said that a bunch of times, dude. And I said it was okay."

"I just wanted to say it again. I was a real fucker at the end of the semester. I treated you like shit and you must have been—"

"Yeah, okay. I got it. You're sorry. Early-life crisis, man. I can dig that. I'm just glad—" He looks at his suitcase.

"Glad of what?"

"You know. That you're okay. 'Cause, I mean, you're a dumb fucktard, but we got two years of school left and you are the only one in this whole provincial state who I can stand looking at. And that's only some of the time, 'cause you're an ugly fuck."

I sigh. "Well, I just felt like I should let you know. That I didn't mean—"

"Being repetitive is a sign of autism."

"I thought my diagnosis was OCD."

"Dude, that was so long ago. I've been reevaluating you. Taking notes. For a while I thought it might be OCD, but that wasn't it either." He smiles. "Wanna hear my final diagnosis?"

"Sure."

"Well, my final diagnosis is this. You are a dicktard. *Dicktard disorder.* I discovered it. I'm gonna be famous. They're gonna put me in scientific journals."

"Great. Now I know." I shuffle my feet. "Anyway, I'm sorry for everything."

"It's okay." I can tell he means it.

"So. August. We'll be juniors."

"Yippee kai yay," he says.

"The best years of our life."

"Yeah, it's gonna suck pretty hard. But at least they'll have the new fall menu at Taco Bell. That should be pretty rad."

"I'm gonna miss you, man," I say. We stand there for a second, looking at each other.

"You aren't going to hug me, are you?" asks Dingo, making a horrible face. "That would be so gay."

"Fuck no. Asstard."

I haven't been to the mall since the day I quit my job. It has only been a few months, but it feels like a lifetime ago. Penn Square looks smaller than I remember, like when you're a kid and you go back to your elementary school or the jungle gym where you used to play, and it seems microscopic compared to how it is in your memory. It still smells the same, though, and the synthesized Muzak version of "Free Bird" is playing on the loudspeaker, which, to my surprise, sucks even worse than hearing someone do it on karaoke.

I pass Aunt Betty's. Some guy I've never seen is working behind the counter. The mall is pretty dead and he looks bored. A few weeks ago Roger called and asked if I was interested in a managerial position. He got promoted to the corporate office. He said, *I always thought you were a great worker and your lifestyle choice, whatever it is, is no business of mine.* I told him thanks, but I had to focus on my schoolwork, which was true. I'd missed so many classes I had to bust my ass to get my grades up, especially considering the deal I'd made with Mom. Roger said it was okay, *you have really great potential in the customer-service arts and if you ever need a recommendation, I'd be pleased to write you one.* I almost wish he were here because I'm wearing a green shirt. He'd like that. He'd tell me the nonverbal cues green relays to potential buyers.

My mom says this shirt is hunter green. She says it brings out the gold flecks in my eyes. I like it. It looks good on me. I stopped wearing black. It wasn't a decision exactly, just something that happened one day. I was sick of it. I got new boots too, though I kept my old Converse with the writing on them. I think they're under my bed somewhere.

I stand outside the window for a long time, watching Laurilee behind the counter. She's laughing with her coworker about something while she sorts bows into different containers. She looks just how I remembered, down to the plaid skirt, except now she's wearing an extralarge sweatshirt over the jumper and the streaks in her hair are bright red. I wonder if that uniform gets dirty. I wonder if she has more than one. I can't decide what to do. I might leave. It was just an impulse, stopping here. I don't have to go in, but I could if I wanted. I can do anything I want. I'm just not sure what I want at this very moment.

I don't have to make a choice because she spots me watching through the glass. She stares for a second, narrowing her eyes. Then gives that big grin I remember and runs for the door. "Doug!" she yells, and throws her arms around me like I've been away at war. "Oh my God! Kid! Where the fuck have you been?"

"Hey," I say, laughing. "Hey."

She steps back and looks at me. "You look different."

"I do?"

"Yeah. Did you get taller? I can't figure it out. You just look different."

"Is that bad?"

"No, you look good." Then she hugs me again, pushing her chest against me. I think about her breasts smushed against me. Those breasts used to have a lot of power over me. They still do. I mean, tits are tits after all, and they are a pretty miraculous invention. But they are just breasts, if you think about it, like so many other breasts in the world. So many future breasts to hold in my hands, to squeeze, to press my face against. Breasts connected to faces. Girls' faces. Amazing girls with amazing thoughts. Girls who I might love. Or just fuck. Or maybe even, one day, both love and fuck at the same time.

Laurilee, I remind myself. *This is Laurilee.* She is smiling up at me, like she can read my thoughts.

"Where the fuck have you been? One day you were just gone, kid. I asked your manager. He said you quit. I didn't know what happened. I didn't know where to find you." *You could have asked Roger for my number. You could have looked in the phone book.* "I missed you, kid," she says. Then she cocks her head, just like how I remember, and it reminds me of old times. I was so young.

We lean against the railing overlooking the second-floor water fountain that the mall calls Inspiration Falls, even though no waterfall is involved. A few people gather around. Fifteen minutes to every hour it squirts in rhythm to "God Bless America." It's pretty exciting if you're under two years old.

"Yeah, I missed you too," I say. "How are you?"

"Same old, you know. Terrance got fired. They found out he was spying on women while they peed in the lower-level bathroom. He had a whole Peeping Tom room set up in a supply cabinet."

"Are you serious? Gross."

"I know. Wow. You look really good, kid. Did you get taller?"

"I don't think so," I say, laughing.

"Something is different. I just can't figure out what."

"I guess I finally went through puberty," I say, and she punches me on the arm.

For a moment we are silent. It isn't weird or anything, just one of those moments when you realize how much time has passed and how important everything seemed when it wasn't as big deal as you first thought. It's kind of sad, those moments, but kind of happy too.

I look at her knees. They aren't anything special. They

are just knees. I look at her stick-out ear. She smiles. The fangs are still there, but they don't make me feel like they used to. I keep waiting for it to come back. That flood. That tidal wave of Laurilee inside me.

"Laurilee."

"Doug," she says, and laughs. Then her face changes. Sparks are under the skin of her face. Or maybe not. Maybe it is just grease. "Oh my God, I haven't showed you!"

"Showed me?"

"Remember? How I was going to do something drastic?"

"Sure."

"C'mere." She takes my hand. She pulls me into an alcove between Trinkets and the white-trash jewelry store where you can buy a diamond for $55.99. "Look," she says in a husky whisper. She turns and pushes down the cut-out neck of the sweatshirt on one side with her thumb.

"Wow. What is it?"

"A tattoo!"

"I can see that. But what is it?"

"Can't you tell? The state flag. It's got everything on it. The peace pipe, the shield. Even the feathers. You see the feathers?"

"Yes. But I thought you hated Oklahoma."

"I know. I do. But I always liked the flag for some reason. It's kinda trippy, right? I had planned on something else. I had all these ideas. A Celtic symbol for the in-between place. Or, like, the Chinese character for strength.

Then he had the needle out and all my ideas seemed, I dunno, silly. And it just came out of my mouth. It was crazy. I said, 'I want the state flag.'" She turns her head and rests her chin on her sharp, bare shoulder. "Well? You like it?"

I reach out and touch her with one finger. Trace the swirl of smoke coming out of the pipe. "It's beautiful." I feel her shiver under my finger. I see goose bumps rise on her back. "And it makes sense. Because Oklahoma gets under your skin."

She shifts suddenly, turns, so she is facing me. Our faces are almost touching. I've never been this near to her.

"I like the way you put words together, Doug. Did I ever tell you that?"

"No." And I know I can kiss her. She wants me to kiss her. But for some reason I don't. It wouldn't be as good as I'd imagined. I just know. I'd rather remember the *wanting to kiss her* part.

"That," I say, "is drastic." Her eyes are half closed. I can feel her breath on my neck. "I have to go, Laurilee."

Her eyes pop open. She looks shocked. She looks disappointed. "Not yet! Just wait a few . . . hey, I can go on break. You want to go smoke? Like old times? We don't even have to hide now that Terrance is gone." Her eyes are shiny.

"I can't. I only have a couple of minutes. I'm going away for the summer."

"Are you serious? So we can't even hang? I've got so much to tell you."

"Maybe when I get back."

"When will you get back?" she says.

"Late August."

"Shit, kid. You disappear, then show up, then disappear. At least give me your number."

"Okay." She runs in the store to get a pen. I wait outside the window of Trinkets. She runs up to me. She writes my number on her forearm with a Sharpie.

"I really got to go. My ride is waiting."

"Okay," she says, pushing out her bottom lip. "That sucks, but okay."

Then, like in slow motion, she stands on her tiptoes and kisses me quickly on the mouth. Her lips are chapped.

"I'm going to call you, okay?" she says quietly. "I missed talking to you. You're a good listener, kid. Did anyone ever tell you that?"

"Not that I remember."

She hugs me. We smile at each other, and it seems so crazy, everything I did. She is just another girl. She could be any girl in the world.

"I'll talk to you soon," she says.

I walk away.

I don't feel much of anything, and that feels just fine.

"Hey," she says from behind me. I turn around. She looks so little there, in the cavern of the mall. "I didn't even ask. Where are you going?"

"I'm not sure. But I'll tell you after I've been there."

• • •

Trevor is waiting in the parking lot. "How was it?" he says, when I get in the car.

"Anticlimactic."

"Is that good or bad?"

"Neither. It just is what it is."

He nods. He's still handsome, except that he's got fat since rehab. He eats all the time. Candy, chips, extralarge slushies. Fatass, I call him. Lardo McLardenstein.

"*It is what it is?* God, you sound like AA talk," he says, pulling out of the mall parking lot. "Hey!" His face lights up. "I forgot to tell you! Guess who was at my meeting yesterday?"

"Who?"

"Mitch Dwight Thompson III."

"No fucking way!"

"I swear to God. He looked okay. He's at step eight."

"You were so obnoxious at eight. 'I'm so fucking sorry, everyone. I'm such a douche bag. I'm so fucking sorry.'"

Trevor looks embarrassed. "Yeah, well. I was sorry. I am sorry."

"Don't start with that, 'kay?"

"You know what else? He thanked me. Mitch thanked me."

"For what?"

"For calling the hospital. After they bandaged him up, they sent him straight to rehab." Trevor smirks at me. "Thing is, I never called the hospital. I forgot."

"Oh, yeah," I say, laughing. "I called them. I remembered a day later, after you were already in detox."

"So he was by himself for a whole day? Fuck, he probably went through detox before they ever came, poor fuck. Without any stuff, since we took it. Hey, did I ever tell you about the charcoal?"

"Charcoal?" We are near the highway.

"You'll like this one. You can put it in your novel. When they pump your stomach, they shove charcoal up your ass. It absorbs the toxins. You shit black stuff for a week. It's pretty fucking nasty."

"Nice," I say, laughing.

"So. What else do we need to do?"

"Well, we got gas. Beef jerky. Water. We could go back and say good-bye to Mom again."

"Fuck no," he says. "God, I couldn't deal with another scene. All those tears. Did you know all the art-class hyenas are coming over tonight so she won't feel lonely? They're going to watch *The Bridges of Madison County*. She made me get it at Blockbuster while you were packing."

"You are officially Mom's bitch."

"I know. I'm just glad she's letting me go."

I laugh. "You should have heard the speech she gave me last night. About my duty to protect you. Hey, set your watch for eight. That's when we are supposed to call her. And Big Dave. To check in." Big Dave is Trevor's sponsor. When he first introduced me to him at a meeting, and he held out his meaty hand to me and said, "They call me Big Dave," all I could say was "Of course they do."

"Yup. He's a little sarcastic fucker," Big Dave said to

Trevor with a grin, "just like you said. But I heard you're a talented little fucker too."

"I still can't believe she's letting us do this," Trevor says, and grins at me.

I light a cigarette. "Well, I think she's kind of sick of us anyway. Besides, I've proven myself to be a good chaperone. I've gone to every one of my NA meetings, I raised my GPA, I'm seriously considering my collegiate options—"

"I'm the fucking survivor here, Jihad. Don't you forget it."

"I didn't know being a dick was one of the twelve steps."

"Fuck you, Cheeks."

"Fuck you, fatass," I say.

We are a block from the highway at a stoplight.

Trevor turns to me. "So."

"So," I say.

"Where should we go?"

"I haven't decided."

"We could take Route 66," he says, "like Kerouac."

"Nah, he was headed to Mexico. Fuck Mexico. What's the opposite of Mexico?"

Trevor thinks. "Canada."

"Yeah. Canada sounds cool. That's where we'll go. Montreal. They have really great jazz clubs there and all the chicks have French accents."

"Montreal?"

"Did I stutter?"

"Montreal," says Trevor, pulling onto the I-40. "Canada. Okay. And where else?"

"Let me think."

"Somewhere you've always wanted to go but never been. You get to pick the first one."

"I've never been anywhere."

"Me neither. Not counting Iraq."

I think about it as Oklahoma City streaks by my window. "I got it! You know where I'd really like to go? A strip club. I've never been to a strip club."

"Well," says Trevor, "then we should stop at the Red Dog on the border. They'll let anyone in there. They don't even ID."

"What about the bar?"

"Ha! There isn't one. Because it's full nude, so they can't have liquor. They sell 7UP and root beer. More dollars for the G-strings anyway." He grins at me. "Besides, I got my chaperone with me, don't I?"

"The strip club, huh?"

"Sure. Why not? The road is our open canvas, right?" He smiles. "We can do anything we want, right?"

"Right. We can do anything we want."

GALLERY READERS
GROUP GUIDE

HIGH BEFORE
HOMEROOM

MAYA SLOAN

INTRODUCTION

Doug Schaffer is ordinary. He is also hopelessly bright, hopelessly in love with a girl named Laurilee, and feeling hopeless about life. His father isn't in his life, his mother is emotionally absent, and the love of his life has a thing for "bad boys." To add to his angst is Trevor, his very popular, good-looking and adored older brother away in the military serving his country.

Determined to fit in, get noticed and be like his hero Jack Kerouac in *On the Road*, Doug concocts a plan to get everything he's ever wanted: Attention from his mother, attention from girls, but mostly especially attention from Laurilee. With great wit and punchy observations, author Maya Sloan takes us on the road with Doug to find what he's always wanted.

DISCUSSION QUESTIONS

1. Mediocrity is a theme in the novel. Discuss some of the places it comes up. Talk about the lengths people go to stand out. Talk about how scared people are to deviate.

2. From Amy to Angela, Doug's mom to Laurilee, how are the women in the novel portrayed?

3. Often, appearances are seen more important to parents than children, and women than men. How does this novel turn those conventional ideas around?

4. Doug gets noticed all the time, just not in the ways which are important to most sixteen year olds. Discuss some of the positive ways he gets noticed. Talk about some of the negative ways.

5. What types of myths does Doug create about manhood and sex? How much of this do you think is influenced by the Jack Kerouac stories and how much do you think is influenced by his missing father?

6. From Roger to Mr. Prescott and Trevor, Doug hardly respects any of the men around him. How do you think that furthers the plot? Do you think this is influenced by his father leaving?

7. The love of Doug's life doesn't notice him the way he wants to be noticed and neither does his mother. Do you think that he has a misplaced need for attention?

8. Doug often has very elaborate fantasies, most involving being seen and recognized. Some of them come from what he's experienced watching television, or reading books. Talk about some of these fantasies. What do they say about both Doug's desires and fears?

9. The author uses vivid imagery to describe the meth lab. Talk about the sights and the sounds.

10. When Trevor returns from the military, what is revealed about him? How is this different from Doug's description?

11. Doug makes a reference to the "Okie caste system." How are his caricatures of people similar in other parts of the country?

12. Do you think Doug is a reliable narrator? Can you trust all of his judgments and his perceptions of people?

A DISCUSSION WITH THE AUTHOR

Q: Doug is very smart, but he makes many bad choices. How did the voice of Doug come to life?

A: Doug is a teenager from Oklahoma. I *was* a teenager from Oklahoma. For years I'd only write about places I lived after I left my state—New York City, California. Places I thought were more romantic and interesting than where I was raised. Then, one day, I decided to try and write about Oklahoma. Just like that, Doug showed up. And he wouldn't shut up. He basically wrote himself. He's a lot like I was at that age, only in guy form.

Q: Why did you make Jack Kerouac such a strong influence on Doug? Are you a fan of the author?

A: I went through a serious Jack Kerouac stage. And even today, no matter where you go—big cosmopolitan cities or little rural towns in the middle of nowhere—you'll probably still find some teenager in a coffee shop pouring over *On the Road*. Like so many other teenagers in high school, I figured I was *different than everyone else in the entire universe* and *no one would ever really get me*. And here are these Beat writers who reveled in being outcasts. They didn't seem to care what anyone thought. I *wished* I could be that way. The characters in *On the Road* create their own lives and identities. They have these crazy adventures, travel, pack up and take off . . . they did all the things I could only imagine doing while I was stuck in my high school cafeteria eating chicken fried steak and cramming for a sixth-period Spanish quiz. Of course, in reality, many of the Beats burned out young and died way before their time . . . but I didn't see that part of the story until I was much older. All I saw was the Beat legend—total freedom. At some point I moved on to other writers, but those books will always be a part of me.

Q: Part of the subtitle reads, "the perks of being perfectly ordinary." Why do you think people, particularly teenagers, feel so bad about being ordinary in the first place?

A: Nobody wants to be ordinary, I guess. And being a teenager, you feel so awkward and strange and full of questions . . . all you really want to be is normal. But then again, you're a confused teenager and you know that probably won't happen. Even if you appear normal, even if you are the most loved, popular kid in the school—some part of you is probably still questioning yourself. *Who am I? Am I a fraud?* Those years can really suck.

Q: How much research did you do on meth labs and meth culture? Are there any books or articles that you utilized?

A: I did a ton of research. I believe in research. But at some point you throw all that away and let the character take over. Ultimately, the book isn't about meth as much as it is about Doug himself. But the thing about research . . . if someone asks me if I've done meth, I take that as a compliment. If I'd written about being a prostitute, and some asked me if I'd really worked the streets, I wouldn't be offended. I'd take that as a compliment too. That means I've succeeded as a writer.

Q: You capture the language of teenage boys, displaying both their aggression and sexual fantasies. Can you talk a little about how you developed the voices of Dingo, Mitch, and Trevor?

A: It helps that I've taught teenagers and young adults for many years. I've gotten to hear their views on everything—literature, politics, pop culture, religion—at some point I started to understand the way they think. And in understanding them, I could see myself at that age reflected back at me. And that was bitter-sweet, and fueled many of my characters. I love how young adults view the world. I've noticed that they may not have the same references as their parents and teachers do, but if you really listen to them, they have an insight we often lose as we age. They call stuff as they see it. Their lives are an emotional roller coaster from day to day, and they remind me how exciting the world can be at that age. You feel like you are experiencing stuff no one has *ever experienced before*. You feel like you invented sex. You feel like—if the politicians would just listen to you—than you could solve every world crisis. You are finding your passions and recreating yourself every moment. I've learned a lot from my students, and they made it easy to fall into Doug's skin.

Q: **The women in your novel, although mostly thematic, are in a lot of pain. You allude to Angela having been sexually hurt in some way. Laurilee knows she's messed up, and Doug's mother is absent and totally obsessed. This novel seems like warning for female destructive behavior as well. Is it?**

A: Yes.

Q: **Speaking of women, can you see yourself writing a female lead in the future?**

A: Doug is actually one of my first male narrators. I mostly write from the female perspective.

Q: **What are you working on next?**
A: I've got some ideas brewing for another novel. But if I told you, it'd just sound crazy. So I figure I'll just write it and see what happens.

ENHANCE YOUR BOOK CLUB

1. Check out the book *On the Road* by Jack Kerouac to get a better perspective of Doug. How does your interpretation of the book differ from his?

2. Doug spends a lot of time discussing Oklahoma's class layout. Take a look at a map of the state and see if you can find any of the neighborhoods he mentions?

3. Think about or visit your childhood bedroom. What do your posters say about you? How do they differentiate you from someone "ordinary"? Have the posters on your wall(s) always been the same? Have they changed as you've gotten older? How?